May 12th, 1874

My Dear Mr. Macgregor,

It has been a pleasure working with your firm and the fine town of Sweetwater. As you know, there were several places considered along the railway line but I thought Sweetwater held the most promise for growth and prosperity.

It is my opinion we will benefit one another as time passes. First National Bank prides itself on being a good neighbor and partner to the towns and cities it resides in. I can see the future of mutual respect and congeniality as we move toward a new century.

I also look forward to meeting you and the fine members of your town's council. Forward thinking men who know what is needed for the future. Men who can see and prepare for growth. I was impressed by your town's recruitment of a midwife and higher-education teacher to help families feel comfortable and welcome. Families are what make or break a town more than any other component. I cannot emphasize that enough.

I plan on arriving during the first week of next month. You will receive a wire as to the exact date when it becomes evident.

Thank you in advance for your help with this project and I look forward to meeting you.

Sincerely yours,
Paul S. Weaver, President of Expansions

New Banker in Town
&
Happy Endings
by

Susan Payne

Sweetwater

This is a work of fiction. Names, characters, places, and incidents are either the product of the author's imagination or are used fictitiously, and any resemblance to actual persons living or dead, business establishments, events, or locales, is entirely coincidental.

New Banker in Town & Happy Endings

COPYRIGHT © 2020 by Susan Kay Payne

The Wild Rose Press, Inc.
PO Box 708
Adams Basin, NY 14410-0708
Visit us at www.thewildrosepress.com

Publishing History
First Cactus Rose Edition, 2020
Trade Paperback Print ISBN 978-1-5092-3207-9
Digital ISBN 978-1-5092-3208-6

Sweetwater Book 4
Published in the United States of America

Dedication

This book is dedicated to my husband of fifty-four years whose sense of romance still takes my breath away.

New Banker in Town

SWEETWATER, KANSAS 1874

CHAPTER 1

Paul Weaver wiped his brow and replaced his black Derby onto his sandy brown hair as gray eyes surveyed the painted train platform. His gaze passed over two pretty girls talking with a tall, muscular man wearing a sheriff's badge on his shirt and a gun strapped to his leg. Paul thought it boded well the sheriff appeared as if he could take care of any problems that might come up.

Walking towards him was another tall man of about twenty-six, with auburn hair exposed under his Stetson and clear green eyes showing a keen intellect.

"Mr. Weaver? I'm Jeremy Macgregor, the architect and engineer on your bank." He held out his right hand, a warm welcoming smile on a tanned face. "I'm glad to meet you."

"It's nice to finally meet you, Mr. Macgregor." Shaking the man's hand, he continued, "It's good to put a face with the many letters and wires we've sent back and forth."

"I'll show you to the hotel so you can rest, sir."

"I'd rather you show me the bank. I'm rather anxious to see how it came out since it is so close to being finished," the older man said, not actually that much older, more in experience than years.

"Not a problem, sir. It's actually on the way to the hotel," Jeremy informed him noting the military bearing, mutton chop side-burns and neatly trimmed mustache of the man in front of him.

1

"Please, call me, Paul. I only use Mr. Weaver when I'm actually in the bank," he replied as he limped keeping up with the younger man.

Jeremy led the way to the steps down to the street. "Then call me, Jeremy. There are a lot of Macgregors in Sweetwater and more on the way, as I hear it."

A few yards behind the station, they stood in front of the impressive marble front two-storied building with Corinthian columns and Federal styled pediment over the front doors. The impressively sized windows were edged with wide fluted trim covered by decorative wrought iron gates. Dark gray granite of the exterior walls abutted the black and white marble tiles covering the interior floors, which they could see through the large glass panels in the doors.

Both men took a moment to soak in the majesty of the building and then Jeremy broke the silence by explaining, "We planned on the building being the closest one to the station so it would take only a couple of guards to bring or take the money bags to the Wells Fargo's safe on the train."

"That was one of the points we liked about the site right from the beginning. The less exposure to non-controlled areas the better our chances of preventing robberies."

"I had consulted with Mason, our sheriff, since he has experience protecting Wells Fargo deliveries. He was very impressed with the vault you sent to be installed. I was, as well, and the installer who arrived with it really knew his business." Jeremy complimented Paul's decisions.

"Yes, I've worked with them before. This will be the third bank I've opened for First National and I have no complaints with the Mosler-Bahmann Company. So, there were no problems?" Paul asked to make sure he needn't follow up with Mosler.

"No, they sent someone out right after the building began to be framed and, of course, I had the engineering requirements for the foundation already. That thirty-eight-hundred-pound vault was placed and we built the building around it. It's not going anywhere," Jeremy confirmed.

"I never underestimate thieves. They are a lazy bunch and that means they try the lazy means to get what they want, even if it means blowing-up an entire building. That's not to say they will get the vault open or out of there but by the time they figure that out, the damage has been done."

"Well, I was kind of interested in the interior of the safe unless that would be giving away too many of your security secrets."

"The experienced bank robbers know too much about the vaults now anyways but I would appreciate your confidence. I have the combination memorized and the keys with me so lead the way." Paul bowed waving Jeremy through the front door.

Once inside, Paul took a few moments to appreciate the fine marble on the floors and halfway up the walls and decorative plastered ceilings. The finished woodwork was precise with each metered corner matched-up. The polished wooden counters where the tellers would stand had brass fittings holding the cage doors in place. Jeremy unlocked the heavy door to the teller's area and Paul seemed impressed with the extra hinges and intricate locking mechanism. He handed the keys to Paul who went toward the massive shiny black safe standing in the center of the room.

Paul peered appreciatively at the safe then bent and used the combination to open the first part of the lock. Pulling out another set of keys to open the large full-sized door, he revealed over a dozen safety deposit boxes, each with their own two keys hanging in their locks. The bottom had an interior of highly polished nickel-plated steel with a copper clashing finish. Several locked drawers were there, too, for gold and silver deposits.

Jeremy was admiring the mechanics of the door bolts. "The engineering on this is amazing. I saw how easily the door swings and I can tell these hinges and bolts are of the highest-grade steel. I'm always being surprised by how man can overcome so many obstacles and come up with ways to make new things. I guess that's why I became an architect. To be part of those new ideas and put them to work."

"I've seen quite a bit of change in the last ten years. I think the war spurred some of those inventions but we need to find a peaceful use for them. The manufacturers that pushed out guns and cannons now need to make steel for things like this safe. Men need work and the knowledge that once made the Gatling gun will now make steam driven plows." Paul hated the flash of painful memories accompanying these thoughts.

"Let me show you the best part." Jeremy turned toward a door near the rear of the building. "I've put a urinal in the men's necessary room."

"I have to see this. You don't know how much ribbing I had to endure when this came through on the invoice. Some not very nice things were said about my aim," he told Jeremy confidentially.

"I, for one, am now a complete convert. I will try to design them into every public building I plan." Jeremy showed off the ceramic item hanging on the wall.

Both men took time to examine the offices and other security devices built into the building to dispel would-be burglars from thinking the Sweetwater bank was going to be easy pickings.

On the way to the hotel, the two men met Matthew St. Michaels, a relatively new-comer and prosperous business man in town, coming from the Mercantile with his mail. Jeremy introduced Matthew who offered to buy Paul dinner that evening at the hotel's restaurant, the only establishment that served meals. Jeremy was invited, also, so the men could discuss the new developments of a growing Sweetwater.

Paul excused himself to check-in to the hotel and see to his luggage. He unconsciously rubbed his leg just below the knee to ease the strain of being on it for so long at one time. He knew it would be bleeding by now and he wanted to get the pressure off the pad and rest it in his room. Hating to allow his injury to alter his life in any way, he found he had to give it rests more and more lately. He didn't want to think it was due to his getting older, as well.

He approached the pleasant-looking young man behind the front counter and then saw the young woman who had been talking with the sheriff on the train platform. She was still wearing the stylish though somber dress with the high bustle although she had removed her gloves and hat. Brown ringlets cascaded down the back of her head from a high pile of curls on top, which bounced as she smiled a welcome. She stood back and didn't say anything to Paul leaving the registration process to the male employee who was efficient and precise.

Letting pride get in the way, he hoped the attractive young lady didn't watch him slowly step up each stair to get to the second floor. He did, at least, prevent himself from rubbing his leg again although it was screaming for attention.

Paul reached his room, unlocked it, and gratefully sat down to press his hands around the aching limb or partial limb, in his case. Removing his coat, he slid the suspenders off his shoulders then stood to push down his trousers, exposing the hated wooden prosthesis with all its leather straps and cotton batting.

Just as he thought. The pad, saturated with fresh blood, would need to be changed. He would need to use a crutch again. If he hated the prosthesis, he despised the crutch. He had seen too many soldiers on both sides needing them and the fact his body was still weak even after almost ten years made him angry. He wasn't angry at the cannon ball and its accompanying debris of nails and metal fragments but of the inability of his body to overcome the injury. A weak body means a weak man and a man with only part of a body, well, that speaks for itself doesn't it?

Molly watched the handsome gentleman climb the stairs slowly. His limp particularly more pronounced now than it had been on the train platform where she first saw him waiting for someone. She had been speaking with Mason, the town's sheriff and Faith, one of her sisters from St. Michaels Foundling Home in New York City. Faith had been instrumental in getting Molly to leave her job as housekeeping manager with the Winston Hotel in New York and accept the manager position at the Sweetwater Hotel, which was owned by Mason and a married couple, Mr. and Mrs. Whitehouse. With the town expanding, the work was getting to be too much for the older couple and they wanted to cut back on the number of hours they put into the business. To do so, they needed to select someone from outside the town since there were no good candidates locally.

So far, Molly saw no glaring irregularities in how the front desk was run and housekeeping simply needed a little additional overseeing. The women who came in to clean every day needed a more accurate list of other duties to keep the common areas neat and presentable. Now that there were more guests and some of them not the hotel's usual type of clientele, cleaning and refreshing would need to be more frequent.

With the town growing, men working in the construction trades came to the hotel for their living choice. The only other option was a Loane Brother's tent out by one of the many construction sites. She wasn't sure where that would lead once the harsh winter winds began to blow.

Molly complimented the clerk on his method of checking in Mr. Weaver and then went to watch the kitchen prepare for dinner. There were many areas a hotel manager needed to cover. Although this establishment was functioning profitably, the change in the town and the clientele would alter the operation of the hotel. Breakfasts were wanted earlier, hardier meals for a working man and the fine dining may get lost with the influx of customers unused to using a napkin let alone being served on a tablecloth.

While on the train to Sweetwater, she had made a short list of changes she hoped to implement that would alleviate some of the strain on the kitchen. But after seeing the buildings and how they were attached to one another, Molly felt her new plan would work out very well for all concerned.

Mason stopped in for a cup of coffee and to see how Molly was doing. "Everything meet your expectations, Molly?"

Molly liked this big blond man who wore a badge yet was vested in the prosperity of the town growing like so many others along the train tracks. He had dimples when he chose to smile which was often, thank goodness. Otherwise, he had a grimness about his mouth that could be frightening if one didn't know him well. Faith, Molly's closest friend from the orphanage, assured her before she came that Mason was trustworthy, honest, and loyal to the bone. Molly trusted Faith's opinion.

"Yes, everything is pretty much as I expected. Better in some cases."

At Mason's questioning expression, she continued. "The cleaning staff is very good with the rooms and the bedding is all first quality. I think having the Chinese laundry doing the linen saves us money and time and lets our cleaners do the important job of keeping the guests' rooms immaculate. The next most important thing is, of course, the bathing rooms, which I think need a little more care. The moisture in the rooms allows mildew build-up in the crevices. I think I have a solution to that problem which won't cost very much money."

"That works for me," grinned Mason. "Although if there is need of some investment I'm not opposed. I would just like to see the plans before you spend anything significant."

"I agree. The owners are in charge of the policies

and investments. I am here to guide you through these transitional times. I can see what you were and I can see what you are becoming. This hotel will have duel purposes until boarding houses and apartments catch-up with the need."

Molly was getting excited about being part of the expansion of the country. "Towns like this one aren't going to be able to stand still. It will need to change as all these new people, mostly men, come into town. The families will follow afterwards and that means more housing."

Mason smiled at her enthusiasm. "Well, I think Faith helped me find the right person to take on the challenge. Let me know if you need anything. Otherwise, Vicki and I will expect you about six o'clock for dinner."

"Thank you very much, Mason. I should be able to make that just fine." Molly had met Vicki earlier in the day when Mason had taken her home to meet his wife and to put her luggage into the spare-room of their apartment. The Whitehouse's had one side of the back apartments and Mason had the other. The hotel was booked solid so Molly had to use the room in Vicki's home.

Molly went into the kitchen and watched Oliver, a long-time cook with experience in a southern fine-dining establishment, and Mrs. Whitehouse, prepare the evenings' fare, which smelled wonderfully. Molly wouldn't need to worry about the food's quality merely quantity at this point. "Before dinner, may we have a talk, Mrs. Whitehouse?"

"Certainly, dear, I merely want to get this bread in the oven and Oliver can keep an eye on it. The soup will be fine as it is," said the older lady with a pleasant smile.

She wore a flour dusted apron over a simple dress and her gray hair was in a plain bun on top of her head.

"I will be in the office going over some notes so come whenever it's convenient," Molly replied.

Molly wanted to tread carefully with any changes, especially with the bill-of-fare for the hotel's dining room. When Mrs. Whitehouse came in, Molly approached the change she saw that was needed and proceeded to convince Mrs. Whitehouse.

"I noticed there were over one-hundred and ten items available for both dinner and supper at the hotel plus the breakfast items. I think, with the type of guests we have occupying the rooms right now, we should cut back."

"Oh, but dear, we are the only dining establishment for the whole town. People come here to enjoy themselves, celebrate a special birthday or anniversary. They expect to have a wide variety to select from," Mrs. Whitehouse replied worriedly.

"And I think those times will return and soon but the rooms are filled with up to four workingmen each. That means there aren't rooms available for those people who spend more for meals. The men who are here are coming in, ordering the least expensive option, then not leaving gratuity, not ordering desserts or beverages other than sometimes coffee." Molly tried to explain the business aspect of running a hotel. That it was things such as wine and extra incidentals which increased the income of a restaurant.

Molly realized the older woman didn't want to cut back on what she considered a proper hotel's offerings so she approached it from a different view. "Mrs. Whitehouse, your usual patrons spend close to two dollars a person when dining here. Your present clientele makes little more than that a day working and then they have to pay for their room. There isn't anything left to send home to their families which, of course, means they will leave town. Abandon their jobs."

"I noticed the nicer entrees aren't being ordered and we are throwing out more to the pigs but what can I do? I mean, people expect us to have a certain level of quality," Mrs. Whitehouse repeated blinking rapidly.

Molly tried once more. "What I am suggesting is instead of so many cold meats, we cut back to only those we have from the previous supper which means cutting back to, let's say four - beef roast, chicken, ham and pickled tongue. Some evenings we will have corned beef or pork roast depending on availability. I noticed we offer both lamb and mutton but I checked past sales and neither really sells in this cattle town so I'm suggesting we take these both off the menu until we get more guests from the East."

She watched Mrs. Whitehouse, the white brows still creased in worry and tried to ease the blow. "I'm still depending on your excellent cooking skills. The quality must not lessen and the dining experience must seem flawless. I am having the bill-of-fare printed daily if need be until we have the perfect offerings."

"That sounds nice, dear. I'm sure Oliver and I can come up with new, interesting offerings while keeping the same inventory items. I've been waiting to use a recipe I received from Callie for a ratatouille, a kind of vegetable medley of summer produce. Oh, and an apple cider dressing for leafy greens." A perkier Mrs. Whitehouse said excitedly, "This may be fun. Oliver will have some ideas, too, I'm sure."

"As long as we work towards cutting the number of inventory items and still offer a decent number of selections, we will get through this change in our guests without losing money. Thank you for being so understanding with these adjustments," Molly told the older lady sincerely.

When she was once again alone in the office, Molly thought, well, that is one tricky hurdle completed, now only a few more to go. Sighing, she returned her attention to the figures on the ledger.

CHAPTER 2

Paul sat in the saloon after dinner, trying to find the fine line between being drunk on his ass and not feeling the pain that intensifies as the day goes on. He had cut himself off from the whiskey and was now drinking the less potent beer, allowing himself to continue to drink until it was time to go up to his room. He watched with interest Mason, the sheriff and his deputy, both standing at the bar with their right foot on the brass rail and their elbows on the polished wood.

Wilder, the deputy, was dark in more ways than one. He wore all black, from his snake skin boots to his Concho hat with its silver buttons tied on with leather strings and a pistol on his hip at the ready. His face was clean-shaven and his jaw strong but his eyes were what would make a man stop dead in his tracks. They were silver-blue and aware of everything in the saloon, constantly taking in everyman's movement.

A man, more drunk than sober was entertaining his buddies at a nearby table with tales of his rooming house that evidently was also a brothel. "This Miss Lily that runs the place is an original Hooker's girl if ever I saw one and believe me, I've seen more than my share. And she weren't any spring chicken even then." The table roared with laughter as drunks usually did at the simplest things.

Paul saw the sheriff stand and slip his badge into his pocket then turn to confront the drunken man. "You want to rephrase that? After all, you're willing to sleep in her house and eat her meals for a very reasonable cost. Do you think it proper to repay Miss Lily by talking this way about her?"

The man, not to be shown-up in front of his pals, stood and swaggered over to the much larger sheriff. "What's it to you? The old whore your mother or something?" Then glanced back to see how his friends were enjoying his bravado.

The sheriff dropped his head and kind of shook it, not believing the stupidity of the man. He stared the drunk straight in the eye, pulled back his right fist and landed a punch on the man's jaw. The inebriated man twirled and landed, bent over the table while his friends looked on in fear and amusement.

The drunk stood up, rubbing his jaw and said, a smirk on his face, "Does that mean she's your mother or are you sleeping with the old harlot?"

Now this was a man who had no sense of self-protection when drunk evidently and Wilder, the deputy held Mason's arm from moving forward.

"I'll get this one." Then he pulled his arm back and threw a punch that had the drunk spinning and grabbing for the tabletop to hold himself up. As he turned back to the bar and his boss to finish his beer, Wilder said, "You held back too much. You should have let more of your displeasure show."

Mason glared at the man and said as a warning, "Now I want you to move out of Miss Lily's. If you're paid ahead, too bad. You need to appreciate the kindness of that woman. You'll remember this night while you're sitting in the snow freezing your ass off in the Kansas winters, which are not mild. Now get out of my sight." Then turned back toward his drink again, too.

Paul sat a little straighter trying to ease his leg when

he heard a loud crack and a gun went flying back to the bar where Wilder stood, pulling and wrapping his bullwhip into a coil. The gun was still spinning on the floorboards in front of him.

"Pulling a gun on a man when his back is turned is jail time. Pulling one on a sheriff is a hanging offence out here. Maybe you should think about blessing another town with your presence as long as you're packing out of Miss Lily's place." Wilder stood facing the drunk, his stance that of a seasoned gun slinger. "You got anything more to say?"

The drunk, sobering quickly, rubbed his hand where the whip had left a red welt as it had grabbed the gun out of it. He shook his head and backed out of the door.

Wilder finally turned back to the bar and said sotto voice to Mason, "Well, are you going to explain to Jeremy how we scared off one of his workers or are you just going to let him find out by himself?"

"I think I'll let the banker tell him. He's been watching the whole thing with interest and I'm sure took enough notice to pass it on fairly," said Mason drinking down the last of his beer. "I'm home to Vicki so you're on your own. Don't smoke in the jail."

Wilder drained his beer too, saying, "I never smoke in the jail." Flashing a grin Mason knew meant – and you can't prove it.

Paul made his way to his room on the second floor of the hotel next to the saloon. It was a quiet town and the saloon was pretty well empty by ten o'clock in the evening. He thought about buying a bottle to keep in his room to help him manage the pain through the night but hadn't done so. He fumbled with the door, finally getting the key in the hole and turning it till the click let him know he was successful. Closing the door behind him, he turned toward the dresser he knew was there to light the lamp.

A female voice from the bed said softly, "I'd rather you wouldn't light that."

To his credit, Paul didn't jump or swear but, instead, asked just as quietly, "So I have a guest, I assume?" He wondered who would have ordered him a companion for the night. Macgregor didn't seem like the type and no one else really knew him well enough to present him with such a gift. Could it be, Molly? The sultry voice sounded older than the girl he had seen behind the registration desk would have had.

"I thought you might like a welcome to Sweetwater besides a tour and dinner," she purred.

Paul could make out the shape lying on the bed with help from the moonlight shining through the window and it was definitely a womanly shape.

"I've been told I'm the kind of man who is open to most new things," he said candidly.

"So, are you trying to tell me that having a woman in your bed is new? So difficult to believe a handsome man as you sleeps alone," the mystery woman said.

"May I ask the name of my guest?" he teased trying to find out who his benefactor was.

"I would rather not answer that question," she replied honestly. "Does it matter?"

Not really answering, Paul asked, "Do you mind if I get comfortable? My leg is becoming very painful."

"Certainly, undress, please. I want you to be at ease. Do you need help?" she asked easily.

"And if I said, I did?" Paul asked as he removed his coat and tie. He wasn't sure how much more she expected him to remove before she made her move on him if that was how this was supposed to play-out.

"Please, I enjoy watching you undress. Finish then come and join me. I am sure I can help you feel more relaxed," she assured him.

Pulling down his suspenders, he tugged his shirt out of his waistband, then shrugged the shirt off his wide shoulders, allowing him to push down his trousers as he sat on the bed.

"I have to take off my prosthetic leg to get undressed," he said waiting to hear the woman's excuses as she left the room upon finding out about his missing limb.

A pause, then finally she offered again, "Do you need any help?"

Paul relaxed after the hardest part of becoming intimate was out of the way between them. "No, I have a lot of experience with undressing alone."

She could hear the humor in his voice. "That is a shame. A fine specimen of a man, such as you, should not have to undress himself. If we knew each other better, I would never let you undress alone," she purred, moving her legs behind his buttocks, nudging him slightly.

Paul fumbled with getting the wooden leg removed. "I find I'm a little clumsy tonight. Must be I imbibed overly much since I didn't realize I had company waiting for me."

He finally got the leather straps unbuckled and the prosthesis loose so he could allow the contraption drop to the floor followed by his trousers. He removed his sock. Now Paul had to face his fear and turn to his bedmate with a sense of humor asking, "Do you prefer the right or left side?"

"I prefer the bottom," she said with humor in her voice and pulled him towards her, lying back, allowing Paul to reach her mouth and placing his upon it.

Paul took over from there, finally realizing this was actually happening, that a lusciously shaped woman was in his bed and willing to stay there for some time.

Between kisses, she asked, "Is there anywhere I should not touch? Anywhere that would hurt?"

"You can touch me anywhere you want. I'm beyond feeling any pain," he said truthfully, wanting to feel her hands on his body, anywhere, everywhere. She stroked his chest then his back as he covered her.

The woman seemed to revel in Paul's attentions. Her naked body pressed to his like a limpet. He covered her lips with his own, seeking and receiving permission for his tongue to enter. She used her tongue with experience, fencing with his, being aggressive as she followed his lead.

His hand had been stroking the long length of her body, feeling the indent of her narrow waist and the rise of her hip so close to his own. He cupped one breast and then without hesitation covered it with his warm mouth, teasing the peak into a hard pebble. The woman responded immediately, pushing her hips to his stiff erection, urging him to join with her.

Paul didn't need much prompting. It had been years since he had felt this way with a woman, this need to unite and become one with her again and again. He felt her warm breath against his neck, the little pants as she got closer and closer to her release, as he got closer and closer to his. His body waited for her, knowing instinctively when she would reach the maximum pleasure and spiraled with her, savoring the rippling of feeling as it went to the outermost parts of every cell in his body.

He rested his chin on her head not saying a word, after all what could mere words express that his body hadn't already? After a few moments, the woman pushed on Paul and he rolled reluctantly to his side knowing she was going to leave him, as everyone had left him.

"I must be going now. It was nice to have met you, Mr. Paul Weaver." Then in the dark she dressed quickly, slipping out the doorway, the light from the hall inferior to his need to see her as she left.

Paul lay in the rumpled bed, thinking about the time years ago when he loved a woman like that, when he made love to a woman in that exact same way. He lay looking up at the ceiling and asked aloud, "How the hell did you get yourself all the way to Sweetwater, Kansas, Colette Dubois?"

CHAPTER 3

Colette Delmar was a French beauty with rich black hair and dark brown eyes that reflected her emotions. Her generous mouth a firm line as she thought about last night. She was restacking the negative plates next to the camera standing in the center of the room she used to take photographs. She had a very popular trade at the moment with the local ranchers wanting photographs to commemorate births, weddings and even deaths.

Tin types had been popular during the war but the modern negative style photographs added a whole new dimension to the field. One photography session could result in several negatives that could be used over and over. Sending them across the country was possible making it easier for family members back east to make copies for their own albums.

Looking across the street toward the hotel, Colette was still regretting her impulsive actions of the evening before. She had gone to take her weekly bath and saw Paul having dinner with Matthew and Jeremy. A short visit next door had Jeremy's wife, Faith, more than willing to talk about the new banker in town.

While in her bath, she reminisced about what she and Paul had shared more than ten years ago, before he went to fight for the Confederate Army leaving Colette alone and under her father's control. It had been less than six-months after Paul's leaving when Colette's father arranged an engagement to a Creole plantation owner, an older man her father knew and played cards with weekly.

Colette later found she had been a payment of a card

debt but it hadn't surprised her. Her father would get into trouble again and Colette wondered what he would bargain with then since he had already sold his only daughter.

Her husband, Pier Delmar, wasn't unkind to Colette but a little disappointed she had not produced the much-wanted son, which was the main reason for his marrying her. She always thought if he had not been wasting his seed with every lady of the evening in New Orleans, she might have had a better chance of fulfilling his desire for a child.

Colette held out hope for the two years she was married before a poisonous spider bite took him to his grave. Colette wore black and grieved but swore to herself she would never return to her father to be used to pay off a debt again. Instead, she travelled up to Charleston and faced the Northern army. She changed her name and heard first that her father had been shot in a fight over cards and then Paul Weaver, her only love, had been killed on the battlefield.

Only that rumor had been false because the man she had sworn to love forever was right across the street and she had easily seduced him last night. And he hadn't even known it.

Still, it would be a night she would remember always. The one last time to say goodbye to her girlish dreams and wants and first love. Colette's eyes misted. When she raised her gaze to look over at the hotel once again, it was to see Paul coming across the dusty street, his limp barely noticeable. Colette tried to find somewhere to hide but then realized Paul was going into the newspaper next door. She exhaled the breath she didn't know she had been holding.

Sneaking into his bed in the dark and waiting for him was one thing, having him approach her in broad daylight was another. Colette relaxed, convinced Paul had not recognized her voice from the night before. Her body had changed, she was well aware of her larger breasts, perhaps wider hips if she were honest. But his body had changed too, not so much in size but he had lost his leg.

Opening the door to the newspaper office, Paul was met by the smell of ink, paper and machine grease all in equal parts. There was also a lovely young woman Paul had been told was Jeremy's wife.

"Mrs. Macgregor?" he asked as he approached the counter. The young woman with strawberry-blond hair piled in curls on top of her head and a heart shaped face looked up smiling. Her simple peach colored shirtwaist and tan skirt showed off a very attractive figure.

The smile became even wider as she said, "Call me, Faith, please. There are a lot of Mrs. Macgregors around. And you must be Mr. Weaver, our new banker."

"I am, and please call me, Paul. I was told you were the one to help me with my printing needs," he said returning the smile.

"We can do most types of printing. We only publish the newspaper once a week right now and use the printer the rest of the time for posters and the printing for the hotel."

"Good, then I hope these won't take too long. I would like to get everything before the bank opens its doors. I jotted down a list of what I'll need and the number of each. Can you read my scratching?" he teased as she read through the list.

"We will need to order some of the paper but it

shouldn't take too long to get it from the distributor."

"I understand Matthew St. Michaels was going to be finishing up on a distribution center here in Sweetwater soon. That should help get things quicker," he said to make small talk.

"I don't think Matthew is going to try to handle paper and printing needs. There is such a demand for farm machinery parts and household goods right now, anything to make the jobs around farms and ranches easier to increase productivity. The women used to come out with their husbands and then after a year or two, returned east to their families, most often taking their children with them. It ended up leaving a lot of lonely men." The sincerity was evident in her tone as her mouth turned down. "Matthew thinks if the women could get the same items in the territories as the women have back east then they will be more content. I believe he's right."

"Well, I know we need the women to stay if a town is to grow and prosper. Families are what strengthen a community. And the addition of the school should go a long way to establishing the town, too. That came as a surprise when Jeremy wrote to tell me about the combination civic building and school. A town this size having something like that is really a good investment." Paul complimented the woman's husband for his forward thinking.

"And Hope St. Michaels, the teacher, is setting up a library. There isn't much to do in the evenings and winter months seem very long so reading for pleasure will give us all something to look forward to. I know she has already received *Frankenstein* by Shelly, which I've been too frightened to read, but Hope assures me I will enjoy it. Then she has Jules Verne's newest book *2000*

Leagues Under the Sea, as well as, *Five Days in A Balloon* and *From the Earth to The Moon.* She has quite a few books on the shelves already and more on the way."

"St. Michaels? Does that mean she's related to Matthew?"

"St. Michaels is the name given to children who didn't know their family name as orphans at St. Michaels Foundling Home." Her chin rose slightly. "I was a St. Michaels before I married Jeremy."

He mentally nodded in understanding with this new information and thought he could wait till later to figure it all out.

"So, I take that the library will be popular with a lot of people? I may have a little money to donate towards books in my grand opening budget. It would be a good use of funds that would reach all age groups in the community," he said, thinking out loud.

"Oh, that reminds me." Her smile was back as was her business acumen. "The Chronicle would like to do an article right before the bank opens so people will know a little about you. I was hoping to talk you into having your photograph taken and then we can place it alongside the story. We may also reprint the bank announcement we ran a month or so ago."

"I guess I can get home-office to send the negative of myself from storage. I've been in print before."

"Oh, I was hoping our local photographer right next door could take a new one. Colette is ever so talented and she could use the business. She is so generous with her time and often doesn't charge the poorer families for the photographs she does for them."

Paul casually said, "Colette, hmm? So, I take it this

photographer is a female. Quite an unusual occupation for a woman, isn't it?"

"I'm afraid I am quite the feminist, Mr. Weaver. Colette's a widow but I think a woman can do anything she sets her mind on and many things better than a male."

"I don't disagree at all. I've seen women handle tragedy and death far better than many men and I'm sure you are all better at handling certain things that would make a grown man faint."

"Now I think you are trying to placate me," she accused smiling.

"Not at all. I sincerely believe if childbirth was left totally up to men the human race would have died out centuries ago." He tipped his hat anxious to go next door and confront his mystery woman of the night before. He thought it would have taken much longer to find her.

This time Colette was caught off guard, thinking Paul was unaware of who and where she was. He entered the door to the photography studio and gazed directly at her. She knew immediately he had recognized her from the evening before. She opened her mouth and then closed it unable to formulate any comments upon seeing him this close in the bright light of day.

"I didn't think you would remember. I was, I merely wanted to say goodbye properly, I guess," she said to his unasked question.

"Do you really think I would have forgotten you? The way you taste and smell? The way you touch me? The way we fit together like we were made only for each other? The way we make love? I could never forget any of those things and I truly thought you couldn't either until I returned to New Orleans, wounded and hurting to find you married and gone," he said, anger rising surprisingly as if it hadn't been ten years before. As if he hadn't grown used to her deceit long ago.

"I didn't want to marry anyone else and I never wanted to leave but I had to or my father would have sold me to another man to pay for his gambling debts. When I became a widow with a little money, I fled north to Charleston and then to Chicago after the war ended. I needed to be away from the South and all I thought it had taken from me. It had been reported you had been killed not just wounded," she told him, justifying her leaving.

"I wasn't able to go home right away. I was held in a prison camp for months where I was more dead than alive. The only thing that kept me going was thinking you were waiting for me. I returned home to find you had married a wealthy man and lived in luxury while I lay in pain and torment." His eyes burned with the remembered physical agony.

"It's too painful for either of us to relive the past. For what we lost and can never recover. The years changed us. Not only the war, although that had a big part in it. Last night was a stupid idea I had to make up for the way we parted, a salute to the life we could have had if everyone hadn't interfered," Colette said, tears for the loss they both shared yet blamed the other for.

"Is there someone else, then? Another man you're interested in?" he asked quietly waiting for the answer that would be like a sword thrust to his heart.

"What kind of a woman do you think I am to slip into your bed while being involved with another? Is that how you always viewed me? I know I went up in flames every time you touched me but that was only with you. You are the only one to affect me like that and it was much the same last night," she said the last few words almost as a whisper.

"What about your husband? Was he good to you?" Paul asked hating himself for not being able to resist asking the question.

"Pier was kind to me but of a different generation. We had nothing in common and he went into town often, staying with friends, while I remained on the plantation." She didn't want him feeling sorry for her so added, "I didn't want for anything material."

"But he died? Then what? You weren't anywhere I could find you when I finally made it home," he half accused.

"When Pier died, I gave the slaves their papers. Although by then they were already free by Yankee law, I wanted them to have the papers. Then I gave them the bill of sale for the fishing and shrimp boats so they could continue to make a living, of sorts. I moved to Charleston to help that town recover but found I was recording through photographs the destruction of a city I once knew well. After that, I moved to Chicago which turned out to be very good for me. I could heal in an area that showed no signs of war," she told him remembering the good times meeting new talented people, honing her craft.

There was a short silence while Paul came to grips with what she told him. So different then what he had always thought occurred. He needed more time to consider this new information, information that could change the rest of his life. He tried to get their relationship back to non-confrontational.

"I came to have you take a photograph for the newspaper but I think I should come back at another time. We are both too raw with emotions. I didn't sleep last night for thinking, trying to figure out what you were playing at… How you came to be in the same small Kansas town as I was. Nothing came to me that made any sense."

"I was escaping the big cities. Chicago isn't the same since the fire. I got tired of the competition and the noise and simply all of it." She shrugged letting the movement say what words were failing to say. "I have been happy the few months I have been here and have begun to be established in the community. You are here for what? Six months, a year, possibly? I hope we can be in the same proximity without drawing attention to our animosity to one another."

"If that was animosity you were displaying for me last night, I'm all for more of it anytime. And I think you misunderstood me, Colette. I don't want to ignore you. I want more of you. Last night awakened old feelings I thought I had dealt with but now find I hadn't. You've told me new information I didn't understand but now, I think I do. Let's go slowly but I think much of the pain and hurt can be healed for both of us. I feel very protective about you right now," he said quietly, standing next to her, smelling her fragrance, noting the agitated rise and fall of her breasts as she listened intently.

"Are you going to be in my bed again tonight?" he asked as her gaze shot daggers at him. "I simply wanted to know if I should curtail my drinking since it may hinder my performance," he teased before kissing her on the forehead and leaving.

Colette went into the back of the building where her private quarters were and poured herself a sherry, drinking it down in one gulp. What had her impulsiveness gotten her into? Was Paul serious about starting up a relationship with her at this late date or did he merely want a bedmate for the few months while he was here? And what did Colette think about either option.

CHAPTER 4

Molly opened her accounting book and marked in the proper amounts taken in and spent that morning. The butcher's bill was one of the highest followed by the laundry cost, although that wasn't a bill due every day plus, they delivered which was another savings.

The evening before, Mason had made the mistake of asking over dinner what Molly thought the changes should be and she told him - all through the meal. She was sorry Mason's wife, Vicki, would feel left-out but then Vicki said Callie Harrison had taught several of the other St. Michaels's graduates in Sweetwater how to cook for the ranch hands. That meant tasty, inexpensive food in large quantities.

Vicki even had some of the recipes she had cut down to serve two or four people but said she could rewrite them to their original quantities. Then they could be used at the hotel just as Molly had been describing to Mason.

One main problem the hotel was facing was the men coming to work in town didn't have the money to pay for a room as well as the higher prices of a hotel's restaurant. Since there didn't seem to be anyone wanting to open any other restaurant in town, yet, Molly had devised the solution of serving a square meal in the saloon. Meals that were less expensive but nutritious and the men wouldn't feel out of place wearing their work clothes in the saloon as opposed to the usual dress requirements of a hotel's dining room.

Molly walked over to speak with Faith since she was one of Callie's sisters, also, and instrumental in getting

Molly the position as hotel manager. Faith had also worked out at the ranch for a few weeks and might be a help with the bill-of-fare for the saloon cum restaurant.

"I thought the saloon served food already, although I've never been inside," Faith said as she took Molly upstairs to the apartment, she shared with her architect husband, Jeremy, until their new house on Second Street was completed.

"The bartender said he has only had pickled eggs on the bar and no one much in during the day at all. He closes before midnight even on Saturday, a bit different from what I am used to. The Winston Hotel bar served till two or three in the morning including food, and then there was the room service and special orders. And the dining room had no less than five courses, one hundred and fifty items along with a selection of desserts and after dinner liquors.

"In New York, every chef was trying to make their specialty the talk of the town, drawing the rich and powerful into their restaurants. Sweetwater's needs are simple, comparatively," Molly told her friend as they settled at the kitchen table to talk.

Coming from the stove with boiling water for the teapot, Faith said, "Callie's meals are delicious, well planned and leftover foods are used in other dishes. She has it planned out by the week and uses the produce and meats as they're harvested. I was impressed and intimidated, at first, but then once we, Charity and I, began it all fell together. I mean, you have roast chicken with celery stuffing, potatoes and then the bones left after carving are placed into the soup pot along with any leftover vegetables you have around and fresh onion for a filling soup the next night. I still make that one," Faith explained browsing through the recipes in front of her.

"That sounds good. When I'm able to get my own place, I'll try it." Molly asked, "Can you remember the weekly plans so I can approach Mrs. Whitehouse with a list? There will only be a single or maybe two offerings at the saloon per meal except breakfast. We have to keep it simple enough not to take a lot of labor and yet be tasty and filling enough to keep the men happy eating in the saloon. Those workmen simply don't want the dinners the hotel is known for serving. The offerings are too complicated and take too long to prepare after the guest orders. It's all right for those with nothing else to do, when dinner is their main entertainment for the evening. The working men want to get a full belly and move on, usually to the saloon."

Faith nodded. "Give me a day or so and I think I can get most of them together. I mean they're made to be flexible, turkey or prairie chicken instead of chicken, venison instead of beef. But I can get them directly from the horse's mouth. I usually visit the Harrison ranch every week or so."

Accepting the cup of tea being offered, Molly asked, "May I go with you next time if I'm free? I would love to see Callie again and meet her husband and son."

"Of course, I'll ask Jeremy when we can go next," Faith told her friend, excited about being able to help.

A few days later, Jeremy drove Faith and Molly to the Harrison ranch. He pointed out the Macgregor family's ranch on the way but continued for more than another half-hour before they saw the large compound of Callie's new home. It consisted of a large two-story wood structure with stone foundation and fireplace and wraparound porch with a wide front door. There was another smaller single storied building that looked much like the main house as well as a bunkhouse with front porch, a stable and barn along with several out-buildings.

They greeted each other in front of the cookhouse. Callie, her bright red hair and gamin looks unchanged by the years or motherhood. The two women threw themselves into each other's arms in welcome and tears mingled with the smiles as each renewed a friendship that had never ended.

"Oh, Callie, you haven't changed at all. I had trouble picturing you married and with a baby. Somehow, I thought it would transform you, make you look like one of the nuns or something. You still look like a girl. How do you do it?" Molly was amazed at how little felt changed between the two of them although their lives had taken such different paths.

"Well, I enjoy every minute of life so that must be the answer. But look at you, that dress is simply elegant. I might not have recognized you on a big city street," Callie said admiring her friend's dress with buttons down the front to the waist and then the skirt's material pulled up to cascade down the back in a waterfall of a bustle. Ribbons and bows trimmed each fall of material with wide lace at the buttoned sleeves and high neckline. The hat a French creation if Callie was any judge and Callie was a very good judge of hats.

Charity, one of the other orphans Callie had invited out to work on the ranch brought out glasses of lemonade with ice. Jeremy had wandered off to find Seth, Callie's husband, and had left the women to gossip, as he politely put it.

Faith asked her best friend, "So how is married life treating you, Charity?" Charity was a petit woman having wispy, blond hair that framed her small face and wide-set blue eyes. She was wearing a gray shirtwaist and skirt with a crisp white apron over it, the uniform of the ranch cooks.

Blushing, she said primly, "It is as you have all explained it to me. I certainly can't complain about anything." Then the others, except Molly, laughed at the inside joke. Charity went on, adding, "Seth gave us the foreman's cabin since Sully, the ranch foreman, is unmarried and has always stayed in the main bunkhouse. It has its own kitchen and everything but we eat in here since I'm cooking and then Will helps me clean-up."

Callie added, "He's been helping clean-up since you moved in here. He was making eyes at you from the beginning. I'm just glad you both decided to stay on so I have you until you start a family, too." Turning to explain to Molly, Callie continue, "I lose most of my cooks to the lonely men around here."

Molly said, "I did notice a lack of females of any age. It seems like in a town there would be more single women."

"I'm afraid not. Callie and I write to some of the others to let them know there are jobs available, even more now the town is expanding. Instead, the growth seems to have brought in more men. Not that I'm complaining but I hate to see a good man go to waste," explained Faith which caused all the ladies to laugh and agree.

Molly decided to broach the reason for the visit. "Callie, Faith said you had some meal plans I could possibly use to feed the construction men in the saloon. The hotel dining room is simply not big enough or inexpensive enough. I want to be able to offer a different bill-of-fare in the saloon, something that will fill their bellies without emptying their wallets."

"I can copy some over while you're here. I may need to alter some because beef and veal are available to us free as ranchers but you'll be paying full price for it. I'll copy the weeks where I've used the less expensive cuts and then we'll see how many different offerings we end up with." Callie stood and limped inside to get paper and pencil. Her birth defect not hampering her ability to run the cookhouse or keep the records.

Just then Mary Margaret, another graduate from St. Michaels, came down from the main house. "I'm sorry to be late but I wanted to get Warren down for his afternoon rest or he turns into a bear." Then she hugged both Faith and Molly in welcome.

"We were hoping to see him before we left," coaxed Faith.

"Oh, he'll only be down for an hour or so. He doesn't take a morning rest at all anymore but the midday one is still very much needed. Maria, the housekeeper, will bring him down when he wakes up," Mary Margaret explained.

The ladies all went through the front doorway of the cookhouse to find Callie busily transcribing her menu plans and Mary Margaret sat down beside her to do the same.

Molly picked up the detailed weekly plans and as she read, said, "I can see where you used your experience as a cook for the orphanage to plan these meals, Callie. You wouldn't want to move to town to be my chief cook and bottle-washer for this project, would you?"

Callie stopped writing and gazed speculatively at Mary Margaret, saying casually, "I couldn't, of course, but there might be someone else that would." She peered directly at Mary Margaret.

Then all three women stared at Mary Margaret who glanced up and asked, "Who, me? I, I like it here and I love taking care of Warren."

Callie said kindly, "And I loved having you here and, of course, Warren, will miss playing with you but I think I've kept you out here on the ranch long enough. I know there were a few men from the neighboring ranches who seemed interested but you sent them on their way. If you ever want a family of your own, you need to move into town where you'll have more exposure to the young men coming into Sweetwater. All the ranch hands here love you but I think they're too much like family now for you to make a romantic connection."

"And you've been listening to all the married female talk and know what to expect and how to participate. You're much more prepared than when you first came out to Kansas," Charity said covering the most frightening part of marriage that she had faced.

"If I go into town, I won't be going to trap a husband. I do know Callie doesn't need my help as much now that Warren can be brought down here when she needs to help out. But I'll need to figure out a place to live and maybe transportation. It will take a while," Mary Margaret explained.

Faith spoke up saying, "Now that Hope and Wilder have moved into the schoolhouse apartment, I have a bedroom downstairs and you'd have full use of the kitchen and can eat with us."

Molly added, "She'll probably eat at the hotel and I'll furnish the uniform. Much like what Charity is wearing will be perfect. Professional and modest so the men won't get any ideas you are on the bill-of-fare, too." The ladies laughed but knew Molly was right.

Mary Margaret looked at Callie and asked, "You're sure? I don't want to desert you and Warren."

"I know my time with you, my sisters, is limited here at the ranch but you will only be an hour away. As always, you are all welcome at any time but most importantly, I want you to feel this is your family home. Always come and visit with each other on holidays here. You are all Warren's aunts," Callie said with heartfelt emotion.

At that reminder, the women all teared up and it took a few minutes to get back to copying the plans. Then Mary Margaret went into the bedroom at the back of the cookhouse and packed her few personal possessions, getting ready to return to town with Molly and Faith.

Warren, now over a year old, was brought to the cookhouse for all the ladies to fuss over. He had a toy horse that seemed to be the favorite to put in his mouth and drool over along with several wooden blocks with hand painted pictures of farm animals on them.

Mary Margaret played with him, explaining she was going to live with Faith but would come out to visit him. Of course, the baby didn't understand her but it made Mary Margaret feel better that he'd been told she wasn't abandoning him.

After a late lunch, Jeremy and Seth Harrison, one of the tallest men Molly had ever seen, came up to the cookhouse. Tall, blond, wearing the traditional ranch hand's outfit of long-sleeved shirt, tan trousers, boots and ten-gallon Stetson, he scooped his son into the air and then went and stood next to his petit wife, making

Callie seem even smaller.

Molly felt his love for his family clear across the room. A little envy and pride that Callie had found her true soulmate seeped into her mind. Perhaps there was a chance for her, too, just as there was for Mary Margaret. Finally, a family of their own.

Then it seemed in a few moments they were all in the buggy driving out of the gate and back towards town. Jeremy explained he wanted to stop in to his family's ranch which they had passed on the way. About half an hour later and the buggy pulled in front of a larger house than Callie's but was more stone than wood. A large porch went around three sides with a wide front door right in the center. Jeremy got down, told the ladies he would be right back and climbed the steps to the porch two at a time.

Two women, wearing stylish dresses, slight bustles showing off their narrow waists, came onto the front porch each with a baby on her hip only much younger than Warren.

Mary Margaret waved from the back seat and called out, "I'd like to introduce, Molly McGuire, a sister. Molly, this is Mavis and Emily Macgregor, Faith's sisters-in-law and their children, Aileen and Elliot."

The two women on the porch, one with dark brown hair pulled up with curls on both sides of her head and the other with lighter brown hair pulled back in a plain bun acknowledged the introduction. The children, both wearing baby dresses, were like two peas in a pod at this point, both red-haired with large blue eyes.

Mary Margaret continued, "Molly has come to manage the hotel and restaurant. I'm going into town to help with the restaurant so I'll be living with Faith for a while."

Faith added, "We'll be moving into our new house in a few weeks and then Mary Margaret will have the whole apartment to herself. I'm inviting you now to a house warming and you can help me decide what other furniture I need. I want to wait until I live in the house for a while before I order anything more. I hate to think what this is all costing Jeremy."

Jeremy came out and kissed his sisters-in-law on the cheek before returning to the buggy. Meanwhile, his brother Jamie, went directly to Mavis giving a little finger tap to the baby's nose to make her smile. A big bear of a man stepped onto the porch making his two brothers look small and they were anything but. He went and stood behind the diminutive woman with the bun and put his big arms around her and the baby she held.

Jeremy said casually, "Molly, my brothers, Jamie and Mac. They drive me to distraction but are loyal and the best brothers a man could have."

Jamie, humor shining in his bright blue eyes, said, "You're laying it on a bit heavy, little brother. We already said we'd be there with some men to help you raise those rafters."

"And I appreciate it. I'll furnish the beer and the food." Jeremy said climbing onto the seat. They all waved as the buggy was again back on the road heading toward town.

CHAPTER 5

Sitting at a table near the window, Paul watched the storefronts across the street. Specifically, the photographer's studio where one lone lamp shown through the window. But Paul knew the living quarters were in the rear of the building. He sat sipping the whiskey since it was still early in the evening. His eyes ached with the strain of staring, afraid that if he blinked, he would miss seeing her through the glass.

Taking a long swallow of his whiskey, he emptied the tumbler then pushed it near the edge of the table. The bartender, a slender man of about twenty-four or so, came over with the bottle and poured the glass half-full. Paul placed his hand on the bottle and the bartender left it.

Finally, most of the lights were extinguished on the far side of the main street and Paul was fruitless in his search for Colette crossing over to the hotel. The bottle was empty and the bartender kept glancing over at him, the only patron left. Paul got up, placed a coin of the table and limped out the door to the boardwalk. Seeing two people entering the jail, Paul wondered what business kept the sheriff working such long hours.

Sheriff Mason chuckled as he pushed his wife up against the wall next to the jail cell and held her hands over her head, giving him ample access to her womanly charms. He had unbuttoned and removed her shirtwaist to find she wasn't wearing the constricting corset. He tugged her camisole out of the waistband and pulled it off over her head freeing her hands to do so. Vicki answered his every move with one of her own, undressing him with the same enthusiasm. Finally, Mason molded her breasts while he kissed and sucked his way to them, lowering his hand on her body even more.

Vicki pulled his head to her breasts as he woke the nipples with his seeking mouth, his hands now busy under her skirt, massaging the eager bud waiting there. Vicki had been unbuttoning and trying to remove Mason's trousers, his shirt gapping open, his bare chest glistening with the energy it took to make love standing up.

Raising his wife up enough to lower her onto his erection, the soft sigh as he filled her body had Mason responding even more strongly than he had been. The plan was to take her slow and long but as usual, she had tricks that made him throw out all his plans and just work toward their mutual fulfillment.

Within moments they were kissing as he snuggled, into her neck. "You still get to me, love. How am I ever going to be in control when you make me so hungry for you?"

Grinning, she shrugged. "We can spend the night here. Molly won't know and you won't need to hold back. No one will hear us," Vicki said as she kissed his chest, rubbing her tongue over his taught nipples and then lower.

Mason was of two minds but both had him buried deeply into his wife again and soon. Without saying anything, Mason and Vicki walked together into the jail cell and removed what was left of each other's clothes, leaving them in a pile on the bare floor.

Mason swung the cell door closed. "This is getting

more and more like what I fantasized about that first night I arrested you."

"I wasn't sure what you had in mind but I think this comes close. Only then, I wasn't sure what it was all about. I thought you were angry at me." Vicki continued returning his kisses. She stroked her hands over his muscular chest and shoulders then down over his hips, enjoying the liberty of touching this man everywhere.

"No, love, I was never angry with you - maybe at myself. I should never have kissed you back then. I was misusing my power and my strength. I don't want to think I ever forced you to do anything you didn't want to do," he said pushing Vicki down on the cot, moving his mouth over her body then down between her legs as he eased himself onto her and apologized in his own way for ever mistreating her.

The sun was beginning to lighten the sky when Mason heard the keys in the jail's door. "Damn, we fell asleep, Vicki. Wilder's here."

And that's when Deputy Wilder came through the door to be met with a naked Mason face down on the jail cot and a grouchy order, "We're a little busy here, Wilder. Why don't you go away and get some coffee or something?"

Wilder grinned but looked away from the cell and his boss's naked buttocks. "Sure thing. I'll be back in half an hour." He turned to leave.

"Wilder, make it an hour," ordered Mason.

Wilder thought a minute. "If I've got an hour I'll go home and say good morning to my own wife." Then closed the door as Mason dropped his head into his wife's neck, chuckling.

"I feel like a teenage boy caught with his hands in

his pants." He kissed his wife on her lips than asked, "You got the keys to these damn cuffs or am I going to have to wait for Wilder to get done and come back?"

Coyly, Vicki asked, "What you going to do for me if I unlock you?"

"Just unlock me and I'll show you. I don't think you'll have any complaints," he told her, leaning down to lick her nipples as they puckered, waiting for more of his threats.

CHAPTER 6

Molly woke before the sun was even up, excited about getting her first project started. She didn't hear either Mason or Vicki so she quietly left to get a cup of coffee at the hotel's kitchen and check on how the day was going to progress. Oliver and Mrs. Whitehouse were already there, the breakfast meats and biscuits in the oven. A single waiter was preparing the tables by placing out jars and bowls of preserves and honey.

Mary Margaret, arriving to meet with Molly came into the kitchen, pleasantly surprised by the equipment available there. The two stoves and ovens. Although only one was being used at this time, both had water reservoirs and warming racks. There was also a hand pump, two sinks with drains evidently leading outside.

Clean pots and pans hung on the wall and over the central preparation table in the center of the room which was also where completed plates were placed for the waiters to pick-up. A stack of clean plates sat on the side of the warming shelf and the large pot of coffee was ready to fill the urns in the dining room.

Molly motioned Mary Margaret to follow her out of the kitchen. "See this dining room? It's set up for fine dining with linen and crystal. That has always been good for the hotel's usual guests but these men are sleeping four to a room simply to be able to afford to sleep inside instead of a tent. The town has some growing pains to get through and I'm hoping to help a little with that pain."

"I think the kitchen looks big enough to run two

restaurants out of with a little practice but where is it that I'm supposed to serve this food?"

"Right through here." Molly led her to a solid wall off the hall from the dining room. "On the other side of this wall is the saloon. I'm planning on getting Mason to agree to open a doorway between the two. Otherwise, its outside then back in. Probably through the back door or we can put a cook stove in the saloon's back room and keep foods warm there. Possibly cook breakfasts if we keep them simple enough. The saloon uses its backroom for kegs and there's not much of it. Surely not enough to keep foods for very long, at any rate.

"Besides, part of keeping the meal inexpensive was being able to use leftovers from one meal as a basis for another and using Oliver as the cook. It will help with the main dining room's food costs by allowing us to use up something that would have otherwise gone to waste."

Mary Margaret nodded. "Callie drilled that into us. She said the concept could be used weather we worked in a kitchen or our own homes. Nothing goes to waste, everything is used. We cooked the peach skins after canning peaches to make peach butter, the same as apple butter. Just squeeze the cooked pulp through a cheese cloth and there you have it. I started feeling a little sorry for the pigs and chickens because there was so little waste coming from the cookhouse kitchen. Of course, the men's appetites took care of most of the food so there really wasn't too many leftover's, either."

"I'll let you go over to the butchers once they've opened. We have a standing order for the dining room and you can pigtail unto that. Just keep the costs separate. Can you do that?" asked Molly.

"Again, Callie made sure we knew how to cost out

every plate we made. Of course, by the time I got there most of the meals were already done but every once in a while, we re-did them if prices changed. What was really fun was when one of the hands brought in some venison or prairie chickens and then the costs would drop. We felt like we struck gold because we had more money for the Christmas party," Mary Margaret said excitedly.

"The Christmas party?"

"Callie always wants us to be together for the holidays and we have a big Christmas party for the hands and all the neighbors. We take any savings from the meals and keep it to buy special items like smoked oysters and caviar. Exotic foods the men would never get a chance to taste. It's a lot of fun and, as you can imagine, the food and beverages at this party are out of this world. The housekeeper, Maria, brings in Mexican dishes and each of the rest of us makes our favorites plus candy and taffy and fudge. It's several days of eating more than we should and we sing and play games. You'll love it, I'm sure."

"It sounds like I've struck a good bargain hiring you then, didn't I? Just price out one of the weekly plans using the costs the hotel pays for things. Don't worry about purchasing spices and basics. Those we'll share for now."

Paul had his breakfast at the hotel, waited about an hour and felt it was a decent enough time to visit Colette, weather she was ready or not. He tried not to stomp since it would be paid for later with pain. Still, he reached the front door sooner than he thought would be possible and tried the handle to find it locked. He knocked and waited, then knocked again, thinking about going around to the back of the building and trying there.

He knew Colette could hear him and was simply trying to ignore him until he went away, but that wasn't going to happen with them ever again. Since being a young man in New Orleans, he had learned to speak his mind, not be so polite when he had an opinion. It had made for some uncomfortable times during his service but he had felt in more control. Taking orders but not necessarily agreeing with them. Changing his commanders' minds when placing a well-thought-out reason in front of those men had saved lives and he had become more assertive and self-confident because of it.

Just as he raised his hand again, Paul could see Colette coming from the back room.

She opened the door saying, "I've been to the butchers. Would you like me to cook you an egg or two to go with the ham?"

"You're actually offering to cook for me? Since when did you learn to do more than steep tea?" he asked, surprise evident in his voice.

"Many things changed during the war, *me amie*. I learned to do many things for myself. I had to as you must have had to also, *oui*?"

"I forget sometimes. It has been so many years and I've tried to get on with my life and not think about how it used to be. How I used to be." He looked down at the leg that was no longer there.

"You are right. We both should forget and go on to live our lives, *ne'st ce pas*? It will be for the best. We are different people and need to live in the here and now. So, do you want an egg?"

"No, no, thank you, I just finished with breakfast. I came over because I thought you could take that photograph Faith wanted for the paper," he said as all anger drained from him now that he felt himself relax in Colette's company. "You know, I could use a cup of coffee if you have it and keep you company while you have your breakfast."

Colette hesitated to accept then said, "Certainly, two old friends sharing a little time together won't be talked about." She led him down the short hall to her private quarters.

Mason entered the jail to find his deputy with his feet up on the desk and the chair tipped back, leaning against the wall. Wilder looked at his boss, who had high-color in his cheeks and asked, "Are we gonna need some kind of code or signal on the door so I don't barge in on you two again?"

"It's not going to happen again," said Mason. At Wilder's disbelieving expression said, "We'll think of something." And felt his cheeks flame even more while Wilder chuckled.

"So how do you think we can keep peace in the tent cities that are popping up? I heard there were gun shots out by the river last night," Mason said trying to get back on a proper topic. "If these men get laid-off due to weather or their jobs end...there could be problems. With the country in a depression some of these men have travelled hundreds of miles for this work. I can't see it lasting forever. Not unless Jeremy or Matthew have more up their sleeves."

"I'm not sure. I know the town pays us and the town doesn't go out that far so how does that affect our jurisdiction? I mean, when I was a bounty hunter, I had no limits but I know you did," Wilder said, a thin piece of wood he was chewing on sticking out the side of his mouth.

"I have to let a sheriff or marshal know if I'm in their jurisdiction but this is kind of no-man's land which usually means the closest lawman handles it. Of course, the Federal Marshall for the state can go anywhere. I guess we'll just keep treating it like an extension of the town, going down only when we need to. Call in the Marshall if it gets beyond us." Mason said reasonably searching for a clean cup for his coffee.

He continued, "The two of us won't be enough if we have to actually patrol it or something. We may have to bring Jeremy into this. He hired guards for the bank as it was being built, maybe he'll have to do the same with the tent cities. After all, they're his men."

"And with the other buildings going up, the houses on Second Street, for example, means these men are here for a while. I don't want to dig out any frozen bodies from the snow this winter. Half of them don't even own more than one set of clothes so getting enough to wear may become an issue. If they try to steal from one another just to stay alive..." Shaking his head, Wilder thought of other possibilities for problems.

"One problem at a time, Wilder. I don't want to get too far ahead of ourselves. Maybe Jeremy has a plan since he doesn't want the men to leave before he's done with them. And the town council will want some input on this, too, since it's their money paying us." Mason adjusted his hat and went out to find Jeremy.

Paul finally left Colette's after she chased him out and after she agreed to have dinner with him that evening. He headed back across Main Street to the hotel, wanting to ask someone about what wines the hotel had available. He was pleased to find they had a relatively wide range including many of his favorite California wines as well as French Champaign, which he would save for a more important celebration. One where he and Colette were back together.

After speaking with the waiter and explaining what he would like at dinner, he went to the front desk to get his mail. He had a discrete conversation with the young male desk clerk and then left the hotel, going past the jail, past the stables and turned on First Street where he found the large two-story house the clerk had described and climbed the steps to the front door.

After tapping on the door, an elderly woman with white hair curled and styled, and wearing a dress of excellent quality opened the door. She had a pleasant motherly smile. "May I help you?"

Feeling foolish, Paul glanced around saying, "Ah, sorry, I might have been given poor directions." And he started to back away.

"Oh, you've been sent by someone. Well, we don't get many afternoon visitors but I can get the girls to come to the parlor so you may talk with them. Our boarders don't get home till after five so you'll have plenty of privacy," the kindly older lady said, waving him into her immaculate parlor.

Not wanting to be seen hanging around on the porch of the local bordello, Paul removed his hat and entered the house. He could feel his face flaming. My God, was he actually blushing speaking with this grandmotherly woman about his needs? "I need, ah, I was hoping to need, I mean… I wish to buy a Goodyear."

"Oh, you need some protection. Very wise of you and very thoughtful. I have them right here in the drawer." She took the small packet and handed it to him.

Paul took the proffered item and still trying to get

his aplomb back, asked, "Could I purchase two, please."

"Of course, that will be a quarter," the kindly lady said. Then patted his hand saying, "This gets easier." Then showed him to the door.

Paul was back to the hotel when he realized he was still clutching the important little packages in his palm. He swallowed with difficulty and thought it sure as hell better get easier or the next time may kill him.

After lunch, Paul was more himself and sent a wire before going to the bank to work. He had some correspondence to see to and then sat back and thought about dinner with Colette.

Later that evening, he went to escort Colette across the street to the hotel. She was wearing a very attractive dress under a short cape and a little hat of feathers and netting that he felt suited her perfectly. After untying the ribbons at her neck, she handed the cape to the waiter who was standing there to take it. She sat elegantly as Paul pulled her chair out for her like he had done a hundred times before in another place - in another time.

The dress' décolletage was riveting, forcing Paul to memories of when they had been young and foolish and in love. When everything seemed to be sunshine and parties and long rides in the country. Before the war tore everything apart, destroyed their way of life, destroyed their love.

The waiter brought the California wine as Paul had ordered earlier that day and Colette was surprised at the quality. "I wasn't sure they had wine like this in Kansas. I find I don't think of even ordering wine with dinner very often. I find wine is better with friends, *ne'st pas?*"

"I always enjoyed wine more with you than anyone else so I guess I drink wine because it reminds me of you," he told her candidly.

"Really, Paul, you are such a flirt. I liked that about you right from the first time we met." She laughed and took a sip of the very good wine.

"And I loved you right from the first time we met," Paul told her honestly.

"Now, no more of that. It will only lead to recriminations and hurt feelings. Let us begin as we mean to go on. As new friends meeting for a nice dinner and evening of conversation," she said easily and raised her glass in a salute.

"So, the welcome I got the first night I was in town wasn't how you plan to go on?" he teased.

"I have apologized for that poor judgment. Please do not keep bringing it up," she said rather coolly.

"I hate to hear that, Colette. I found we are just as compatible now as we ever were." He held her hand across the table.

"Because, it is as you said, *me amie*. It makes you think of the past and that has been agreed to be left in the past," Colette reminded him of their pact.

Paul took his glass and held it up. "Then let this be for our new relationship and wherever that takes us."

Colette looked at Paul for any hidden meaning but raised her glass. "And to you."

After dinner, Paul reluctantly walked Colette home, getting a brief kiss on his cheek for his troubles. He limped up the stairs to his lonely room and empty bed and after undressing lay on the bed rubbing his wounded leg. He wished he had made more of an effort to hunt her down after the war ended but he hadn't had the energy. Nostalgia they had said. Soldier's Heart they called it. Irritable Heart Syndrome. All names for his melancholy that almost drove him to the end. At least, he had never gone far enough to have acute mania and end up in the Governmental Hospital for the Insane in Washington D. C. but not for lack of trying.

Between his physical pain and his mental anguish, it took him years to recover and then years to rebuild himself and his life. His new life without the woman he thought would wait for him. The woman who had filled his waking days with nighttime dreams.

Whatever it had been called, it was years before he felt alive and not just one of the walking dead. That was about the same time he had his permanent prosthesis fitted. Maybe becoming whole again made more of an impact on his life than he had realized. Now what could he do to help Colette begin to live again, too?

Colette lay in her bed naked, as she had always slept since hot humid nights of Louisiana. She didn't want to remember herself as a malleable young girl. Why hadn't she stood up against her parent and told him she wouldn't marry a man old enough to be her father or tell, Delmar, the man she was to marry, that she had already lain with another and was pledge to him. She had choices but she found she couldn't think without Paul being close.

She had given up living when he got on the train and left to join his unit. That was the last day she had felt anything except a deep loss. How had she not realized she had stopped living and now it was all too late? She almost wished that she hadn't found Paul again – almost. But even she couldn't lie that well to herself.

Now that he was so close, all she could think of was the two of them when they were so in love it hurt. And she had lived with the pain for years. She had finally put all that behind her. Made a new life but never a new love. Men had tried but she couldn't get over the loss she felt over losing Paul. Or thinking she had lost Paul.

She thought of the other night and how good it felt to lay with him. To touch him and know he was alive and real. A bit older but so was she. And wiser. That was why she knew she had to prevent herself from falling into a trap of her own making. Fall in love all over again only to be hurt when his time here in Sweetwater ended. She didn't want him to compromise his life for her. He hadn't the first time and she wouldn't expect him to this time. She wouldn't survive losing him again. Her heart had too many scars to live through another heartbreak.

It was best to leave it as it was. Simply knowing he wasn't dead should be enough of an answer to long lost prayers. He was hale and hearty and a man who seemed to have everything in hand. She should take that to her heart and hold on to it in the years to come.

CHAPTER 7

Molly looked excitedly at Mary Margaret saying, "Well, this is it. The bill-of-fare is printed on the chalkboard at the door and I'll help dish up if you get behind. Good luck."

"I feel like I'll need it." Mary Margaret stood in the empty saloon. The bartender had come in early to help in case he was needed and was setting out mugs for beer orders.

Franklin, a man of about twenty-four and well-built from years of hauling kegs around, had sandy brown hair and blue eyes and was considered very attractive with a strong jaw line and straight nose. He was wearing a long-sleeved shirt rolled up to his elbows and black and gray striped trousers. He had already dispensed with his vest since the day was turning into a scorcher. It was going to mean a long day for him but he was sweet to get up this early just to come in to get the lamps lit and act as a buffer if he was needed.

The first couple of men came in from the hotel, sitting at a table and looking around as Mary Margaret came up and asked them which they wanted for breakfast from the plates being offered. Today it was biscuits with sausage gravy, a large sausage patty, fried potatoes and two eggs or a slice of ham, two eggs, fried potatoes and slice of white bread for a nickel.

Neither man had read the bill-of-fare on the sandwich board as they came in and Mary Margaret got the impression they couldn't read. She was going to need to verbalize the selections and that was going to slow her down.

Both men ordered the same meal of sausage and Mary Margaret left to get them. The doorway had recently been cut through the wall so she was able to go directly into the kitchen from the hall and called out two sausage plates for Oliver to fill. He added the eggs right on top.

Mary Margaret took the plates and faced three tables full of hungry men, all eyes looking eagerly toward her as she returned to the saloon.

Franklin was busy pouring coffee for everyone and smiled encouragingly at her. He called out he needed five sausage and six ham plates. Mary Margaret nodded and turned back to the kitchen as soon as she placed the plates in front of the first two men.

She called out the needed order as she entered the kitchen and Oliver started putting them together. Then she carried a large tray to the saloon, passing out the plates as she placed them in front of evidently happy customers. It was extremely busy for about half an hour. With everyman fed and departed, she glanced at Franklin as they both laughed in relief.

"Well, tomorrow will go better," Mary Margaret said as she cleared the now empty plates and cups.

Franklin, with a wide grin said, "What do you mean tomorrow? These blokes are going to be back at noontime and probably with more men from the tents if word spreads."

The shock must have shown on her face because Franklin went to her side saying consolingly, "Don't worry, I'll help and they'll probably want beer at lunch so that means no pouring coffee. They were all happy when they left and they waited a lot less time than they would have if they had ordered in the hotel's dining room."

"I guess you're right but I hate to just be better than something worse. You know what I mean?" she asked, discouraged by the poor service she felt the men received at breakfast.

"We'll get better. I think the way that luncheon is set up, there will be a faster time for men to get their food and back out to work. It's certainly faster than the hotel's dining room. The men don't get an hour for a break and I know a hungry man can mean a grumpy man, and a hungry, grumpy man doesn't make a good worker," he told her trying to show her how important what they were doing was for everyone.

"I hope your right, Franklin. And I want to thank you for helping." She thought out loud. "I think if I place cups on the tables I can fill them as they sit down. If it gets too busy, I'll set a pot at each table for them to fill their own cups. This isn't fine dining."

"See. Now you're already thinking of ways to make the job easier. I knew you could work this out. You're in the planning stages, yet. And these men just want their food. Getting a good tasting square meal and at a bargain price should be considered a bonus."

Mary Margaret tried to agree but was still trying to figure out how best to get the service time down.

Franklin was right. Noontime was busier and having everything made ahead worked out well to get the men fed quickly. The men realized they needed to form a line, accept their filled plates and then get seated. Biscuits, butter and honey were on the table already and Mary Margaret came around placing their choice of dessert in front of them. They called out to Franklin if they wanted a beer which almost all of them did. There was coffee available for those who didn't. Since dinner was a more substantial meal, it cost ten cents not including the beer and the men flocked in.

She had just returned from taking the empty stew pot back to the kitchen for the scrub boy to clean when Franklin called across the bar, "See, now that wasn't so bad, was it?"

"No, that went as well as any meal at the Harrison ranch. Once the men get used to the system, I guess, we'll be fine. Now I don't want to run out of food and have to face an angry mob," she confessed with humor.

"These men are pretty tame comparatively. I've worked places where there were knife fights every night. Mason wouldn't allow that here which is one of the reasons I stayed on in Sweetwater," he admitted.

"So where are you from and how long have you been here?" Mary Margaret asked as she wiped off the tables.

Franklin leaned on the broom and thought. "I guess I came here about five years after the war ended. I'm originally from Ohio but I lost both my older brothers in the war and then my Ma died so I thought I would travel west where everything is clean and new. It still seems that way to me. Sheriff Mason and Mr. Thompson pretty much built this town. I mean, when I got here the buildings across the street weren't there at all and then Thompson brought a crew of men in and the next thing, we have a Main Street with stores and buildings and almost everything you may want to buy."

"I noticed everything looked pretty new. Not as fancy as you find in the big cities but nice and clean. I didn't realize that was one of the differences," she said as she stood from wiping the last table.

"Mason even sends Andy from the stable around to clean-up the streets of droppings every day. It's those kinds of things that made me want to live here and not move on."

"Well, again, I thank you for the help and I, for one, am very glad you didn't move on," Mary Margaret said as she turned and left the bar.

Mary Margaret prepared the meal selections for the supper, which would be the costliest of the square meals at two-bits not including beer presented in the saloon, but a lot less expensive than in the hotel's dining room.

Molly had been checking on Mary Margaret's progress all through the day to make sure she wasn't needed so when the two passed in the hall, Molly asked, "Still doing all right?"

"Yes, but I'm a little worried about the food getting cold before the men have all been fed. I mean, I don't think running between the kitchen and the table is a good thing but I'm not sure serving from the line is best with what we have on offer either."

"We can use the dining room's plate covers. I don't think the dining room is going to be so over-whelmed now the men are being fed in the saloon."

"Oh, like pie tins turned upside down over the food? That should work out. I'm afraid this is going to become more popular than we first envisioned. Many of the men were from the tents and they said they were tired of eating beans out of a can. They want meat and potatoes and apple pie," Mary Margaret repeated their requests ticking them off on her fingers.

"I'm glad that's what's on the stove then. If we run out, they'll have to be quicker in tomorrow night," said

Molly thinking about the profit margin.

"The men said Maria's husband, Carlos, has been selling enchiladas with rice and beans out by the river tents but he never has enough for everyone. The men have been pre-ordering and Carlos takes it out to them, fills their plates and then goes home. So, there is another source of food for the men."

That evening the men came in right from their work, excited about the new 'restaurant' in town that catered to them. The room had been separated, with most of the tables pushed toward the hotel side set with coffee cups and salts. The other side was for the bar patrons which were nil at this time of day now that Mary Margaret was serving a full meal for two-bits.

Approaching the first table that sat, she told the men the bill-of-fare for the evening. Vegetable soup and a choice of pork roast or ham or corned beef each being served with boiled potatoes, glazed carrots, succotash and rolls with apple or berry pie for dessert.

Hurrying back to the kitchen, she placed the order with Oliver then filled the soup bowls, delivered them and took the next table's order. By the time she returned to the kitchen with that order, the first was ready to place in front of the hungry men. She ran back and forth until all the tables were served and by then the first table was ready for their dessert.

The pie was already plated so she took a tray and disbursed them as the men finished their meal. She ran out of apple pie but the men didn't seem too upset about that and accepted the berry pie with equal enthusiasm. Most of the men hadn't had dessert since coming to town due to the expense so were grateful for anything.

As men finished, they moved over to the bar and

ordered another beer and she cleared then wiped down the tables. Some of the men stayed at the table where they had eaten and leaned back to give her leave to wipe the table in front of them.

Franklin kept a close eye on the men whenever Mary Margaret was around. When one man started saying things he shouldn't, Franklin took a piece of wood out from under the bar and gave him a man-to-man look. Everyone quieted down. Mary Margaret didn't enter the saloon after the meal was cleaned away so was unaware of the new house rules Franklin imposed on the men.

Basically, if they liked the improved food and liked the new prices, they had better curb their swearing, dirty stories, spitting, and keep their eyes where they belonged. And no one, not anyone, should take leave to touch Mary Margaret even by accident. Each rule was emphasized with the baseball bat hitting the bar top loudly.

Sheriff Mason had arrived in time to hear most of the rules and he tipped his hat at his bartender and left knowing that the new meals in the saloon seemed to be working out just fine. On the way out, he ran into Jeremy which was unusual since Jeremy never drank in the saloon. Jeremy didn't imbibe much at all.

"Mason, I want to thank you for allowing Mary Margaret to set this restaurant up for my men. It's hard enough to get men to travel all the way out here to Kansas but then to be unable to meet their living needs makes it difficult to get them to stay. I'm already paying top wages, two dollars and seventy-five cents a day and bonuses if the buildings get done on time," said Jeremy, one businessman to another. "If you need me to subsidize the food, I'd more than gladly do so."

"According to Molly, the women have that worked out. We should be making money over all, just not the same profit as we do in the dining room. But these men don't leave gratuities so the waiters do the work but get less pay when the construction men eat in the hotel." Mason explained the problem knowing Jeremy would appreciate the need to change locations.

"I'm sorry to hear that. I never wanted to be a problem, you know, getting Sweetwater growing. I'm not sure these men or men just like them aren't going to keep coming to fill the jobs that are here. Right now, I'm in competition with Chicago where the fire damage hasn't been replaced, yet. Even with the nation-wide depression it isn't easy to get experienced workmen and as long as contractors are needed back East, it will be harder to draw them here."

"I understand." Then thinking about it said, "Why don't you talk to the butcher's wife. I've been speaking with Thompson about leasing the building next to the butcher's shop and converting it into a boarding house with sleeping rooms upstairs and a few down with a kitchen and dining room. The butcher's wife doesn't speak English very well but there is a daughter and son who speak it just fine."

"Do you think this woman can handle a boarding house?" asked Jeremy. "I mean there's a lot of work there."

"It's a hard-working family and, like I said, they have almost grown kids to help. She's a good cook and keeps an immaculate home. It could handle maybe twenty, twenty-four men. That means a lot less tents," Mason advised. The two men went their own ways, both thinking about what the other had said.

Paul limped to the bank's big doors and had a smile ready as he opened them to find Jeremy Macgregor outside. "Well, Jeremy to what do I owe the pleasure? Come in to my office, the furniture arrived yesterday but then you probably knew that."

"I did. So, does that mean the grand opening is about to be announced?"

"It does. I plan on having an article in the paper and the photographer down here to commemorate the ribbon-cutting ceremony with the mayor and, of course, yourself," said Paul affably.

"I wouldn't miss it. But does that mean you can't talk business, yet? I have a proposal to put to you."

"No, I can talk business. I just don't have any tellers or an assistant manager, yet. I have some men coming in for interviews so I hope I can select someone from those candidates," Paul explained as he led Jeremy back to the office.

"My concern is that winter is coming and there are a lot of men living in tents. I don't want any casualties. These men, some of them at least, have families they want to bring out here to Sweetwater but there aren't any homes for them. I plan to build some modest single-story houses with an attic or loft space for children to sleep in. About the same size as the one the midwife lives in down across from the church."

Always looking for a good investment, Paul asked, "What do you think these houses would cost? And how many do you think you'll need?"

"I could build them for between three-hundred and three-fifty with a well and privy. The land belongs to the town and I think they will donate it to enlarge the tax rolls and to get homes for these families. Population seems to be power in the township wars of the state."

"So, do you need money for the lumber or labor or what were you thinking?" asked Paul, leaving Jeremy's needs to be told to him.

"I can cover the labor for the most part but not all the lumber and other building supplies. I was hoping you could offer some low interest loans to the men who want to remain in Sweetwater and buy the homes," Jeremy continued with his whole plan.

Peaking his fingers beneath his chin, Paul nodded slightly. "If the man has steady work, a skill-trade would be best, I would lean toward giving the man a loan. With unemployment at over fourteen percent men will probably jump at getting a job here. I think I can stand clear to offer mortgages at about twenty percent. That sounds high but it is about three to four per cent less than other banks will be charging."

Jeremy didn't hesitate. "No, I think that's fair. Hopefully some of these men are able to set some money aside to put toward the house and that will help lower the monthly payment. I'm going to build the houses as reasonably as I can and still have a decent product. Some of these men can finish the house off inside on their own and that could help keep the price lower, too."

"As long as the bank is happy with the collateral, there won't be a problem. Let me know how you progress and we can write up a formal commitment as soon as we have all the facts. Anything more I can do for you? What about your own home?" Paul asked knowing there were two large houses being built on Second Street for the Macgregor families.

"I built that out of my savings so I won't need a mortgage, thank you. Jessie's done the same. The houses should be finished in a week or two depending on the weather staying dry. Plaster won't cure if it's too rainy or humid and you can't paint until it's completely dried. My wife has changed her mind several times over the color of some of the rooms so I'm hoping it gets dry and painted so she can stop worrying. Any of the colors she's chosen would be good, but she needs to see it done. Once it's up on those walls though, it's there to stay."

Paul, after meeting with the men applying for his bank's positions, was happy with his final selections. All of them were going to work out well. He also realized the problem Jeremy was having housing new employees was also going to be his problem. These men would want to bring their families or at least not live in the hotel as he was doing but there were no houses. He would need to see if the buildings with upstairs' apartments along Main Street would be available for lease. He must remind himself to ask Jeremy about them.

That evening Paul tapped on the door to the photography studio with a bottle of Bourbon in his hand. When Colette opened it, he asked, "Do you mind if I come in? I need to oil my knee and I don't wish to drink alone again tonight."

"It sounds to me as if you have already been drinking," she said smiling as she walked back to her private quarters, Paul limping along behind her.

"Isn't there something more to be done to help you, Paul? I mean, it's been almost ten years."

"I know exactly how many years it's been. Who would know it more than me?" He sat down hard on the wooden chair next to the small table. Placing the bottle down, he asked, "Do you have a glass handy?"

"Of course. I see you at least drink the good stuff

and not something that will rot your gut," she said as she handed him two glasses.

Paul poured them both half-full and immediately drank his down, grimacing at the strong liquor or the pain in his leg. Colette couldn't tell which.

"It's funny but drinking actually makes me remember the war - not forget it," he said as he refilled the glass. "We drank so much between battles, justifying it because, hell, it may be the last good drunk we had in us, you know? For many of those young men it was. Every time I made it off the field, every time I saw all those graves, I thought why them. Why not me? Why Robert? Why Brian?" Then a pause, "Why Phillip?"

"Oh, Paul, don't think those thoughts. Your brother chose his own way. He would not have wanted you to take his place. He understood your views even if he did not agree with them. If people could take another's place in death, alter fate, then every parent would volunteer to replace a child who had died. What parent would want to live if their child was dead?"

She looked away from his tortured face and continued, "There should never have been a war but you and I disagreed on that from the start. You said the states should have worked out a proper agreement, learned to run the plantations without slaves, found a way to use paid labor, instead. It took four years, three weeks, six days to end a way of life that had taken centuries to create."

"I sneered at Phillip when he was one of the first to enlist, fight for the southern right to run their own states. Snubbing his nose at Washington and those who dared to interfere with his chosen way of life. I never got to tell him I admired his strength, his commitment to leave the comfort of our home, to live in the filth and stink of the battlefields. I had no idea what he endured fighting for what he believed in," Paul said before drinking down another glass of bourbon.

"Don't you think you have had enough?" Colette asked quietly, concern in her voice.

"Never enough," he told her. And took another mouth full.

"Paul, you must forgive yourself. After all, you fought for the South even though you did not believe in their fight. I guess that is why I did not understand why you left me voluntarily, to possibly die for something you did not believe in." She peered at him but saw the much younger man from her youth.

"I did go to die. I had no other thought when I left you. That's why I didn't ask you to marry me, to wait for me. I never thought I'd make it back to you and then when I did, you were gone," he said morosely.

"I would have waited if you had asked," she said, knowing that was the truth.

"It doesn't matter now, does it? Here we are and you won't commit to me, will you, Colette? Isn't that why I'm here and drunk and talking to you as if we might never see one another again?" he asked slightly listing from the chair.

"Let me help you, Paul. You said the other night taking the leg off, removing it helped ease the pain. Are we not good enough friends that you could do so here in the privacy of my home?"

"No, it's all right. It always gets like this after a long day and I walked to the train station several times today meeting prospective interviewees." He pressed at the top of the wooden leg where his own leg hurt the most.

"Let me, Paul" She reached over to him.

Paul was afraid to let her touch him while at the same time wanting her touch so badly.

"Do you need to lie down to remove it? I can help if…" Colette began.

"I'd loved to convince you I needed to lay down. Preferably, with a naked lady beside me to ease the pain but that wouldn't be the truth. Well, at least not the whole truth. I would feel better if the lady were you," he teased trying to ignore the burning pain at the base of his severed leg.

"I would do so if it would help but I think you are teasing with me so I will not do anything so foolish again. Now let me see it, in the light. Perhaps I can make it feel better by laying a cool cloth on it or perhaps a massage. I learned some techniques most recently."

Paul looked at her skeptically. "Why the hell not. You'll either accept me as I am or go running off into the night screaming. Your choice, I guess." He stood and began taking down his trousers, suspenders and all.

"Really, Paul. Take your coat off first, I do not know how you dress yourself each morning," she tut-tutted.

"Well, I'm usually sober by then so that seems to make it easier," he said handing her his coat and vest then pulling his suspenders down again, this time with success. He hesitated when he got to the trousers saying, "This is much easier when the woman involved is getting undressed, as well. Are you sure you won't join me?" He smiled a little boy smile that almost broke her heart.

"No. Now sit back down and help me take off this contraption," she said as she looked at the leather and cotton straps holding the prosthesis in place. The cotton pads fell away, showing the bright red stain of fresh blood.

"Oh, Paul, this cannot be right. To bleed after all these years. There must be something wrong. When was the last time a doctor looked at this? It needs to be tended to not simply ignored until it hurts so much you have to drink to get through the pain," she said kneeling in front of him, looking up at his agonized face.

"It's a lot less than many men had to endure. Now if you don't mind, I want to go back to the hotel," said Paul a lot more sober now than he was a moment ago.

"Paul, you have more than paid for your brother's dying on the field while you remained in the city. It does not balance out anything to keep living in pain. Phillip would not have wanted this for you and neither do I. Will you not try to see if a doctor can fix this? At least keep it from bleeding?" Colette pleaded with him.

"You don't know what I do or do not owe. I was wounded like thousands of others and I will live with the decision to go to war no matter what it costs me." He put his prosthesis back on pulling his trousers and suspenders up as he stood. He tipped his refilled glass to his lips and drank the glass down. Flipping his jacket over his shoulder, he left by way of the back door.

Colette stayed kneeling on the floor and the tears she feared to let flow while Paul had been there made rivulets down her cheek. She had not cried in years and almost ten years since crying for Paul but here she was again, in love, in pain and crying over the same man.

The next evening, Paul found himself with a message in his hand, delivered to him when he returned from the bank. Colette had sent the note and had made it sound like an emergency. The front door to her studio was open and she met him in the hallway looking calm and as beautiful as always.

"What happened? What did you need me for?" he asked gazing into her clear brown eyes.

"I have an offer. A tit for tat so to speak," she said coyly.

Paul smiled, hoping this wasn't merely a game Colette felt like playing. That possibly she was going to give him a reason to use those condoms he had in his drawer at the hotel. He leaned against the wall saying, "I'm listening."

"I want you to do something for me and then I will do something for you," she said, still an enigma.

"What are these 'some things'? Are they at least equal in some way?" he asked willing to play the game if he got the prize he wanted in the end.

"I think they are equal in their strengths of desire of both of us," she replied still not showing her hand.

"I think you had better get to the crux of the matter because my leg is beginning to ache," he said tiring of the game so soon. The pain interfering with what he really wanted to do.

"I want you to come with me for a few moments and then I will go with you where ever you want me," Colette said knowing she was gambling a lot on a little.

"Let me get this straight. I go with you and then you go with me? Anywhere? To do anything?" he asked to make sure he hadn't heard wrongly because his heart started beating much more rapidly as soon as the proposition was out of her mouth, her beautiful luscious mouth.

"Do you agree to the terms, Paul?" she asked seriously.

"Do I need an attorney to write this up or are you

trustworthy?" he asked still unsure of the game or the consequences.

"I am completely trust worthy. This is not something to hurt you," she confided.

"Now I'm frightened and intrigued. I will collect on this agreement, you know. It's something I've been dreaming of since the first night I was in town." He stared directly at her trying to discern any deviousness. But that had never been her style and he smiled, held out his hand saying, "Deal."

As they started to walk down First Street toward Miss Lily's house, Paul began to have second thoughts. Now what was Colette up to, to lead him to the only brothel in town? But to his surprise, she crossed the street and walked down the far side to the dark and closed Chinese laundry. Colette guided him to a hidden door, which opened before she could knock.

The house portion was small and crowded with unusual furniture, many things strange and exotic to the Westerners. A Chinese man with a little dark beanie hat came forward and bowed as Colette returned the bow saying, "*Ni hao*."

Then the man turned to Paul and bowed again. Paul followed Colette's lead bowing, also.

The other Chinese, all women from what Paul could discern, scattered into the bowels of the home, doorways covered by brightly colored fabrics and ribbons. The older man indicated they should sit so Colette and Paul sat on a type of couch, soft and covered in a beautiful silk embroidered scarf.

Colette said, holding Paul in place, "This is, Dr. Woo." She held tightly until Paul's first reaction to run was under control and he said between his teeth, "Is this the tit for tat, then?"

"You promised me. Now it's your turn to stick to your guns. Let Dr. Woo look at your wound to see if he has a possible cure or medicine to help," she said quietly trying not to let Dr. Woo know how much Paul wanted to leave.

But Dr. Woo, aware of the conflict between the two of them, was letting it work out to its conclusion.

When Paul relaxed back onto the cushion, Dr. Woo then indicated he wanted to see the amputated leg. Paul stood to remove his coat then his suspenders and pulled down his trousers to reveal the prosthesis. After removing that, he sat back down not looking at Colette.

Dr. Woo nodded as he examined the seeping wound, pressing on the flesh where the surgeon had cut off Paul's leg. Paul held his mouth firmly, not showing the touch was causing him pain.

Then the older man went to a table, pulled down jars, dried roots, and began mashing them in a pestle. Colette didn't say anything to disturb the quiet. Holding her breath, she hoped Paul would think the reward worth the pain and humiliation of having to expose himself to yet another person who looked at and prodded his injury.

The old Chinese man came back, smeared the paste mixture onto the wound, and made a pad of silk material using it in place of the cotton. Then he indicated Paul should put the prosthetic back on while handing Colette the rest of the mixture.

Before Paul could stand and leave, Dr. Woo held up his hand to stop further movement. He tugged on Paul's shirt to show him he wanted it removed as well as his trousers.

Paul   glanced   at   Colette   and   she   smiled

encouragingly. "I promised," she said reminding him of his reward.

He removed his shirt and lay face down on the cushioned couch as Colette moved to a nearby stool.

Colette leaned down and whispered, "I don't think you should watch this part. Just trust me it will help." She brushed her hands over his eyes to close them.

Paul wasn't going to let some voodoo doctor take advantage of him so he opened his eyes to see the reflection of Dr. Woo, Colette and himself in the glass case across the room. He almost got up demanding to be let go but the promise, his reward for doing 'this something', was still there holding him to his pledge as he would hold Colette to hers.

And voodoo doctor came very close to what Paul thought was happening. Dr. Woo selected a long needle from a case and inserted it into Paul's back just above his buttocks. Colette looked away, seemingly unable to watch him used as a pincushion. Then another and another, needle after needle inserted and then manipulated, turning and twisting with little to no pain to Paul.

Paul remembered hearing about the voodoo dolls and pins inserted to cause the victim distress and pain and sometimes even death. He had always thought it was only a story to keep the slaves from hiding in the swamps and bayous since that was where the voodoo always took place. He watched entranced with the sight of pins sticking out of him like the back of a porcupine.

He wondered if Dr. Woo was planning on putting so many needles into him there wouldn't be any more places to put one more but suddenly the doctor was pulling the needles, one by one, carefully out of his back and legs and even shoulders. Paul stayed still waiting to be told he could move so Colette couldn't claim he hadn't honored his part of their bargain.

Dr. Woo indicated Paul should redress and then bowed. Colette bowed also and said, "*Xie, xie*. Thank you so much, Dr, Woo."

As Paul and Colette were walking back towards her studio, Paul asked, "Should I have offered him some sort of payment or something?"

"No, Dr. Woo feels he owes me. I was taking photographs of his family doing the laundry and of his granddaughters playing. He asked if he could have the children's photographs. I made copies and gave them to him and I took one of the whole family and did the same. He sent them to his parents who are still living in China so they could see their great grandchildren. I was very moved that he wanted them to know they were doing well and what they looked like."

"I'm not sure I would have gone with you tonight if I had any notion what Dr. Woo was going to do, no matter what you promised me," he said teasingly. A few steps further he said, relenting, "No, I think I would have. I'd do anything to have time with you. Even letting some crazy old man stick pins in me."

"You looked! How could you. I certainly couldn't when he did it to me," she confessed. "But I knew they did not hurt, either."

"Do you mind if I go back to the hotel and rest? Can I claim my prize later?" he asked seriously.

"Certainly. Paul, I hope this will give you some respite from the pain."

"It seems to be already working." He leaned down and kissed her on her mouth, opened her door for her then turned back to the hotel.

That evening Paul's nightmare came back. Finding himself wandering through the fog-covered battlefield, stepping over bodies of young men, their faces blurred. Some wearing blue uniforms and some wearing gray, all having large stains of blood covering them.

He finds himself calling out, over and over, "Phillip, Phillip." Never getting an answer, never getting anyone answering him. They are all dead and then they are all gone. The fields are empty except for the cannons and guns and bullet shells, leaving only the smell of gunpowder and blood, two smells categorically linked in his memory.

Paul cries out for his brother again, "Phillip, Phillip." But he never finds him, he never finds his body. He wakes in a cold sweat, sheets twisted off his body but there was a difference this time. This time his leg wasn't in agonizing pain.

Paul rolled to his side, letting his partial leg lay on the whole one as he marveled the leg was free of pain. He would need to make sure to use that mixture everyday if just one use worked this well. Perhaps there could be some peace between him and his missing limb. It would be the first time in ten years if it were so.

The next evening Colette anxiously opened the door, glad Paul felt well enough to visit her. "I've been on pins and needles all day, dying to know if your pain is better."

"Now that's funny." He followed her inside. "Actually, I've felt better than I have since before the war. It's seven o'clock at night and my leg isn't hurting. I am sober and feel energized and somehow stronger. It's hard to explain but it's like I've awakened from a long nap or that I've been rejuvenated. I want us to renew ourselves, too. Were you serious about my reward or do you want me to accept my good health and painless day as reward enough?" he asked, his eyes beseeching her not to turn him away.

"I always pay my debts, Paul, and being with you can hardly be considered a hardship." She led him to the back of the building.

"Do you want a drink? I have the bottle you left the other night or sherry," she offered as a good hostess.

"I don't want anything to dull the memories of tonight, if you don't mind. If you need something, please go right ahead."

Colette smiled and took his hand leading him to the darkened bedroom.

"Going to bed before it's even dark out?" he teased.

"I want to enjoy as much of the evening, too. Do you have any particular fantasy you need to unburden yourself of?" she asked as she helped him remove his suit jacket and vest. As she untied the ribbon around his collar, he reached up and took her hands in his.

"I'd rather watch you undress if you don't mind."

"A promise is a promise." Smiling, she began to slowly take off her clothes.

He placed his hand over hers as she unbuttoned the top of her dress. "Don't do it if you're only fulfilling a promise. Do it because you want to be with me."

"I want to be with you, Paul. You know if I wanted to, I could have gotten you to Dr. Woo some other way. This is for both of us. I want to be with you again, perhaps for the last time," she said mysteriously.

Paul didn't like the last part of that comment but he'd deal with it later. Tonight, he was planning to enjoy his time with her. He continued to remove his shirt while sitting on the bed, removing his shoe and sock. Watching Colette remove her clothes one by one - the bustle and corset already on the floor next to the chair. Paul knew this was the happiest he'd been in a long time. She turned showing him her figure still covered by a lace camisole with burgundy ribbons.

"Do you want me to take down my hair?" she asked, both hands raised to the pile of curls at the top of her head.

A hissed, "Yes-s-s." It was all Paul could muster for an answer.

So, Colette pulled the pins out one by one letting the long tresses of hair to tumble below her shoulders, curling when it reached her waist.

"Don't tease me anymore, Colette, I don't think I can take it." He reached out towards her.

"Just let me remove this last little piece...."

And she didn't finish because Paul had pulled her unto the bed and was ravishing her mouth, cupping her breast through the sheer muslin and making humming noises, enjoying his attainment.

Finally, the ribbons were undone and the camisole pulled over her head to land on the floor with the rest of her clothing. Paul lay next to Colette, enjoying her body fully as he hadn't been able to the night in the hotel.

Kissing her mouth, he covered her lips, seeking entrance with his tongue, tasting her as if for the first time. He leaned down and placed his mouth on the most womanly part of her, feeling her startled reaction. He gentled her then placed a kiss using his tongue to learn about this new, more mature Colette.

Paul was taking his fill of her and she was allowing

him full control of her body and her pleasure - and this was pleasure, one she had not encountered before. She held his head, petting it as he brought her to completion.

He climbed up her body, kissing her breasts then her lips, using the same movements to lay claim to all of her, to re-claim what he always felt was his. He took a moment to put on the condom and entered her warm satiny channel, beginning the intensely satisfying stroking he knew he craved and she loved.

This wasn't going to last long. It never did between them. The feelings were too intense, too close to the surface, too enticing to be put off for long. And then they reached that point, the no going back point.

Paul thrust one last time as Colette cried out, "Oh, Paul, I love you."

Paul stayed all night and they made love again in the morning. It was the first time he had slept with a woman in his bed the whole night since he left to go to war. And the first night he didn't have the nightmares that usually caused him to cry out and wake himself from a sound sleep.

He held Colette and whispered, "I must leave or we will be discovered by some early rising neighbor and I don't want to have to explain anything." He kissed her on the top of her head and sat up in bed to reach his prosthesis.

"Don't forget when you get to the hotel to place some of that mixture on your wound," she reminded sleepily.

"I will, and change the cloth. The silk feels much better against my skin, too." Finally, he felt presentable enough to go back to the hotel by way of the alley then cut over to the stable yard.

As Paul crossed the road to the boardwalk on the other side, Mason came out of the jail. "Kind of early for a walk, isn't it?"

"Depends where you're going, I suppose," Paul answered undisturbed he had been caught coming back to the hotel so early in the morning.

"I don't usually interfere in a man's constitutionals but we take care of our women, especially women who have no other kin to watch over them." Mason said, his drawl becoming more pronounced.

"I don't have a problem with that, Sheriff. That's one reason I'm up so early - taking care." Then continued towards the hotel.

Mason watched the man leaving then to Colette's studio and re-set his ten-gallon Stetson. He returned to the jail apparently satisfied the banker wasn't an out and out scoundrel.

CHAPTER 8

Mary Margaret returned to the kitchen after serving the men their breakfast. As she thought, it was getting easier, now the men knew what to expect and Franklin was there to help collect the money and pour coffee. But she shouldn't depend on him since he still was the one who closed the saloon every night, too.

Molly came in all aflutter, her cheeks a pretty pink. Mary Margaret asked, "What happened? The nuns catch you making eyes at a boy?" Teasing about one of the worst acts you could do when at St. Michaels Foundling Home.

"Almost," she laughed. "I was paying a little more attention than I should to a new guest but I thought he couldn't see me. Then I realized he was watching me in that long hall mirror. I don't know if I can look him in the eyes now, not after this." Shaking her head, she put her hands to her cheeks trying to get relief from their blazing heat.

"Don't worry," Mary Margaret said. "If he was watching you in the mirror, doesn't that mean he was interested in you first?"

Molly stared at Mary Margaret with large eyes saying, "Perhaps. I don't know. I have never been this attracted to a man I've really never even met. He checked in yesterday while I was in my office and then I saw him last night and he nodded and smiled. Oh, he has a devastating smile with little dimples on both cheeks," she added to her friend in almost a squeak. "Then this morning he asked about meal times and that is when I was caught staring at him, probably with my mouth open. Oh, I do feel like such a fool."

Mary Margaret tried to calm her friend. "Look, you're making too much out of this, I'm sure. A handsome man gets used to women looking at them. They expect it even. Now go back to doing what you were doing. He'll probably be gone in a day or two and you won't have any reminders. Personally, I think, as women we should be able to look all we want until someone puts a ring on our finger."

Molly glared at Mary Margaret as if she had spouted blasphemy. "What would Sister Mary Margaret, your name sake, have to say to that?"

"Pretty much what I just said. She told me to check around, appreciate an attractive man but don't fall for a good-looking man but a good man with looks," Mary Margaret explained as she punched down the dough for the rolls she was baking.

Molly went back to the front desk, relieving Martin for his noon break. She picked up the ledger and looked through the few new arrivals. There were two, both with single rooms and both with indeterminate stays. Molly was so involved in trying to figure out which name belonged to the good-looking gentleman, she was startled when a well-modulated voice interrupted her.

"If I get any mail here will you notify me or should I ask each day? My name is, Elijah Winters, but most people call me, Eli."

Molly peered up into the bluest eyes she had ever seen. Up close they were so striking they almost made one stammer. Something she had failed to notice the other two times they had met since she lowered her gaze unconsciously whenever he was around, well, around and able to see her. He was about six-foot and slender but not skinny causing her breathing to increase in an alarming manner.

He had a tan, which may indicate he liked the out of doors and he was dressed in a business suit with vest, white shirt and bow tie. His bowler was held in his hand, allowing the cowlick to show in his dark brown hair. Molly had the strangest urge to brush it back into place.

"Um, we usually put a note in your room but asking here at the front desk is fine, also. We place it right here in the box for you." She indicated a small row of pigeonholes for mail and package deliveries.

"And do you provide laundry service? I have accepted a position with the First National Bank and will be extending my stay, if that's all right?" he asked his lips turning up on the corners.

"Certainly, and that was for Mr. Winters, then?" she said as she made some marks in the guest book as if she hadn't already memorized his name.

Molly's knees actually trembled by the time Elijah, no, just Eli, had left. She wasn't sure what was happening but she had to get over this, this lusting for one of the hotel's guest. She had never had the urge to become more familiar with any guest she had checked in before and she had handled thousands of check-ins.

This was getting dangerously close to a reason for dismissal. A woman in this business, in particular, needed to maintain the highest standards of propriety. It should never appear as if a staff-member were available for improprieties. Molly was very strict with this rule with her staff. Now she had to remember those rules apply to her as well.

Molly almost groaned in her embarrassment, trying

to think over the man's reactions and find any indication he sensed the conflicting emotions going through her every time she saw him. She hoped not, she really, really hoped not. Trying to get back into her work, she had difficulty staying on task.

The next few days passed quickly, with Molly having limited contacts with the handsome Eli. Usually he came in when Martin was on lunch break. Evidently the bank closed at noontime and Eli came back to the hotel for his meal. Molly wasn't sure that was going to be the schedule once the bank opened officially.

At the end of the week, there was to be a ribbon cutting and celebration the hotel was catering, as well as a large decorated cake coming from her sister, Callie, out at the Harrison ranch. There was to be a band, too. A different kind of ending for summer.

Paul entered the studio hoping to find Colette there but the room was empty. He called out, not wanting to intrude upon her personal rooms until they were more formally attached to one another. He wanted Colette to feel as if she were in control of how fast they moved towards becoming a couple again. As long as she didn't push him out completely, Paul thought he could wait.

Of course, knowing she was only across the street from his room and in a big bed by herself was playing havoc with his sleep but it was better than the nightmares he used to have. Now when he closed his eyes, he saw a beautiful naked Colette - not the stench and decay of a battlefield days after the generals called a halt to the killing.

Colette came through the back door, saw him standing in the front and quickly came to meet him, "I'm sorry, Paul. Did we have an appointment?"

"No, I wanted to ask if you would be my personal guest this Friday, you know, a sort of hostess?"

"I do not think that to be wise, Paul. I will be there to photograph the festivities but not to participate in them, *ne'st pas*? I will enjoy everything through my camera," she said hoping to take the sting out of the rejection.

"I was merely being optimistic and eager to visit with you again. A dinner and then some time alone, reminiscing."

And Colette was under no delusion as to what he wanted to reminisce.

"Paul, you know I planned on that being a onetime reunion. I was merely paying a debt, one that I enjoyed most thoroughly, I admit."

"Why can't you let us have a chance again? I've changed since coming here. You helped me get my wound healed. It no longer hurts or swells as it did. It feels firmer and the skin looks healthy, like new skin almost. I don't know what that voodoo doctor did but I've actually been back to him and let him poke me full of holes again. Do you know what that silly old man did? I laid out a twenty, ten, five- and one-dollar pieces in my hand for him to take his payment for the treatment and he took the dollar. I tried to pay him more but he refused to take it. It was the darnedest thing. I mean, I would have given all my worldly goods to be free of that pain and he takes a dollar."

"Dr. Woo is very humble in accepting payment for his abilities. I think he feels he owes it to people to help where he can."

"Well, I'm a believer. I've never felt so well or so, mmm, let's use the term, amorous." He leaned down to nuzzle Colette's neck.

Colette jumped back away from him. "Stop that. Someone could walk by and see us through the window."

"You win for now, Angel, but don't plan on sleeping alone forever." He replaced his hat then left smiling.

Colette stood for a moment. Angel, he had called her, Angel. She hadn't heard that endearment from his lips since the day he left her crying in New Orleans, the day he left her to get himself killed.

It felt like yesterday. His leaving after days of arguing and recriminations. Tears as well as shouts and demands as well as promises. Nothing kept him from what he felt he owed his brother, Phillip. Simply because the brothers hadn't agreed on what should be done about the war. About their state succeeding from the union. Joining the Confederation and settling how the citizens would go on from there.

Phillip took less than a day to decide to go to war. To fight the North in the War of Southern Rebellion. A righteous and virtuous war to save the South's way of life. The right to have and keep what is theirs. The right to decide how to manage their property and livelihoods.

She remembered the arguments between the two brothers. Remembered hearing the final argument as Phillip told Paul he could stay home and ignore his duty. That Phillip would uphold the family honor and, in a few months, when the conflict was over, Phillip expected his younger brother's apology for arguing against the Southern principles. A way of life that had given them everything they had and owned.

That argument, those words, rang out and echoed between their city homes. Being neighbors had made the two families close, at least the children and Colette had known both men as young boys. But it was Paul who won her heart and hurt her as no other could ever do.

Having seen so many march off to war, she thought Paul the one male not dominated by the need to fight in battles. How foolish of her to think that. Once news of Phillip's death came back in a letter sent by the commanding officer of his regiment, Paul's only thought was to replace his brother in battle. To take up the arms he had avowed as unnecessary and against common sense.

Her last memory was of him getting on a train taking him to the front while she tried to argue he needn't go. He didn't need to leave her. That she didn't care if others had left their wives and loved ones.

What hurt the most was that he never expected her to wait for him. He never asked for her to wait for him. Her finger was as ringless that day as it had been since birth. There would not be a commitment to return to her or for her to be waiting when he did. It was as if he had decided there was no future for them even after she had given him her virginity. Even after she had begged him to stay at home with her.

CHAPTER 9

Colette, fully clothed, sat in the dark cavern of Dr. Woo's home waiting, not sure how to explain her malady. She wasn't exactly sick but she didn't feel well, either. She was hoping it wasn't a side effect of any other illness or that it was an indication anything was getting worse. Her worries were interrupted by the old worn Chinese gentleman.

He looked closely into her eyes. Pulling the lid up. Then he sniffed her breath and Colette immediately felt embarrassed thinking her breath might smell from something she had eaten. Then he lifted her wrist and smelled that. For some reason, Colette was more embarrassed at this intimate exploration than she had been when she was stark naked and the doctor was poking those sharp little needles into her skin.

Dr. Woo said something in Chinese and at Colette's dumbfounded look called out for his granddaughter, Mei. The pretty young woman came into the room and bowed to her grandfather and then to Colette.

Dr. Woo said something in Chinese to Mei and then she smiled at Colette saying, "Be be."

Looking at the girl, Colette said, "I'm sorry, I don't understand. What is be be?"

Mei smiled widely and said, "Bebe." Then folded her arms as if holding an infant and rocked them.

Colette's eyes went wide as she said, "No, oh, no, that is not possible. I mean, I never could have, I mean, I cannot...." That is when she remembered her impulsive behavior and Paul's enthusiastic welcome his first night in town.

Walking home in a daze, she thought she waved to Miss Lily on her porch, but now wasn't sure. Oh, if this was true it was the worst and best news she had ever gotten. Now what was she supposed to do? Go back and hide in Chicago? She still had friends there who would stand by her. Artistic types that had a different set of mores they lived by.

She was sure some of her new friends she had made in town would stand by her, too. But that didn't make it easier for the child, especially when it got to be school age. And what would Colette do if her other secret was discovered?

Perhaps coming to a small town hadn't been the best plan for her after all. But then, if she hadn't been in Sweetwater, she wouldn't have met Paul again and she wouldn't be in this situation. Colette went to lie down, she had too much to think about and none of it sounded good.

A baby, a child. Being a mother of a child, she never thought to have. And the father was the one man she thought it could never be. Her life had taken another dramatic turn and she couldn't be sorry about this one no matter how she looked at it. She would be a mother and she would cherish the gift. How could she ever not cherish this child? It was as if someone searched her heart and found the one perfect reward to replace all the pain and loss she ever felt.

A calm came over her and she knew she wouldn't run and hide. Couldn't run and hide, not again. No matter what the outcome of anything else, Sweetwater was where she would raise this child and live everyday as if it were her last. Her new friends would see her through and help her, she knew without hesitation.

Paul, even though she knew him to be busy, came down to help Colette move the camera and equipment to the front of the bank. There were bunting and large American flags flying in the breeze. It was going to be a sunny day, which was good for Colette as long as the people didn't need to face into the sun and end up squinting. But this was still morning and the sun was going to be perfect for taking photographs with the bank building in the background.

Setting up the easel, she explained what she was doing to the children who were starting to collect around her and the equipment. She didn't mind their inquisitiveness as long as they didn't touch anything. Little finger prints in the wrong place could mean disaster later. She waved to her friends, Hope, and Callie Harrison, who were setting up the refreshment table with a large cake and pitchers of ice tea and lemonade.

It appeared Jeremy had let the construction workers off work to come to the celebration and reap the rewards, so to speak, for finishing the building in a timely manner. They seemed to be a friendly group and blended in for the most part with the other working people of the town. Her new acquaintance, Mary Margaret, stood on the boardwalk in front of the saloon but didn't come down to the end of the street. She was probably watching things on the stove and couldn't get away.

Paul came over to ask solicitously if there was anything, he could do for her and she wondered if, somehow, he knew what Dr. Woo had told her. But she dismissed that idea. Paul was merely being considerate since he had hopes of visiting her bed again.

She wondered if he would be as willing to do so if

he knew she was expecting and would be getting fat and ungainly in a few months. She smiled at what she imagined she would look like and then shook her head, trying to clear the image. She had to pay attention to the here and now. One day at a time, like she promised herself when she got her first prognosis.

Soon the band started-up an opening song. The people, who had been milling about, gathered to listen to the speeches prepared by the mayor and then, Jeremy, and then, Paul. Every man said what a proud and happy day this was for the town - a day to put the town on the map, a day to celebrate the town's prosperity because only a prosperous town would have a bank like this one. Only the good people of Sweetwater could make it happen.

Colette had heard similar speeches before at every kind of grand opening from town halls to schools to hospitals. All important milestones in a town's life, each to be commemorated in photographs, all putting a little money into her pocket.

Pulling herself together, Colette tried to stop being so cynical. It couldn't possibly be good for the baby. Stopping a moment, she realized she had already accepted the child as a human being she would be responsible for. She smiled to herself, knowing she was going to be a mother after all and what a truly wonderful thing that was.

After the actual ribbon cutting, Colette took time to visit with the towns' people she knew and to meet some of the new ones. Which included the very handsome, Eli Winters, who had every female eye on him although he didn't appear to notice. He was talking with Molly, the hotel manager who was pointedly ignoring him. He didn't seem to notice her snubs, either, so Colette thought there was more there than what was showing.

Colette gathered her equipment offering a penny to one of the older boys to help her carry it back to the studio. When she got there, she took off her hat then undressed and lay down on the bed hoping the strange feeling would settle or go away.

She woke up to Paul replacing the damp cloth on her head with a cooler one, a worried expression on his face. "Are you all right? Did it get too hot for you in the sun? I always think woman are foolish to kill themselves for fashion. Why cinch yourselves up in those damn corsets and then add a bustle as well as a hat and gloves? My God, its ninety degrees out there." He brushed the stray strands of hair from her forehead while staring into her eyes.

"And that coming from a man wearing a suit with shirt, vest, cravat, drawers, socks and top hat?" she replied drily in return.

"Maybe we both have too many clothes on." He began to undo his tie.

"Wait," Colette ordered. "Don't get any ideas. Making love in the hot afternoon is the furthest thing from my mind, right now."

"Oh," he said in understanding. "One of those days is it? I can wait…again." And he leaned over and kissed her. "Is there anything I can get you before I need to return to the bank?"

"No, I'll be fine. Just maybe a little too much sun is all," she lied knowing that her body was reacting to the new little person she was growing.

"I'll check in with you later, anyways. Maybe bring you supper?"

Then he left the room, left Colette feeling more ill than before his talking about food at a time like this. Colette would need to visit Rebecca, the midwife in Sweetwater, to make sure she knew what to do as a first-time mother.

She had liked the idea of making love in the afternoon with Paul but wanted to make sure doing so wouldn't harm the baby. It would be easier to get Paul to go away now before they started something rather than later, after they had become intimate on a regular basis.

Colette sat on the edge of the narrow cot in the back room of the midwife's house. Rebecca, a competent young woman, said, "I agree with Dr. Woo about the pregnancy. I'd say maybe in about seven, seven and a half months. I would like you to visit me each month. Not that you're too old to give birth to a healthy child but this is your first and I like to make sure my mothers are kept up-to-date on everything. I'll weigh you, check your heart rate that sort of thing. Nothing uncomfortable.

"I also consult with mothers as to how your body will change, how your needs may change over the months. There are many good ideas out there and we should select the ones that will work best for each one of us. Eat milk and cheese, meats and vegetables and fruits. Try to cut back on sauces and bread. I know it's not easy. I can preach but I can't follow my own advice. I gained forty pounds with my baby and it took a while to get back to where I was. I had to give up Miss Lily's cookies which was a true hardship," Rebecca told her laughing.

Colette was unaware of Miss Lily's cookies so was surprised that Rebecca, the minister's wife, actually had contact with Miss Lily socially. Colette had to re-evaluate her thoughts about the midwife and decided she liked the plain-speaking woman. Rebecca knew Colette was a widow, a widow whose husband has been dead for years. The how didn't seem to matter to the other woman. Colette felt this woman would cosset her through this pregnancy and become a very good friend in the process.

When Colette first opened her studio, she became friends with many of the younger wives in town, some with children, while others were still newlyweds. If they accepted her pregnancy as well as the minister's wife had, the possibility of her remaining in Sweetwater was good. The smaller town was still her first choice of where to spend the rest of her life. She had decided that before leaving Chicago and her life there.

Maybe staying in Sweetwater to have and raise her baby wouldn't be too bad after all. It would depend on whether Paul should end up leaving before the baby was showing. She could not stay if Paul was there, it would break her heart. And he…what would he do? What would he expect? Access to the child, at the very least. Family had been the most important thing in Paul's mind at one time. At the time he chose to go to war over remaining with her.

CHAPTER 10

Molly walked quickly and almost had her office door closed when Eli said, "Miss McGuire, Molly, please don't shut me out."

"I'm sorry, Mr. Winters, did you need to see me about a hotel matter?" she asked in her most business-like voice.

"I've been pleasant to you. I've been polite and I've been consistent with my regard of you. So, if you call me Mr. Winters one more time, I swear, no matter where I am, I'm going to kiss you right on the mouth," he warned, tired of having to chase this woman.

Molly started to say, "Mr. Wi..." And stopped. Looking up into the determined young man's face, she began again, "Eli, I am honored with your regard but I cannot be seen fraternizing with a hotel guest. It is a very established rule for all hotels and in place for a very good reason. A hotel guest is exactly what it implies - someone out of his or her home area and living temporarily in another. It is easy to mix loneliness with true feelings and it is up to the hotel staff member to keep the boundaries. A guest is not an acceptable associate."

Eli looked at Molly and then asked, "How many times have you had to give that speech to some little housemaid or waiter? That's not what this is and you know it. You feel it, too."

"It doesn't change the fact, Eli. I can't be seen as if I am showing you favor. It causes all sorts of trouble. Please understand my perspective." She pleaded with her eyes as well as her voice.

"So, if I were to say live somewhere else, like move out to the tent camps, then you will allow me to speak with you about something other than my bill?"

"Yes, I guess so, but you can't move out to the woods in a tent. You are the assistant bank manager, for goodness sakes. What would people think?" she told him, exasperated with his thinking.

"Maybe they would think, hey, that fella must really like Molly if he was willing to live in a tent just so she would talk with him," he teased now she was meeting his gaze when she spoke to him.

"You are the silliest man, I swear. Why can't you see I have to set the example for the rest of the staff? I need to be above reproach or the hotel's reputation could be harmed and that means Mason and Vicki and the Whitehouses would be harmed. I can't be the cause of them losing everything," she said earnestly.

"Neither can I. That's why I'm giving you notice I will be vacating my room by this Friday and moving into the new rooming house across the street. Paul, I mean, Mr. Weaver, has made it possible for the German family to run a boardinghouse since there are so many single men coming to town and we all need a warm place for the winter. I'm planning on having a house built for me so if I can't get it done by this winter, it will be first on the list for next spring, Macgregor said."

"I wasn't aware it was opening so soon. That will help ease the room shortages at the hotel then, too. I know the construction men find living here a little expensive along with buying their meals. Does Mary Margaret know about the change do you think?" Molly worried about the ramifications of opening another place that will serve food to the construction men, too.

"I'm not sure. I don't know anything except they took out an upstairs' kitchen and turned the spaces into sleeping rooms. There will be a parlor and dining area downstairs. No smoking, no spitting and no women were the rules I understood from Mrs. Burgess. And hearing that from her made me feel like my father was giving me my lecture before going off to college." He chuckled at the expression that crossed Molly's face.

"Oh, really, Eli. You shouldn't say such things to me. What would people think if they heard you?" she said as she thought what the nuns would have said about such language.

"They would think I was the luckiest of men because I was talking to one of the prettiest girls."

"Are you Irish by any chance? We had a lot of Irish in the home where I was raised and you sound a lot like one of those boyos and that is for sure," she said imitating a perfect New York Irish brogue.

"I'd like to know more about your growing up, I think, but I have compromised you enough for today." He leaned down and kissed her on her surprised mouth before she knew what he was doing. Then he was gone.

She touched her lips thinking he had tasted pleasant, the only term that came to mind. She would hold that taste in her memory of her first kiss forever. She leaned back against the closed door and smiled.

CHAPTER 11

Colette was sitting in the studio, studying the negatives, which would not stop wavering in front of her eyes. Putting on the tinted glasses the doctors had given her helped but it was no use. She would need to wait for her eyes to be less fatigued before she could choose the photographs to place in the paper. Or she could simply hand them all to Faith and let her do the selection. That sounded like the best idea.

Turning to go to the back to get the eyedrops, she realized Paul was at the door, watching her through the glass. She responded angrily because she was so weary, she hadn't known he was there, "What do you want now? Go away, I am tired and want to be alone."

"And grumpy by the sounds of things. I brought that dinner I promised and not any too soon." He placed a covered plate and bowl on the table, watching her fumble trying to hide the glasses in her hand.

"You do look tired. Do you have a fever? Should I call the doctor over to check you?" he offered as he led her to the back bedroom.

"I don't want to go back to bed. Please just leave me, Paul." She swayed as she went to sidestep him. That's when Paul swung her into his arms and carried her to her bed, laying her on the comforter.

"I'm fine. Simply allow me to lie quietly for a minute. Let the room stop spinning," she said waiting for her stomach to catch-up with her body.

Looking down on the bed, Paul picked up the tinted glasses, looking them over then asked, "What are these for?"

Colette opened her eyes long enough to see what he held then said, too weary to lie, "I use them when my eyes get sensitive to the light. I do not need them most of the time, yet."

"What do you mean, 'yet'?" He jumped on her misspoken word.

"Just what I said. I wear them when I need to and I do not when I do not!" Losing all patience with his questions and the heat and this dizzy feeling that kept making her stomach want to give up its contents, which wasn't much.

"I'm sorry. Rest and I'll be within calling distance if you need me," he said taking the glasses with him.

Paul stared at the little bottle of liquid he held in his hand. The directions were clearly written on the wrapper and he was trying to figure out what exactly that meant for Colette. After an hour, Paul heard Colette moving around in the bedroom and went to the door to confront her.

As soon as he saw her though, all recriminations died and he asked gently, "Are you looking for this?" He showed her the small blue bottle palmed in his hand.

"I, I, yes, thank you. They help rest my eyes." She reached out for the bottle.

"Can I help?" he asked quietly.

"No, I do it by myself easily. It seems a lot easier then strapping on a prosthesis and learning to walk all over again." She threw the ball into his court.

"Touché," he said as he gave the bottle up. "Can we talk about this at least? I went with you to Dr. Woo's," he reminded her

"I had to bribe you with sex," she replied getting

some of her sense of humor back.

"I can offer you the same bribe." He smiled back at her.

Colette put a couple of drops in each eye blinking rapidly as the medicine began to work. "That is better. Thank you for staying but I assure you I am quite all right now."

"Do you get dizzy with this, too? Should you be moving around alone here?" he asked trying to find out how ill Colette was.

"No, that was due to not eating as you said. My eyes are fine. They merely get tired some days with too much close work in the bright light," she repeated the lie easily.

"One thing we always had between us was honesty. I'd hate to think we lost that, too," Paul said sadly.

He was right. They had never lied to one another and this was such a small thing between them. It would convince him they no longer had a chance of ever being together in the future. "I am going blind but it should not happen for a while, possibly years," she stated unemotionally.

Paul took a minute to soak up the information and asked, "You're sure? Can we get another opinion? See someone with more experience?"

"I saw a specialist, a doctor who trained under a Dutch doctor, Franciscus Donders, who has done a long study on this type of blindness. I will get poorer and poorer vision until most of my vision will be blocked out, possibly allowing some peripheral vision of light. They are not sure how long it will take since it usually begins when a person is older but my mother was quite young when she started having symptoms, too," she told Paul not seeking any pity or special attention.

"If I took you to the Dutch doctor…?" began Paul but was cut off.

"*Non, me Cherie*, he cannot do anything either. I fought for the first year, went from one doctor to another trying all sorts of therapies and possible remedies. Even here, I sought out Dr. Woo when I found he did acupuncture, seeking the cure that does not exist," she told him and shrugged.

"But your work, you're so young…." Paul began his arguments once again.

"That's one reason I came to Sweetwater. I was seeking a small town that did not have a photographer and this town came up on the list. I thought I would be able to maneuver around a smaller town. As I lost my sight, I had planned on selling my equipment and business and live upstairs while the new business owner paid me rent."

"I think that was a very sound plan. But now you have me and we can figure out a plan that includes me," he said taking her hand.

"Oh, Paul, you don't want to saddle yourself with a blind woman. I can understand that. I would not blame you for saying goodbye right now. You do not owe me anything and I do not expect anything from you. I will go on after you leave Sweetwater and we will have our memories to live with. I am grateful we had this chance to mend what we had broken so many years ago." She patted his hand but retaking hers, placed them in her lap.

"I won't be saddling myself with a blind woman. I will be choosing the woman I love, have always loved. It's up to you whether we do this as a married couple or with me sneaking in here every night."

"I have a plan," she started to say.

"And a very good plan it was, too, for one person. Now there are two of us and that means we need a new plan. It doesn't mean we have to throw out the old one but it may need adapting."

At the mention that it was now two of them, Colette was shocked into reality. She was already 'two'. In essence, he would be making plans for three but did she want his pity to save her from living her life blind and alone. Or could she envision them as a family? This was something she needed more time to figure out.

"I'm still tired. Would you mind letting yourself out?" she asked playing on his sympathy.

"Of course not. Are you sure this tiredness isn't related to the other?" he asked concerned.

"*Non*, it is just that time of month." She grabbed the first excuse that came to her, strengthened by his original misunderstanding earlier that day.

Paul leaned down and kissed her forehead. "I'll speak with you tomorrow then, good night, Angel."

Undressing, she slipped on a light muslin nightgown. She thought she was well-rested and would take this time to think on what Paul had said. She tried to think about what to do with her life now she was to become a mother but before she had formed any conclusions, she fell asleep again.

Molly was working in the office after dinner the next afternoon when Mary Margaret came in, excited, almost jumping up and down.

"Faith just told me they would be in their new house within two-weeks and then I can move upstairs. There is another bedroom for you if you want it."

Molly didn't need to think long and answered, "That would be wonderful. I really feel that I am intruding on

Mason and Vicki. I mean, they are newly married and Mason has such a varied work schedule. I stay here as long as I can in the evening but eventually, I need to return to their home. It is a little distracting having that big handsome man there. Not that he has eyes for anyone but Vicki, it's simply that I cannot sit and complain about woman stuff because Mason could be coming in at any time."

Mary Margaret said, "You don't need to explain anything to me. I, at least, can slip away downstairs so I don't have to watch Faith and Jeremy bill and coo at one another all evening. They're just waiting for me to leave and then I hear them head for their bedroom. It's rather embarrassing if you think about it so I try not to think about what's going on. Sometimes I think they're in the bath tub together. Maybe it's to cool off?"

Both girls thought about that for a moment and then glanced at each other shaking their heads and laughing.

Mary Margaret said, "We have to get into a place of our own. I remember Callie trying to explain these things to Beth and me. I wasn't understanding anything and Beth was next to horrified. Now Beth is all blaze` about married life and I'm here growing into a spinster."

Molly stared at her friend in disbelief. "You are not a spinster by any means and if you wanted to be married you certainly could be, I'm sure. You put up some kind of wall or something to keep men at a distance. Open up a little. With all these men around, one of them should meet your exacting standards."

Looking to get some information out of her friend, Mary Margaret said, "Well, there is that good-looking stud here at the hotel. Mr. Winters, I think his name is. Works at the bank, clean and always so respectably dressed. I wonder what he looks like with fewer clothes."

Molly had been getting redder and redder as she listened to Mary Margaret speak about a man, she had been pushing away for the past few days. She didn't like the thought of Mary Margaret thinking about Eli in that manner – undressed that is.

"I do not think we should be discussing gentlemen, dressed or undressed, if they are guests at the hotel. We are employees and should respect the privacy…."

"I understand, Molly, hands off. All you had to do is tell me and I would have left him alone," interrupted Mary Margaret as she got up to leave the office. "I was only teasing to see if you would respond and you did. I wish you the best of luck with him."

Before Molly could think up anything to say in response, Mary Margaret was gone and she couldn't get the picture of what Eli might look like with fewer clothes on out of her mind.

Colette thought things couldn't get more complicated until she looked up to see Thom Thompson entering her studio. He was the son of the mayor and also the son of the nosiest neighbor in the world. The young man had shown particular interest in Colette before returning to Topeka to work for a senator there a few months ago.

"Why, Thom, it is good to see you looking so healthy. City life must agree with you." She put out both hands to clasp his and to keep him from leaning in for a kiss. Colette air-kissed both of his cheeks but he didn't seem to feel rebuffed.

"The capital is great. I mean, it's still growing and there are exciting amusements. The circus was recently there and is now heading to Washington. They have special train cars for the wild animals and everything. Then the opera house has had something new almost weekly. You'd love being there, I know you would," he enthused.

"I'm glad you find it so enlightening. I actually prefer Sweetwater. I had enough of the other when I lived in Chicago, before the fire, of course," she said to keep the conversation going along these nonpersonal lines. When Thom left weeks ago, he had indicated he would come back and have a more sensitive offer for Colette then, after his job was secured in the capital.

"Mother wrote me. She said the new banker was taking an interest in you and I felt I must come back to make sure you knew of my intentions, you know, between us," he said brashly.

Colette was at a loss. She never meant for Thom to assume she was waiting for him to declare himself. She had decided, although Thom was a very nice man, he wanted different things from life than Colette did. His mother would be the mother-in-law from hell and having a blind wife would not be to a politician's benefit. But the most obvious misconception was that she loved him.

"Thom, I thought I made myself clear before you left. Although I find you attractive and an entertaining companion, I wish to live here in Sweetwater just as I am. A single business woman."

"But Darling, really, the capital is the place to be and this little business of yours is well, it can be a hobby. You know, taking photographs of our children and perhaps our friends' children. I'm not saying you can't take photographs. I'm merely thinking that with everything else going on you'll be too busy." He smiled that friendly open smile that had made him so attractive to her in the first place.

"It is more than a hobby and I hope to be able to take photographs for many more years, but that is not the point. I…."

She was interrupted as Thom jumped up saying, "Darling, let's go over things at dinner. I'm late for a meeting at the hotel so I will have to leave you. Wear something daring, will you? I've missed you terribly." Then he left as Colette was still trying to find the way to tell him he had it all wrong.

Now Colette was not only committed to having dinner with Thom, she was no closer to making him understand she wasn't going to marry him.

That evening Thom came to escort Colette to the hotel dining room, graciously holding the door open and offering to take her wrap once inside. Colette was dressed nicely but not in a dress with a low décolletage, not in the dress she wore when dining with Paul.

Thinking of Paul must have conjured him up because as she entered the hotel's dining room, Paul looked up from his meal and a smile immediately formed as he saw her, welcoming her. Then it disappeared to be replaced by a cold expression, his brows drawn together in deep thought as Thom followed her in and helped her sit at the private table he had reserved.

Colette tried to collect her thoughts. She hadn't realized there was a possibility of her running into Paul. She thought he ate earlier and would be gone from the room by now. Instead, she had to concentrate on Thom and what he was saying, try to get her chance to make Thom realize she had only friendship in mind. And to try to do so under the watchful eye of the man she once loved was somewhat daunting.

Colette could not remember afterwards what she had even eaten. She knew it was good and that she picked at the last couple of courses, her appetite completely gone. Thom continued to tell her about all the plans he had in Topeka and how fast he was moving up the ladder. Whenever Thom approached anything remotely like plans for them as a couple, Colette would remind him they were not a couple and she was not going to be in Topeka at any time.

Finally, Thom began to hear the reminder over and over. "Well, we are not in session all year around. That gives us weeks of time to be here in Sweetwater. Mother and father have plenty of room and we can spend the summers here, visiting with everyone before going back in the fall when the houses are back in session."

"Thom, please walk me home. I think we need to be alone for you to hear this," she said getting up without his assistance with her chair.

Colette had her wrap and Thom was helping her down the boardwalk onto the street when she finally said, "Thom, I am not going to marry you. I am not going to marry anyone. I have my life planned out and it does not include anyone else. This is my decision to make. Do I have to hear you repeat it back to me before you understand?"

Thom gazed into her eyes, almost pleading. "Mother wrote you were showing interest in another man. I should have come home sooner. But I thought you understood my regard for you. Won't you give us a chance? I know we would be good for each other."

"I think you are a good man but not for me. I told you the truth before you left. I have no plans to marry any man and I am sorry if you made any plans with me in mind. I thought we were simply friends."

"Mother thinks I'm too polite. She says women need a stronger hand." He stared at his feet as he confessed this.

"You are perfectly fine just as you are and you are a lovable man. Some day you will find the right woman and then I expect a thank you note for turning you down. I wish you the best in Topeka," she told him as she turned towards her door.

"So, there isn't a chance? If I agreed to stay here? Live in Sweetwater?" he asked beseechingly.

"Thom, think about it. Would you be here now if your mother had not written to you about another man taking me to dinner? Tell me and yourself honestly that you would have left all the delights of the capital and travelled hours by train simply to see me because you missed me," Colette challenged him.

"I guess the letter did stir me up a little. I thought it was because I loved you and wanted you with me."

"But those were not the reasons. The part of your plans you are concerned about right now - you can plug almost any reasonably attractive woman into it. You do not have real feelings invested yet because when you do, you would never need to make plans, they simply happen to you. Love is entirely unplanned. Love makes things completely messy, so, I guess you know you are in love when your life turns to *merde*." She was surprised at how strongly she believed that.

Tom's mouth fell open at her uncouth comment and then he snapped it shut saying, "I think I understand now. I wish the best with whomever you care for and wish I could help in some way."

"That is the other thing about love, it only involves

two people when it is done right." She went up on tiptoe and kissed his cheek before entering her studio.

Colette dropped her wrap on the chair and kept walking toward the back and the lamp she left burning. She was completely dragged out. The emotional evening having taken all her reserves of strength as she walked listlessly to her room. A shadow that should not be there moved and Colette jumped away before realizing it was Paul.

"You don't know how lucky that son-of-a-bitch is, not to have come in here with you. I had it all planned out. How I was going to smash his face in, knock his teeth out and then wipe the bloody floor with his body," he growled, unable to hold back the graphic images.

Colette said, "Thom is merely a friend. He doesn't even live here. He lives in Topeka."

"That's not what I was told. I had someone local fill me in while you were dining tet-a-tet and I was drinking alone. I can drink a lot pretty quickly when I have anger to fuel my thirst," he continued to growl.

"We were simply catching up. Thom knows I am not interested in him in that way," she said, starting to take the pins put of her hair and shaking it loose, almost moaning with the relief of not having her hair pulled tight any longer. The slight headache she had beginning to dissipate.

"He doesn't look at you like a friend. I was afraid you were on the menu after seeing him watch you like a hungry hawk tonight," Paul said churlishly.

"I didn't notice," she lied, trying to sooth his temper and get to bed.

"Why didn't you tell me about him? You said you weren't involved with anyone," he accused.

"I told you, we are simply friends. I have male friends and that does not mean I am involved intimately with them," she said trying to find a way to make him go so she could get into bed and get some desperately needed sleep.

"I don't believe you," he stated flatly.

"And I do not care," she said finally giving up and closing the door on her bedroom locking Paul and his jealous thoughts out.

"I'm staying right out here to make sure Mamma's boy doesn't try to sneak in the back door for a rendezvous," he called out as he settled into the chair placing his bad leg on another for comfort and support.

The next morning, Colette woke to find no signs of Paul but a persistent queasiness to her stomach that was threatening her sanity. She dressed lethargically and clutched her reticule before walking stoically to the Chinese laundry. Mei took one look at Colette and motioned for her to come in through the side door.

Colette obliged and fell thankfully onto the cushioned couch as soon as she could. Mei's mother came in with a tea pot and cups and a root of some sort. She motioned Colette to watch as she took the root and sliced thin slivers of the plant and then used the knife blade to scoop the pieces into the tea pot. After a couple of minutes, Colette was offered the small cup. She breathed in the smell of the pleasant brew than drank the cup in little sips.

Mei's mother nodded in encouragement and then said, "*Shi dui*, yes, yes"

Colette felt much better and gave the cup back, accepting the little package of root Mei's mother had cutoff for her to take home.

"*Xie, xie.*" Colette thanked her as she tried to pay for the root but Mei's mother refused to take any payment.

"I will take more photographs, then," she said not knowing if the woman understood or not and left feeling much better.

On the way home, Colette realized she had picked up a stalker. Paul was following a few yards behind but had caught up with her by the time she reached her front door.

"Allow me," he said as he bent in front of her to open the door and she pushed through it, her once calm stomach already wanting to rebel.

"Do I need to ask the sheriff to have a talk with you about bothering me?" she demanded as she pulled off her gloves and removed her hat.

"He already has but that isn't going to slow me down. So explain, why is Dr. Woo giving you medicine if there is nothing that will cure your blindness?" He pointed to the packet in her hand.

"It is not for that. I told you there is no cure. This calms my stomach. I worry too much and I get indigestion," she said half-truthfully.

"I don't believe you." His jaw jutted forward, daring her to keep lying to him.

"I don't care. Now leave or I will do something rash and, and, oh, God…." Placing her hand over her mouth, she ran to the back of the building to be sick in the dish pan in the sink.

Colette was still retching as Paul got there, placing his arm around her, taking her weight in his arms as she finally stopped the heaving that was wracking her body.

"That's not nothing. Tell me what's wrong with you or if I have to go and beat it out of the little voodoo doctor, I will," he threatened.

"No, it is nothing really. Please do not make a scene. I will never live it down if you do." Tears of frustration formed as nothing seemed to be going right for her lately.

"All right, but promise me you'll tell me if it's something important. I don't want to find out bad news later that I could have helped you with," he said concerned, wiping her face with a wet cloth.

"It is not bad news. At least not for me," she said enigmatically.

"Then it is not bad news for me." Taking her onto his lap he sat in the kitchen chair.

Colette tried to stand up as she remembered, "Oh, your leg…."

"My leg is fine. More than fine feeling your rump up against me like this," he said nuzzling her neck.

"Really, Paul, you are utterly incorrigible. I was just sick as a dog and you want to make love."

"Oh, you can feel that can you? Sorry, I started out merely trying to comfort you, I swear," he said lying through his teeth.

"I really ought to rinse my mouth and maybe lie down for a while. I do not have any appointments so I can lock up and rest," she said drowsily, covering a yawn with her hand.

"Mmmmmm." Paul hummed then added, "Can I help you undress at least? I won't try to seduce you, I promise." He was still nuzzling her neck.

"You brat. You are already trying to seduce me. Go away or I will do something drastic, like miss the pan next time and toss up my accounts on you instead."

"All right, you win." He stood letting her feet touch the floor and steadying her before he let go. "Are you sure there's nothing you need me to do for you?"

"Nothing, please simply let me rest. I will feel better after I sleep."

"That's what you told me yesterday," he said with a parting shot.

Paul did not like leaving her like this, feeling so unwell. He knew she wasn't being candid with him and he still thought it had to do with the Mamma's boy. If Colette really had dismissed the other man's suit then the young pup showing up here the other day may have increased her feeling ill. She should not have gone with Thompson and tried to eat a heavy meal if she wasn't feeling well. Paul would try to find more time to spend with Colette so they could get back to a better footing with one another. He hadn't changed his mind about becoming more involved with her.

In fact, if anything, he was even more drawn to her. To begin with he had thought she had some sort of ulterior motive for climbing into his bed but being with her again, spending time together had increased his feelings for her. Brought them back to life after he had been so certain even the embers of the flame that once burned between them so fiercely were well and truly cold. How the past pain and damage was becoming less and less vivid while what they had now, as mature adults, seemed most important.

And it wasn't simply that his leg had stopped paining him although he was sure that was part of it. Being free of the constant ache and throbbing had freed his mind to think of more personal things. Of making love and even carrying Colette as he would have done if not for his missing limb. The other night, he hadn't thought about hesitating and found no waiting pain or aftermath for his chivalrous action. He was back to feeling like the man he was meant to be.

Not that he was falling back in love due to that. He also could see how his actions had hurt Colette so many years ago. How his grief for his brother over-ruled all else, even her begging him to take a little longer before making such a drastic decision. He never explained how being one of the few able-bodied men left in town had made him feel. How hearing about the battles had made him feel powerless to help stop the killing. How he thought he could be a rational voice when all those around him were speaking emotionally. His hubris amazed him now as he thought of it from a different perspective.

He supposed that was his ability to think of it rationally himself, now. To see it as an adult without the taste of grief so strong in his mouth. His need to avenge his brother's death even if it meant losing his own life. And there was the crutch of it, wasn't it? He had basically told Colette that him living for her was less important than him dying for his brother. No wonder she turned to another man for her security, for her future.

CHAPTER 12

Molly wasn't sure she should be allowing herself the fissure of pleasure before settling into the front seat of the rented buggy.

Eli climbed in the other side smiling as he said, "Ready? I'm not sure I'll know when to stop. I mean, Mary Margaret didn't say there was any marker or anything to tell a passerby there was a place to reach the river. We're lucky the weather is still so mild. I've been warned about the winters here and have stocked up on my union suits in case I need to double up on them." And he laughed.

Molly blushed, realizing he was speaking of under-garments. For someone who had been out on her own for several years, she didn't have much social time to simply talk with a man. At work, there was a strict policy about employees fraternizing with one another or with a guest. Either would mean immediate dismissal without a reference and probably banned from working in any other hotel in the city.

Eli saw the blush. "I'm sorry if I've spoken out of turn. I have four sisters so I don't have any control when it comes to talking about, well, I am afraid, about anything. If I start to get too personal or offend you, don't hesitate to tell me to stop speaking. I won't hold it against you, I promise. And it won't be the first time I've heard it." Then he really laughed right out loud. "My sisters tell me that all the time."

"I am afraid I am the opposite. The orphanage where I grew up was segregated much of the times. The girls from the boys except at mealtime or if we had chores together. All of us had to learn to cook, clean, wash clothes, sew and take care of small repairs with hand tools. So, I can paint, use a saw properly and drill out holes for pegs. They thought I was too weak to work on the roofs or I would know how to shingle, too," she explained a portion of her early life. One she had never shared with anyone else. Her only friends had been other children from St. Michaels and they knew all about her early life.

"I am impressed. I can barely cook, if you call it that, laundry and sewing are why stores sell ready-made clothing and I don't think I'd know how to shingle if my life depended on it. I guess I wouldn't be very good out in the territories where a man has to do a little of everything to make it," he confessed.

"So, you need to marry someone who can fill in where you're weak," she said, then looked at him wide-eyed. "I mean, i-if you marry…and i-if you think you want someone like that."

"Don't worry, when I get married, I'll be able to afford to pay someone else to do those kinds of repairs. My wife won't be expected to know how, either," he informed her proudly. "Tell me about growing up surrounded by all those children. I mean, I thought I had it bad with four sisters."

"I don't know, it was simply the way it was." Shrugging, she thought for a moment. "Few of us knew anything different. I had been dropped off by a landlady after my parents died of cholera that swept through the Five Points area where a lot of the immigrants lived. I was kept separated from the others for days until the nuns were sure I couldn't pass it on. I don't remember much.

I was only three but that's why I have my father's name, McGuire."

Then she put the sad past behind her, into long ago memories and smiled as she told him more. "There were some girls I was closer with than others. Sometimes I felt sorry for a new girl brought in and tried to help her adjust but then there were many girls who were adopted and most of them never looked back. Which I hope means they melded into their new families so much that St. Michaels became a dim memory."

"I can't imagine not having my family all around me. I have to admit I'm spoiled by my mother and pampered, almost like a pet, by my sisters. I didn't know how much until I went away to school. Then the other boys treat all the new boys to hazing and all sorts of things I can't discuss with an unmarried young lady. Suffice it to say, though, that most of the things I went through, I got to pass on to the next new class."

At Molly's shocked expression he explained, "It was nothing hurtful. Just a little reminder they weren't at home any more with their mother taking care of them."

"Didn't you want to run back home when it began?" Molly asked almost horrified boys would mistreat each other so.

"No, I think that was what it was all about. It made you want to show the others you could take it, could take getting dropped off out in the woods, miles from school without your trousers. That you could make it on your own. By the time the hazing ended, you were well embroiled in the school and had bonded with your classmates, brought together by mutual misery sometimes. I still write to most of the men I met there." And then asked, "Oh, here, do you think this track into the grasses could be the place?"

"It looks like someone is used to pulling off here and I can almost smell the cool clean water," Molly said getting ready to depart the buggy as soon as Eli brought it to a stop.

Eli tied the reins to a branch of a smoke tree. "I'll bring some water to the horse in a little while. Let's see what kind of a fishing spot we've got ourselves, should we?"

He held up the leafy branches so that Molly could walk through without dislodging her hat. The two of them watched the swiftly coursing river and smiled in delight. It was wider than Molly thought it would be and she could see where there was a path worn down to the water's edge.

"Oh, it's beautiful. I pictured a little stream of some sort," Molly told him.

"Well, the rains we've had after those summer storms have probably made the river higher than it normally would be this time of year. That's why the crops are so good and even beef will be more plentiful. No loss to drought over the summer will mean more cattle to market. It will depress the price a little but the ranchers will gain due to less expense in feeding them through the winter." Eli said, as he spread the blanket he had brought from the buggy. "I never asked if you've ever fished before."

She watched him as he got the poles ready. "No, not actually. I never thought about it much in New York. Our fish there came right from the boats in huge boxes packed in ice. I never thought about fishing one fish at a time. Do your sisters fish?" she asked wanting to know more about his family.

"Two do and two would much rather do anything else. My parents used to take us out as a family outing after Sunday dinner. We would sit in the sun, fish and read aloud from a book one of the girls would bring. I had to listen to a lot of *Wuthering Heights* and *Pride and Prejudice* but the fishing with Dad was worth it. He was so busy during the week he didn't get home till late many nights and missed taking supper with us."

"That must have been hard on you. I mean, you were the only male in the house most of the time," she said, thinking about that for a moment.

"Yes, but he was definitely still in charge even when he wasn't there physically. I would get a talking to if I didn't behave or if I got in trouble in school. So did the girls, of course, only not as sternly. I think their tears unnerved him and he couldn't contend with them." He laughed at the memories of his father undone by a few fake tears from his sisters.

"Oh, so your sisters pulled the old sobbing routine, did they? That didn't work with the nuns at all. They would say something about tears were wasted if they didn't bring about answers. There was one, Sister Mary Margaret, who said a good cry eased the soul but then you should dry your face and come up with a real solution to your problem. That solution usually began with a prayer for guidance. She was always one to force you to face the problem and fight through it. Tears had their place and then you were to wipe your eyes and trudge on."

Eli baited a hook and gave Molly the pole, showing her how to drop the line into the water. "She sounds more like a military commander. And she was in charge of children?" He wondered out loud.

"Oh, she is wonderful and is now the Mother Superior. She knew that we, that all the orphans, were going to confront more challenges than most do when entering the working world. She wanted us strong and ready and able to face whatever was out there in the streets. I don't think there is a St. Michaels's graduate who doesn't feel they owe their lives to those nuns," Molly said strongly.

"I guess in a way, then, you weren't so much an orphan as that you had a lot of mothers and sisters and brothers telling you what to do," Eli said looking at her, happy in the warm sun, fishing on a bank of a river with her.

"That I did and I didn't realize how much I missed it until I got to Sweetwater. Mary Margaret and Faith and even, Callie, began interfering in my life again." She smiled to take any sting out of the comment.

"Oh, look, your bobber is dipping," he said pointing to the river and showing Molly what to do next.

After the picnic lunch Mrs. Burgess, his landlady, had made up for them at Eli's request, he lay back on the blanket. "This is the most relaxing day I've had in a long time. Thank you for coming out with me. It wouldn't have been as fun alone."

"Well, I made you do all the work. I mean, there is no way I can put a worm on a hook like that and then getting those little fish off? Their little mouths opening and closing like that? Oh, I thought it was pitiful. I am glad you kept throwing them back," Molly told him, feeling sorry for the poor fish.

"Some of those fish were the same ones over and over. Fish aren't very smart. But they were too small to try to clean and eat. There would have been nothing left of them by the time you were done cooking them. It's better to let them grow a little more and then eat them."

"Oh, that sounds just like a man, no sensitivity."

"Oh, no, now you sound like my sister, Bethany. She won't eat meat anymore, at all. Said it is inhuman. While my sister, Ann, eats meat so rare I swear it could be brought back to life by a good veterinarian."

"That sounds awful, Eli. Quit teasing with me," Molly reprimanded him.

"I find you easy to tease. It just goes to show you, I travel three states away from a house full of women only to find my first new friend is female. I know...," he said raising his mason jar of sweetened tea into the air. "Here's to new friends and new hometowns."

"Here, here." Molly mimicked his salute.

Paul sat on the chair in the studio, a book of photographs opened on the table in front of him. "I'm impressed with the number of photographs you have collected and how clear the features are of the people in them," he said as he continued to turn the pages slowly.

Looking over his shoulder, Colette explained, "Oh, they are of the Eskimos brought down from Alaska Territory by the Chicago Museum, I think. Those are the original fur clothing they wear and I know they had to be so hot because at the time it was eighty degrees. They were brought in to highlight their society. The men going up to the territory to mine are changing the migration patterns of the seals and whales and that is what these people hunt to survive. Their chiefs are afraid that what happened to the buffalo will be repeated there. It's such a shame. They were very nice people, didn't seem violent by nature."

And then pointing to another group, Colette

continued, "And those were the group of Greek dancers that came to one of the Chicago theatres and I asked if I could photograph their native costumes. They were so good as to strike a pose and hold it for me so I have some original steps to their dance, also. In reality, the dance is fast paced and riotous in the end." Laughing at the memory she impulsively yelled, "Oompah! It was quite marvelous to watch."

Paul smiled at her enthusiasm, as he pointed to another group of men. "I think I've seen this uniform before."

"Those were the Cossack dancers from Russia. I really wished I could photograph in color but that is not available yet. Soon I think, though. There are people working on a film capable of holding a color and then these beautiful costumes will be immortalized."

She sounded regretful because by then she would probably be blind and unable to catch the bright colors of life.

"I see you have gotten a lot of Indian photographs already." He was gazing at the unsmiling faces in rigid poses.

"Yes, I travelled to catch up with some of them. Mostly chiefs having travelled with wild west shows or circuses but I wanted to catch the true life of the native tribes before it disappears forever. Mason said I am too late for that here. The tribes have moved further west and north. The few that have remained around here have adopted too many of our ways, the men wearing Calvary shirts and hats, even top hats and derby with their feathers and braids hanging from under them. I have some of those photographs depicting the loss of their culture but I would still like to capture the original way of life as it was lived in their camps."

"You know, Colette, that won't be easy for a woman, especially alone." Paul tried to warn her, to let her down easy as to the difficulty of finishing her project.

"I know but I feel that time is running out and I must finish some of these things or face never having accomplished them."

"Do you think your sight will be diminished that soon?" Paul asked worriedly, looking closely at Colette for her reaction.

Actually, Colette had been thinking of the baby she carried. It would be impossible to travel among the few tribes left with a small child in tow. She quickly tried to cover her discomposure. "Look, there are the Woos. They were dressed for some sort of holiday and I came back and grabbed my camera and took these shots of their beautifully colorful costumes. I mean, how fortunate to have seen them just then. Now this is again where I would have wanted the camera to capture the color as well as the subject."

She slowly turned the next few pages stopping at one. "And here is one of Mei and her grandmother boiling the clothes, Mei's mother gathering wood for the fires on her back like a pack animal. It is intriguing to capture their lives on film. Here's Dr. Woo smoking his long pipe. I think he looks so wise there." She tapped the photograph with one finger.

"I think he still looks like a voodoo priest," said Paul looking closely at the old dragon who seemed to take delight in sticking pins into him.

"Really you are still saying such things about the man you admit made the pain in your leg go away?" Colette admonished him.

"I didn't say he didn't fix people. I merely think he and the voodoo priest of the bayous have something in common." He turned from the album and lifted a bottle reading the label. "Let's open this bottle of wine I brought. I remembered you liked a rich burgundy so I hope this meets your standards," he told her as he expertly removed the cork with his personal corkscrew.

"I am sure it will be delightful, *me amie*. Wine is good any time of day," she said, her French accent a little more pronounced.

Paul handed the glass to Colette and smiled, taking a long sip of his, then swirled the glass in his hand waiting for Colette's appreciation of the extra fine wine.

Bringing the glass to her nose to breathe in the bouquet, her stomach did an immediate rolling surge as the scent of the warm buttery grape wine hit her senses. She tried to smile and as soon as she started to say something to explain why she wasn't taking a drink, pushed the glass into Paul's hand and ran from the room, barely making it to the dish pan before she was sick - again.

Paul came to give her aid but she held out her hand trying to keep him behind her, not within sight of her humiliation.

"This is too much, Colette. I'm getting the doctor, right now, and I will not be satisfied until we know what is causing you to be so ill. It can't be healthy for you. I saw strong men wither up and die from dysentery and violent binges of vomiting. Soon they were too weak due to loss of fluids and then they died, laying there, once perfectly healthy men. I'll be back in a few minutes. Mason told me where the doctor lives and I'll get him to return with me," Paul said worriedly.

"*Non*, no, I know what is wrong with me. Well, wrong is not the word. I am perfectly healthy...," she began to say.

Paul interrupted her, denying what she was saying.

So, she continued, "This is perfectly normal. I am with child and this, this sickness should go away in a few more weeks," she said too weak to argue with him anymore. Simply wanting to lay down and not talk of it again.

"You're expecting a child?" he said slowly trying to take this shocking news in. "And you have known this, but didn't say anything? To anyone?"

Colette could only shake her head at each of the last questions. Not trusting her stomach not to react badly to anything more.

"So, you came to my bed hoping I might consider I'm the father in case Thompson didn't come back for you? So, you had a backup plan, those plans you are so fond of making?" he said, his back teeth aching from grinding them together between the words.

Colette glared at Paul, anger in every fiber of his body, back ramrod straight and arms stiffly at his sides, his lips a grim reminder of his military training to show no emotion.

"Don't worry. Thom is making a home ready for me as we speak. You are right but Thom raced home when he thought I might be making another liaison. You will not be linked with this child, ever," she said, the pain of Paul's lack of trust hurting more than anything she had had to bear so far in her life.

"Then I will give you my congratulations now since I don't plan on speaking with you again." Turning, he limped down the hall.

When Colette returned to the studio hours later, the book still lay open to the photographs of the Woos but the wine bottle and glasses were gone.

"Thank God for that, at least," Colette said aloud knowing her stomach was never going to be the same around wine again.

CHAPTER 13

Molly sat in her office after supper, finalizing the day's receipts when Eli entered and nudge the door almost closed.

"Eli, you shouldn't be in here. I could get into trouble," she began.

"From who? The Whitehouses? They dote on you as the daughter they never had. They are so happy with the way you came in here and immediately relieved them of all the paperwork and employee training. They love being the hosts here, welcoming guests into the hotel and raving about the food. And Mason, he's too busy chasing after his wife to worry about what we're doing," he said honestly.

"Eli, I told you not to say things like that to me. It's simply not right," she said blushing at thoughts going through her mind about Mason and Vicki, trying not to put pictures to the sounds she heard nightly.

"Sorry, I keep forgetting. I'm just so open with my sisters I keep forgetting you may take offense," he half apologized.

"I do not take offence but you should not take for granted I understand what you are saying either. I may be from a big city but I am not experienced so if you have some strange idea that I, that we…." And she stopped realizing she was digging a much deeper hole than she could ever hope to get out of.

Eli looked at Molly then smiled. "My sisters aren't experienced either, not in that way, but they understand things of the world. Between men and women."

"I do as well, I think. I had to spend a lot of time on my own but I understand the concept. That doesn't mean I am comfortable speaking of such things or having a man speak of them either," she said sounding much like a nun even to her own ears.

"I didn't mean anything, Molly. I expect as time goes on; we'll learn about these things together. When the time's right, after we're engaged," he said, shyly taking her hand in his.

"So, you don't know? I mean you're not experienced, either?" she asked quietly, not wanting anyone outside in the hallway to accidently overhear their confessions.

"I know the fundamentals. I know some of the female, umm, things but I'm glad I won't have any one to compete with, if you understand me," he admitted just as quietly.

"I'm not sure but I think it means we will learn everything together and that sounds right to me," she said, now smiling, relieved Eli and she were at the same starting point in life and love.

"Just not right now although I'm not opposed …," he began.

Molly interrupted, "No, no, I think we need to know each other better before we try to learn anything more."

Eli relaxed saying, "Well, I meant to come in here to ask you to sit with me in church this Sunday if you can get away from the hotel."

Molly said primly, "I would like that very much, Mr. Winters." Then her eyes widened, remembering the threat he had made weeks ago.

Eli smiled broadly. "I remember that I warned you about calling me, Mr. Winters. Now come and let me punish you properly - or should I say reward." He folded Molly into his arms.

"Someone thinks mighty highly of himself," she replied standing still, waiting for her prize.

Then Eli bent his head and they both knew the moment their lips touched again this was the right one, the right man, the right woman, and the right place to fall in love.

Faith was sitting in Colette's studio. She had come over to see if Colette wanted to go with her, to pick berries for a pie she was going to make. Faith often made extra to give to Colette because the French woman had made it plain early on in their friendship she didn't know how to cook very well and didn't bake at all having had a cook during her growing up years and marriage.

As soon as Colette came in, Faith said worriedly, "All right, what is the problem. I can tell the sound of someone being sick. Is there something I can do to help?"

"*Non*, I will be fine in a few moments. It usually hits me once a day and then is gone," Colette said unselfconsciously willing to let this friend in on her secret.

"It goes away…? Oh, Colette, have you spoken with Rebecca or Beth, yet? They can be so much help," said Faith understanding immediately Colette's condition.

"I have seen Rebecca and we are in agreement," said Colette enigmatically.

"It isn't Thom's, is it? I just can't see you and him and Mrs. Thomson making a good marriage." Putting her hand to her mouth said, "Oh, I'm sorry, if it's Thom you want then I know you'll…." But at the look that came into Colette's eyes, continued, "It isn't Thom. Then who? Oh, the banker, I mean, Mr. Weaver. He's the one." Looking at Colette for confirmation, she found it.

"I do not want anyone to know for a while, at least. I am hoping Paul will be gone by the time I begin to show that I am with child. It will make things so much easier," said Colette and smiled trying to get her friend to think that everything had been settled.

Faith firmed her lips. "That bastard hurt you. I'm going to tell Jeremy to stop doing business with him, drive him out of town. We don't need his type here…."

Colette almost laughed at the fierce protectiveness Faith was showing. "*Non, non ma petit mignon,* I will live just fine. I have lived through worse. Now you asked for me to go and pick these berries? I think I would like to do so. I need more exercise or I will get too fat."

Faith tied her poke bonnet on her head. "I won't speak of it again today but I think we need to make a plan. And I want that scoundrel to understand he can't come to Sweetwater and treat us this way."

The two women went down First Street past Miss Lily's toward the river where Faith knew the berry bushes were ripe. The two women talked the whole way, laughing and discussing the draperies Faith was putting up in the new house. And about the material she ordered to reupholster the chairs for her parlor.

They had not been paying too much attention to things around them when a man jumped out in front of them. He swayed as he spoke.

"Well, well, well, look at what we have here. One for me and one for a spare. I can call a friend. He ain't too far away and maybe we can have us a party? You know just the three or four of us." He made a lurch for Faith as both women side-stepped quickly. Colette wished she had thought to bring her Derringer and knew Faith never carried a gun.

A deep voice startled them all. "I suggest you go and have a party by yourself and leave the ladies alone. Why aren't you working?" Wilder asked, looking more like a desperado than a lawman other than the shiny badge on his shirt.

"I don't got a job," the drunken man growled.

"But you live in the tents by the river?" asked Wilder not liking the fact that hangers-on were now living in the tent camps, too. Men ready to take a good man's pay by cheating or gambling or both.

"I stay there mostly. I'm waitin' for my friend to get back," he told Wilder.

"Then stay in camp. I don't want you on the roads or paths bothering the ladies, do you understand me? And stay sober. You're lucky I'm not the sheriff. You would have less digits than a three toed frog right now."

The man apologized to Faith and Colette then shuffled back toward the woods from where he came.

Faith and Colette started to say, "We'll go back to town...."

Noting the empty basket in their hands, Wilder turned to his sister-in-law and Colette saying, "It would be a sad day when two ladies can't go and pick huckleberries in the morning. I'll just hang around and make sure no one bothers you."

"Oh, we can't let you waste your time following us, Wilder, you must have better things to do," Faith told him.

"My job is protecting the town and its people and right now that means you two," Wilder said matter of fact.

"All right, Wilder, I'll send over some pie to the jail when it's done," Faith told him.

"I like berry pie." He smiled that devilish grin that won his wife's heart for him. "That sounds like a fair trade."

The bushes were heavy with berries and the baskets were filled to almost over-flowing in a short time. Wilder picking berries and eating them right from the bushes as the ladies teased, he would get a belly ache. An hour later they all walked back to town, back to a reality for Faith starting a life in her own home and Colette of being unmarried and pregnant.

Faith promised Colette complete secrecy, which also meant she would have to suffer in silence about what a dog she thought Paul Weaver was and how she gritted her teeth every time Jeremy spoke about him. She didn't say anything but then she also wouldn't welcome a visit from the man or invite him to dinner again.

Colette was the one who had a lot to think about. Debating whether she could continue to live in the friendly town that she had been so welcomed in, everyone being eager to have her become like family. Exposing herself to the possibility of Paul finding out her last secret. The one she needed to keep, the one that meant the most in her life.

Faith and her sister, Hope, had been the first people to invite her to their home and made sure she was fed well when they learned she didn't really know how to cook. Faith, a wonderful baker, always had enough to bring over pies and cookies and cakes for Colette. In payment, Colette took photographs of places and people that would please her new friends.

Now, once again, Colette would have to move on

and find a place where she could raise her child as well as live once she lost her sight. Going back south was too painful, Chicago was too big, and Sweetwater was too good. She didn't want to see pity in her friend's eyes and there was always the problem Paul could return to the town and figure out Thom wasn't the father to her child.

But where could she afford to travel? How far would be far enough and how many years would she have with sight enough to earn her living as a photographer and be able to take care of her own child. The trail would have to be unfollowable, no way for Paul to track her if he should take it into his head to do so. This wasn't going to be easy and she may need to look to her friends for help.

She knew that Faith's brother, Matthew St. Michaels, was experienced in hiding abused wives and women in need and she was considering asking him for help. She wasn't abused but she was in need and that could have him help her with her escape.

But right now, she was tired, so very, very tired and simply wanted to sleep, maybe for days until this dreadful fatigue left her just as the dreadful morning sickness will. She undressed to her camisole and then laid on the cool sheet, listening to the crickets and other night time insects trying to put worry and planning out of her mind long enough to fall asleep.

In the morning she was no further ahead than she had been the night before but was beginning to think leaving town was the right answer. To raise her child as the widow she was. No one had to know when her husband died. A few misleading comments in her new place of residence and no one would know any different. It was the only way to save her child from living with a sin that Colette had committed. Loving too much and for too long. It was time for her to bury her youthful innocent love.

Paul was having another of his nightmares, which had been lessening in the last few weeks. But this time, while stumbling over the corpses in the fog calling for Phillip, Paul actually saw his brother among the wounded. Falling to his knees, he held his dying brother in his arms crying.

Phillip opened his gray eyes so similar to the ones Paul looked into in the mirror every morning, and said, "You shouldn't have come. It makes no difference for me and this was never your war. I never meant for you to feel you must fight in this battle, too. The outcome will be the same. I will die and you will live, that is as it should be, as it was always meant to be. Go back, go back to her and carry our name on with your sons and daughters."

Then Paul woke up, shaken with what was the most realistic dream he had ever had.

He stayed awake, wondering if it were simply another phase the dream was taking or if there was a premonition there as well. He spent the rest of the night awake and thinking about his life decisions.

Colette had been correct when she said leaving her had been his decision, one he made without considering how it would affect her life. He could have left her with a child to raise on her own during a war everyone knew the south was going to lose. The very essence of their southern life-style was going to be destroyed and that was before the confederacy had fallen.

If he thought his life had changed drastically, what of hers. She and her father had lost their home and the family's livelihood as an exporter when the harbors were blockaded and all shipping to Europe was prohibited. Then Colette's older husband ignored her to spend time with his peers and other woman, finally to die and leave her to save herself.

She was brave and strong and independent and he had thrown that all away to go and prove - what? That he was as foolish as his brother? Searching for freedom of the guilt he felt after learning of Phillip's death? Fighting for something he never believed in simply to avenge a dead brother?

When he found himself face to face with Colette once more, he thought himself the luckiest of men - and he was. For the two of them, with all their travels and vagrancies from their original lives to have found each other in a small Kansas town was a miracle. A few weeks one way or the other and they may never have seen one another again, let alone have the time to investigate the feelings they once had when they were both too young to appreciate them.

Now he was old enough to know how very rare such emotions were. He should have told this all to Colette before he let jealousy invade his mind merely because someone else had given her a child before he could. That wasn't her fault - that was his. He should have searched for her instead of feeling sorry for himself and mourning the loss of his leg. It was an excuse to punish himself for living while Phillip had died but he hadn't thought about how it was punishing her as well.

If he could make her listen to him, he would tell her it didn't matter. Everything that occurred before they had found each other didn't matter. And then, as he thought about how she had been in his bed…his feisty, gutsy

Angel. It took his breath away. It did then and it did whenever he thought of that night.

And that is when he realized she never would have joined with him to try to fool him into thinking the child she carried was his. That child was his. Now he had to make her know he could be depended on to honor his commitment to her and his child - but it was about her first, and their family second. She was who he loved, who was the most important person to him. And her child, his child, their child, was the proof of that love.

But how to keep her from running because he sensed she was going to do so, just as she had from the south to escape the war-torn damage, then from Charleston to forget his death, and finally from Chicago. Staying here in Sweetwater where he knew she had strong friendships and support for her future loss of sight had to be incorporated into his plans for their life together. He would use everything he could to convince her to stay with him.

CHAPTER 14

At the monthly town meeting now held in the basement of the new school, Mrs. Thompson was holding court, accepting as her right that everyone coming down the stairs would stop to greet her and compliment her on the decorations of bunting and flags as if Mrs. Thompson herself hung each and every one. The room appeared as if it was election day.

Paul felt that he, too, should pay his respects to the mayor's wife and intended to stay just the moment it would take but what he over-heard her say to the woman behind him made him remain within hearing distance.

"Oh, yes, Thomas writes me weekly. He knows how interested I am in what happens in the capital. I expect to be visiting there much more often when he marries as I'm hoping will be the case soon. He's been keeping company with a senator's daughter whom will remain unnamed at this time. I wouldn't want gossip mongers in the newspaper world to interfere with their privacy," Mrs. Thompson told the other lady peering around as if hoping Jessie, the newspaper editor, was within ear-shot. The woman being told this little bit of gossip showed a sufficient amount of curiosity and respect to be chosen as the mayor's wife's confidant.

As if imparting state secrets, Mrs. Thompson continued, "But I can tell you she is a graduate of a finishing school in New York State where she attended with daughters of federal Senators and Representatives. Even some cabinet member's family. Then she took a year to tour the continent, visiting all the capitals and even meeting royalty, as I understand it. It will be truly a happy day and not too far in the future when I receive the news my son is engaged to marry this fine, fine, girl." She smiled, nodding her head as the other lady appeared as if she, too, were to be lifted in the social strata in some way simply knowing this information.

Paul moved on to find his chair when he decided Mrs. Thompson wasn't going to disclose anything more about her son. He wondered if Colette knew about Thompson's possible engagement and if she would care. He had made a muddle of things with her, aggressively accusing her when it didn't matter who fathered the child. If she would marry Paul, hell, even if she didn't marry him, he would claim the child. The baby was part of Colette and that made Paul love it no matter what happened.

He saw Colette enter and go directly to the far side of the room, taking a seat next to Faith and Jeremy. He could move and sit by Jeremy. It wouldn't cause speculation but he thought it best to remain where he was. The meeting was going to be called to order any moment.

During the course of the meeting, it was discussed under new business, about the housing that would be built due to the need for more living quarters. There was discussion that if these houses were not built, then shanty and shacks, lacking in quality and basic living needs will spring up instead, squatting on land owned by others. Also, there was a criminal element hiding in the camps among the hardworking construction men. A group of men who were there as parasites would be chased out when the construction men moved into town, into proper living quarters and homes, bringing their families and settling in Sweetwater.

The meeting was beginning to wind down when Colette asked to be heard. She stood and explained she would be moving back to Chicago and her building would be available for sale or lease.

There were murmurs of regret from several members of the audience. The mayor stood up and thanked Colette for being an upstanding citizen and business person while she was in Sweetwater and that she would be missed.

Colette thanked the mayor for his kind words and took that moment to turn to leave the meeting, probably trying to leave before people, especially Paul, made his way over to her.

So, in the middle of the town hall meeting, Paul stood up and gazed across at Colette poised to leave the room. "This has been a long time coming, too long. I should have done this ten years ago, before I lost you, before I lost some of myself - but I'm doing it now. I realize you know my failings more than anyone else still alive but I believe my love can overcome all problems between us. Colette Dubois, will you marry me?"

A sigh swept across the riveted audience as all eyes turned to Colette, her mouth in a sad O but she was shaking her head unable to voice the rejection she felt sure she should make.

Paul continued, "I want to be your husband, the father to your children. If you don't marry me then you are condemning me to a life alone, lonely and sad for the rest of my days."

When Paul had first started speaking again, all heads swiveled in his direction but now the faces and the accusing glares swung to face Colette who was pinned to the floor unable to make a respectable exit and unwilling to give an answer in front of so many people she had become friends with.

Then Paul pulled the last arrow out of his quiver. "If you won't marry me, I will have to leave Sweetwater and all its good people and live in a big city in the east where I will die abandoned."

The entire audience, as if as one, turned from the man speaking his heart to again stare at Colette some with accusing eyes, some with curiosity and some with love.

At that point, all Colette could think to say was, "You carpetbagger!" And if dagger glares could kill, he would, at least, be bleeding profusely.

Paul grinned because he knew that was the worst, she was going to call him and even that he could talk her down from. Colette was his, the baby was his and Sweetwater was his.

The audience sat in anticipation of the next move. Paul walked quickly to Colette's side. Taking her hand in his, turned and as any good performer, bowed to his audience saying, "I'm sure you understand that my fiancée and I have a lot of things to talk over." As the couple left the room a chorus of applause and congratulations followed them out to the cool night air.

But Colette wasn't done blistering his ears. "I cannot believe you said those things in front of the whole town. How am I supposed to live here after tonight? It will take me a couple of weeks to pack everything up for shipping. What in the world will be going through their minds?"

"That I am the most romantic man in town and I must be out of my mind with love for you. You are a much-envied woman, Angel, and you should enjoy it

139

because it will be short lived as people forget tonight and place the memory among things gone and done," Paul said trying to minimize the sensation of his very public display.

Then Colette began to shake and admitted her fears, "I thought you were going to mention the baby or Thomas or something to force me to accept you. I was so afraid of hurting the people I have grown to love and respect."

Paul stopped walking and pulled Colette into his arms, holding her close. "This was never meant to cause you embarrassment or pain. I love you. I wanted you to know. I wanted everyone to know I love you. And even if you won't marry me, they will know you were loved and this child is loved. I want you both but only if you want me. If you really don't feel we should marry then so be it. But I'm not leaving you and if you go, I'll follow. I'll love and care for you and our child till I die."

Tears were streaming down her face and Colette was trying to dry her eyes with her knit gloves. "How did everything get so complicated?" she whimpered.

"It isn't complicated. It's the world righting itself. Me and you together, starting a family as it was intended ten years ago before we lost our way. This is simply one time to make it right. If it isn't the right time for you then I'll wait around until you tell me it is the right time. But I warn you now, no one will mistake this child as anyone else's. I'll stake claim as soon as it becomes obvious that you are with child." He wiped her face with his handkerchief and then turned her toward her home.

Paul followed Colette into the storefront and down the hall to her private parlor. She removed her damp gloves then her hat, pushing the pin into the brim as she sat it on the table.

"So, you want to be the father to this child even though you think Thom is the true father?"

"I'm an ass but I wouldn't deny a man knowing his own child. But Thom has nothing to do with this child and I should have realized that from the beginning. Thom was so infatuated with you he wouldn't have walked away, especially if you two had been intimate. You must have driven him away for his own good because you knew you could never love him as you love me. It was my jealousy that made me only think painful thoughts. I was still unable to forgive myself, for Phillip, for fighting in a war I wasn't committed to, for leaving you. I didn't feel I deserved to be happy," he told her, trying to explain his actions.

He pulled Colette into his arms. "I can't apologize enough for causing you pain. I didn't realize how much until tonight. I thought I was the only one hurting, rather self-absorbed of me but you do deserve happiness and light and joy. If I can give you those things then I will do anything for you, for our child, for our life together if you'll have me."

"I believe you, my love. Please forgive yourself, though, or we will be living under a dark cloud and I want only sunshine for this child. Can you do this for me, for our child?" Colette was pleading for him, for their future.

"I will do anything for you. I have already told the town. Now I will live as I have sworn to in front of them." And he kissed his Angel.

Colette said, "Should we go to the bedroom and finish making our vows there, *me amour*?"

"Is it safe, I mean, for the baby? I can wait," he said

pulling her closer.

"*Non*, Rebecca told me before that it is not bad for the baby and often good for the mother."

"I don't think this father thinks too badly of it, either," he said starting to remove his coat and tie.

Soon, snuggled in bed, Paul took his Angel in his arms and kissed her eyes, her lips finding the warm entry to her mouth with his tongue and stroking, feeling Colette's response as she pushed herself closer to his body.

"I can't wait too much either, Angel, but are you sure this won't hurt the baby? It's been so long for us," he asked once more, hesitating, waiting for her answer.

The answer came as Colette rolled on top of him, his surprised smile a reward for her taking the initiative in beginning their love making, allowing herself to envelope him completely.

"I guess that's a, yes, then. This is all for you, Angel. I'll let you take the lead and I'll follow wherever you want me."

And with that directive, Colette began the long slow strokes that brought Paul to the edge of passionate desire more than once but he resisted the urge to take charge. Allowing her control of their pleasure fully and he did enjoy it. Finally, as she increased the speed and stretched each thrust to last as long as she could before lowering herself back onto his rigid staff, she stiffened with euphoric release as he held her waist, held her tightly to him until he too was complete.

Collapsing onto his chest, Colette took little gasps of breath, loving the feel of her fingers in his chest hair. "I love you so much, Paul. I am so very, very happy."

"And so am I but I will be happier once we are

married, which I plan on being very soon." He kissed the top of her head.

"The town will be expecting it and we can't disappoint our neighbors," she said through her smile. Then they both laughed in sweet enjoyment of one another and slept together all night as a couple for the first time.

Happy Endings

CHAPTER 1

Opening her eyes, Hope found her new husband watching her. She stretched unembarrassed that it brought her naked breasts above the light sheet covering her during the night. Wilder, a muscular, handsome man with black hair and bronzed skin smiled, allowing his silver gaze to roam over her body. Pleased by what he got to glimpse but more with the fact he could look his fill any time he wanted now they were man and wife.

Hope, with her blond hair bound up in a long braid to keep it from tangling and heart shaped face with arched brows, gazed at him across the bed. She enjoyed the love and admiration she saw in her husband's eyes, even with her large wine-stain birthmark covering the right side of her face. With Wilder she felt beautiful, loved and desired.

He stroked his hand over the smooth skin on her shoulder and down her back. "How did I get so lucky as to have you love me? I thought after a few weeks the feeling of unreality would settle down, that I would kiss you goodbye and go off to work without thinking twice. Instead, I find I can't leave you that easily."

"I don't know what I'm going to do with you, Mr. Wilder. I need to be in that school room in an hour or all those children will run wild. Now what can I do to make this all feel better for you?" she teased as she flipped him unto his back straddling his naked body with her own.

"That's a good start, Babe. I think you can figure out

something being such a smart lady and all," he said as she settled over his eager erection.

Starting the slow process of making love, Hope refused to be hurried by Wilder in his need of her. She continued the slow, long lift of her body and the slow, long descent as she brought them both to another culmination of sensations and euphoric climax that raced through both their bodies.

A little while afterwards, Hope pushed at her husband saying, "Wilder, get out of here so I can finish getting ready. This is probably why they usually don't let married women teach. They can't get to work on time due to their husbands uncontrolled appetites."

Wilder, misunderstanding on purpose, explained, "I only had two biscuits and some eggs and bacon."

"Out, out right now or what happened this morning isn't going to ever happen in the morning again," she threatened trying to wind her hair up into a knot on top of her head.

"I'm leaving. I may be back at midday." Almost hating the sound of desperation in his voice, asked, "Will I get to see you?"

"Probably." Kissing his lips, she gave him a little push on his chest towards the door.

Wilder left laughing and Hope went to apply the concealing cream she used on her birthmark to make it practically disappear. She heard her husband return as she stood after pulling her shoes out from under the bed. She had kicked them off when she and Wilder fell into bed last night, undressing each other in eager anticipation.

"Mrs. Wilder, can you come out here a minute?" called Wilder just as Hope got up and huffed a breath then went out to the kitchen saying, "Wilder, if you need…."

Wilder stood in her kitchen with two small children, hallowed eyed, both too thin with bare feet. "I thought since these children got to school so early maybe you could find them a couple of those biscuits. Maybe some honey to go with them?"

"Certainly, Mr. Wilder. Now what are your names?" she asked the children as Wilder helped them unto the kitchen chairs.

The children remained quiet, large blue eyes peering around, taking in all the different items in the kitchen and living area of the teacher's apartment.

Wilder placed his hand over the boy's head, saying "This is, Walter, and this is, Corabelle Taylor. Their mother sent them to school while she stayed home with a younger sister."

Hope spoke quietly and asked, "Will you talk with me? I'm going to be your teacher."

The small boy, evidently the older, said, "We can talk to him because he's got a badge and that means he's safe to talk to. If you're the teacher, Ma said to behave real good or we could get a switching and be sent home and not allowed back."

Hope knelt down next to the children after she poured each a glass of milk. "I never switch my students and I can see you're very good children so you needn't worry about being sent away. Do you understand?"

Both little heads nodded as they bit into the biscuits.

"Mr. Wilder, would you please deliver this welcome to Sweetwater basket to these children's mother?" asked Hope as she broke two eggs into the still hot grease in the pan on the stove.

Wilder began, "The Sweetwater welcoming bask...?" Then his brows rose as he nodded. "Sure, I can do that. The kids said they're camping next to the river down First Street, I think."

He watched as Hope placed the ham that he had planned to have for dinner into the center of a hamper lined with a clean towel. Followed by a bag of dried beans, a jar of applesauce, jam, honey, sack of coffee beans, two fresh tomatoes, six eggs and the loaf of German brown bread he had planned to eat with the ham.

Hope handed the heavy basket to her husband giving him a smile that asked him, 'what did you expect'?

Wilder smiled his answer back, saying, "I'll let you know what I find out."

"Thank you, Mr. Wilder," she replied as she placed a cooked egg in front of each child on a plate with a fork, watching their eyes widen at the treat.

It took Wilder a half-hour to find the right tent and wagon the children probably came from. It was the one with diapers hanging to dry on a makeshift clothes line.

A small campfire burned a few feet from the tent flap so he called, "Mrs. Taylor? I'm Deputy Wilder here to speak with you."

There was no answer from the tent but he felt she was in there, possibly afraid he was there to kick her off the land, make her move on to another place so he added, "I have a welcome to Sweetwater basket for you."

A thin young woman, too young to be those children's mother, certainly, but Wilder had been around long enough to know that didn't always mean anything. She was wearing a well-worn dress, too big for her small frame and a pair of men's work shoes. A shawl was wrapped around her upper body and she was holding a swaddled baby close to her chest.

"Are the children all right?" she asked fearfully.

"Walter and Corabelle are fine, ma'am. They're with my wife who's the teacher in Sweetwater."

"So, are you here because of my husband?" she asked seemingly fearing his answer.

"Where's your husband?" asked Wilder, his lawman instincts turning on.

"He left with the horses about ten days ago, now. Said he'd be back as soon as he found a place for us to live. There was nothing here in town so he said he would have to look along other towns and would come back to take me and the children in the wagon. I was sort of hoping he'd be back by now. I sent the children to school so they could stay warmer during the day. It's getting kind of scary with Walt being gone so long."

Wilder had been thinking the whole time he had listened to this poor woman talk. "Well, I can check the other nearby towns to see if he came through there. What does he look like?"

"Well, Walt's five-foot eight-inches tall, thin and he has brown eyes and brown hair getting a little thin on top," she replied slowly.

"Does he have any scars or distinguishing marks?" Wilder asked thinking the description would match too many men.

"He has a small burn on his right wrist. Is that enough?"

"That should be good enough for now. But meanwhile, I have this basket for you as a welcome to our town." He raised the wicker hamper so she could see it.

"Oh, but we're really not staying in town. I mean, as

soon as Walt gets back, we'll be moving on," she explained looking longingly at the food in the basket.

"That don't matter, ma'am. I'm to leave this with you, anyway," he said while placing the basket near the tent flap. Tipping his hat, he mounted his horse and headed back toward town.

Wilder sent off some wires inquiring about any unclaimed bodies with the description or drifter using the name of Walt Taylor. He hoped the man hadn't abandoned his family but it was known to happen. Life gets too hard and a man can get to thinking his family would be better off without him. Or he'd be better off without them.

He walked along the boardwalk to the butcher shop to get another ham and hopefully some of Mrs. Burgess' good brown bread she made each day. It had been less available since Mrs. Burgess opened a boarding house for the constant stream of construction crews coming into Sweetwater.

Wilder was lucky, there was one loaf left and he paid Mr. Burgess taking the items back to the apartment on the backside of the new school building that doubled as the civic building for the town.

Hope, coming around the white picket fence gate after all the children had gone home for the day, spotted her husband lying in a net tied between two trees. "Where did you get that, Wilder? It looks kind of fun."

"It's something I picked up years ago in Mexico and realized I didn't have to sleep in it, just hang it up and swing."

"I think it's going to put you to sleep. You're like a dog in the sun. You simply close your eyes and go to sleep. I have never seen anything like it," she said standing next to her husband.

"Well, I've learned to sleep when I can to make up for the times when I may be on watch. Come, lay down with me and see if you like it. It could be our next best place to make love." And he smiled, his silver eyes glinting in the fall sunshine.

"If this is merely some trick to get me to cozy up to you, Wilder, you'll be sorry," she said trying to figure out how to get into the net without tipping Wilder out.

"Just sit and swing your feet up, Babe. I'll keep it from flipping us over." He pulled her to him, nestling her against the full length of his body.

The swinging of the net made Hope shriek and grab onto her husband, then giggled as she accustomed herself to the movement. "I'm not sure this was meant for two people, Wilder."

"Sure, it is. They make love in it in Mexico. Where do you think all those little Mexican babies come from?"

"Don't be foolish. You're always telling me tales then making me feel dumb for trusting you." She admonished in her best teacher voice.

"I'm not telling you anything but the truth. Most of the Mexicans I saw slept in these things and, yes, they had children." Then more seriously, he said, "Maybe we shouldn't be in it together."

"Why not? I'm beginning to like it." And she bumped her fanny into his hips.

"Because of that. We need to stop doing so much of that." But he couldn't help but push into her soft bottom with his hips.

"Well, we can't really do anything out here. We are well within view of the parsonage and although Rebecca wouldn't think twice about it, I think the Reverend would be scandalized."

"There's more to the good Reverend than you think. He might just stay and watch out the window," Wilder said as he nuzzled her neck, finding the warm area just below her ear.

"So, what are you worried about? I can hear it in your voice, Wilder." Her instincts kicked in.

"The more we…we make love, the more chances you can become pregnant and then you'll quit teaching, which you love, and then you'll start to hate me for taking away what you love and…."

Hope interrupted her husband at that point turning over and facing him. "I love you. And I will love our children. If silly schoolboards want to make it mandatory that only single women can teach then that is their loss. I will teach our children. I will mentor others and I will tutor students for college entrance exams. I will never need to give up teaching. Only if I want to. Now do I have to make all the moves or are we going to make love in this contraption?"

"I think we should go inside and finish what we've started and maybe spend a couple of hours swinging afterwards. How's that sound, Mrs. Wilder?"

"That sounds perfect, Mr. Wilder. I don't know why I didn't think of it myself." She smiled as he helped her get out of the hamaca without tipping them both to the ground.

CHAPTER 2

Molly tried one more hat on her brunette ringlets cascading down the back of her head. Her bright brown eyes examined how it looked in the mirror and her pretty mouth, turned up at the corners in a perpetual smile, agreed it was fetching. Glancing at the clock, she jumped up removing the hat before returning to her job as manager of the hotel across the street.

"I cannot decide, Abbey. They are all so beautiful but I do want a new one for the wedding," she told the owner of the dress shop and milliner of the hats Molly so admired.

"That's all right, Molly. This is a big decision and you may come back as many times as you want to try them on. I am so pleased you and Eli are getting married. Matthew and I really like him and it is fortuitous you both had to come across the country to meet each other here in Sweetwater. I believe in fate and that eventually we will meet the people we are meant to be with. Romantic of me, I know."

Abby was a little older than Molly with dark brown hair and lovely, slightly slanted deep-brown eyes which gave a look of the exotic about her. Her mouth curved in a wide smile as she held up an almost see-through nightgown with lace at the collar and cuffs and trimmed with pink ribbon on the bodice. "I want you to have this as a wedding gift."

"Oh, Abby, I couldn't accept that. It's too precious," Molly said but her eyes never left the lovely garment.

"Of course, you can. Every woman should have

something pretty to wear on her wedding night and I can't see you going to bed in a hat." Both women laughed at the image racing through their minds.

"I understand, I may need to look the seductress," said Molly blushing.

"I don't think Eli will need much tempting. I have seen him watch you walk away from him," Abbey, a long-time married wife, teased the younger woman. "Don't worry, he's a full, red-blooded male and he won't need seducing but it is still nice to feel a little naughty."

"I thank you, then, and I will take it with me the next time I come to buy that hat." Molly pointed to a little white hat with a tiny bird and veil attached that sat nicely in front of the curls she wore on the back of her head.

Molly got back in plenty of time to let Martin, the front desk clerk, leave for his midday break. She watched as Maggie rushed back and forth to the kitchen setting up for the influx of construction workers who would almost overwhelm the saloon next door. The impromptu restaurant had been set-up to serve the group of men brought in to complete the new buildings and smaller homes a less expensive meal than the hotel restaurant could provide.

Maggie cooked most of the food, served it and then cleaned up afterwards. It seemed to be working out although Molly knew the bartender, Franklin, was sweet on Maggie and helped her out with the heavy lifting or if she fell behind.

Finally, Maggie came through with the last of the empty pans placing them in the kitchen for the scrub boy to take care of. Molly smiled in sympathy and nodded for the front desk clerk to take over his duties again.

"Maggie, do you still think all this work is worth it?

I know you're turning a profit but it makes a long day for you and even longer for Franklin," Molly said looking over her friend's face that was still flushed from rushing around. The men only had half an hour to eat before needing to be back on the work site which put stress on Maggie and the kitchen to get the food out and served.

"I keep telling Franklin I don't need him there but he said he is awake anyway. Said he never got used to sleeping in the mornings even after a late night working the bar," Maggie informed her life-long friend who grew up at St. Michaels Foundling Home alongside her.

"I know but things are going to change as the town grows. Right now, we only have an influx of the trades and manual laborers but as we get more businesses or the train begins to stop more often, we'll get more custom for the hotel and the saloon. Maybe we simply need a restaurant for the common man?" Molly teased with some truth behind it.

"I don't know if I can keep the prices low enough if I have to pay rent. And hire a kitchen helper, plus the cost of wood and ice and other things I'm using from the hotel's kitchen," she said worriedly. She was hoping to keep the inexpensive meals going for the construction workers, many of whom lived in tents down by the river.

"We don't need to change anything, right now. I just hate to see you work so hard for so little reward," Molly told her friend.

"I enjoy feeding the men. Most of them are really nice fellas who have families back east. I'm sure if the work remains here then they'll send for their wives and won't need to eat in the saloon."

"I hope they get a good start on those houses off First Street then. Thompson Street, I think it's going to be called. Named after the mayor to induce him to vote for the town allowing the houses to be built on city land. I know the Macgregor's are paying for the land and the town needs the houses so the families can move here, but it makes Mrs. Thompson almost impossible to be near. She thinks we should change the town's name to Thompsonville and if I hear about her son's wonderful, beautiful, rich fiancée one more time I will throw-up, I swear," Molly said still smiling.

"Now, be nice. She's been in control of this town for years. It must be a little frightening for her to realize all these new people are showing up and taking over little bits of the town. She has a reason to be over-zealous in her dreams - so many of them have been lost. Besides, I don't have to deal with her." Maggie waved goodbye as she went back through the doorway to the saloon.

A tall, slender man wearing wire rimmed spectacles entered the hotel's front door, removed his hat, and strode toward Molly standing in the hall, near her office. His blue-eyed gaze never left her face and the dimples that bracketed his smile were right in place. "Could I speak with you about a business matter, Miss McGuire?" he said loud enough for the clerk to hear him.

"Why certainly, Mr. Winters. Right this way."

She led him into the office where he quickly wrapped his arms around her and whispered, "I can't wait another two days till the wedding. I found myself adding up the same two rows of numbers twice and then not putting the totals down either time. You are all I can think of."

"I understand. I've been misplacing things. I still can't find my comb and I can't make a decision, even about a hat." She allowed him to kiss her again, enjoying his body pressing her against the wall.

He kissed her neck and behind her ear. "I know I should leave you alone but I'm eager to be your husband and scared to death of the wedding night." At her worried expression, he confessed, "You know, of letting you down."

"I won't be let down. The girls said it's all about getting to know one another. Learning what each of us likes, what feels good," Molly explained to her fiancé.

"You told the girls? Your friends that I, that I had never been with anyone?" he asked quietly.

"No, never. They know that I have never been with anyone. The other is between us. We'll figure it out together but they have been helpful with hints and ideas to help me make you happy," Molly confessed.

"You make me happy simply being yourself," he said hugging her to his body and then let her go, knowing they had been in the office too long together.

"Do not worry about the wedding night, Eli. The girls said it doesn't have to happen then. It will when we get used to one another, when we are comfortable with each other's bodies."

"You better stop explaining things. Parts of my body are more than ready to be comfortable with parts of yours. At least, I know that much," he told her ruefully.

"And mine are crying out for yours but you are right, we have been in here long enough. Oh, and if you see my pearl hair pins, let me know." She smiled and sent him on his way with another brief kiss.

CHAPTER 3

Matthew, swinging his long leg over the back of the horse as he dismounted, called out to what looked like an abandoned campsite. "Mrs. Taylor? My name is Matthew St. Michaels and I have come to talk with you."

A petit woman, holding a baby, came out through the tent flap asking tentatively, "Is this about my husband? Did you find him?" She faced the tall man dressed in a black suit, white shirt with black string tie and wearing a dark Stetson. His blue eyes and pleasant smile with deep dimples had her relaxing slightly. He didn't look as if he had come to do her any harm but she reminded herself evil can look like anyone it wanted to.

"No, ma'am, but it hasn't been very long since the wires went out to the neighboring towns. I came about something else," he said, knowing he would need to be very careful about broaching this subject. He would have to play to her instincts as a mother, which seemed to be strong the way everything appeared cared for and the grip she had on the baby in her arms.

"What do you want, then?" she asked looking as if she was searching for a way to run if she felt threatened.

"Deputy Wilder said you may need a safer place to stay, you know, before the colder days hit us. That won't be too much longer in these parts. I thought perhaps you should move into town. It would be safer, warmer and your children would be closer to school," he said, laying out the reasons she should chose to go with him.

"I can't. My husband expects to find me here so I'll stay. The children will be fine. Mrs. Wilder even sent some clothes home for them to keep them warmer. And shoes. They never had shoes afore," she told him, trying to justify her staying in the small tent beside the wagon.

"I understand you not wanting to leave this place but it is going to become very cold. So cold the children won't be able to walk to school and that is even before the snow starts to blow. We get snow falls higher than this tent. Your firewood and water will be impossible to get. You can't melt snow without firewood," he told her reasonably.

"I think I should stay here. I got a basket of food stuffs from the deputy just the other day and I'll stack up more firewood," she said glancing at the small pile of branches she had gathered over the past few days.

"I appreciate your hard work but I don't think you understand how cold it gets here," he said trying to think what else he could say to change her mind. "Look, my wife has two young babies, too. She could use your help taking care of them since she wants to sew most of the time for her dress shop. She could hire you and room and board can be included."

The woman lifted her head in interest and Matthew remained silent to let her make up her mind. "I'll think about that. My husband would probably check with the local sheriff if I weren't here, I guess." As if she had made some kind of decision she offered, "Would you like a berry tart? I made them this morning from the late berries over a ways."

Matthew was torn between not wanting to take food from this family that apparently had so little and offending the generosity of the woman. "Just a small piece. I've found that since getting married, I've been eating too well. I'm having difficulty fitting into my clothes."

Mrs. Taylor returned from the tent, evidently having laid the baby down, bringing out half of a tart. She handed it to Matthew on a tin plate with a fork.

Matthew took a bite and then another, saying, "I can't believe you can bake something this flaky on an open fire. Your husband should hurry back to you for your cooking alone."

Mrs. Taylor laughed. The first smile that had crossed her lips since Matthew had been talking with her.

"He always said he married me for my baking. I was the blue-ribbon winner at the county fair for pie and cake baking every year since I was fourteen. Well, not the last one, we were travelling then. I got second place for my breads. I bake an oatmeal and raisin that some say is the best bread they ever ate," she boasted proudly, remembering a better time and place.

"After tasting this tart, I'm sure those ribbons were not misplaced. I'll let you think our conversation over but please know, we only want what is best for you and your family." Then he remounted and returned the wave Mrs. Taylor gave him as she watched him ride away.

CHAPTER 4

The church had some late blooming flowers in vases at the front altar and a row of lamps gave a glow over the somber group sitting in the pews. The early setting of the sun made this unusual evening ceremony special and Molly focused on Eli's eyes, his smile beaming proudly as he watched her walk slowly toward him.

She wore a white dress with lace overlay and lavender ribbons trimming the high collar, cuffs and every layer of ruffles down the back of the slight bustle which swayed with each step. A small hat, hardly more than a whimsy with a veil, perched on top of her hair pulled up and back with fat curls hanging down. She held a small bouquet of pink roses that had come by train just for her.

Reverend Walters began the ceremony with the words that had bound so many of those in the pews together, many of the couples holding each other's hands as they remembered their day in front of him, the sanctifying of their love to one another. Then Father Manuel, the Catholic priest, celebrated a shorter version of a Catholic wedding so all of the St. Michaels' orphans present would feel Molly was truly married.

Although Molly and Eli had only been in town a couple of months, Molly was one of the young women who had come to town as a graduate of the St. Michaels Foundling Home in New York City. That insured her a readymade family as soon as she arrived and they accepted Eli because Molly loved him and it was as apparent that he loved Molly.

As soon as the wedding was over, the entire group headed back to the hotel where there would be some of the best food in town. The matriarch of the group, Matthew's sister, Callie Harrison, came prepared to feed an army. Her cooking and baking skills couldn't be bested, having at one time been a sous chef at a fine dining restaurant in a St. Louis hotel.

Callie, a petit young woman, came over when the wedding party was beginning to wane due to the lateness of the hour saying, "I bet you're glad you accepted my offer to come to Sweetwater now aren't you, Molly? I didn't expect you to find your soulmate so soon but that's the way it is here, I guess. And Eli, welcome to the family. You are now expected at the Harrison ranch during holidays, except Fourth of July which is when we all come to town," Callie explained the rules of the St. Michaels' family's blooming traditions.

Molly asked, concerned for her friend travelling in the dark, "Thank you for doing all this for us, Callie, it was all delicious. You're not headed back to the ranch tonight, are you?"

"No, Seth and I have a room here but don't worry, we sleep soundly and won't be disturbed by anything you two do," she said making her friend blush, as well as Eli, which surprised her a little. "I'm sorry, I couldn't resist teasing. Many happy returns to you both and may God bless you."

"May God bless you, too, Callie," returned Molly.

"He has, in so many ways." She gazed at her husband of close to two years, Seth, as he stood talking with her brother, Matthew, and his wife, Abbey.

Callie and Seth, her tall husband with blond hair and bronzed skin from being out of doors so much of his life, walked up the stairs of the hotel holding hands and murmuring together about their wedding and the ensuing night. "I can't believe how ignorant I was that I had to get information from Mason," Seth confessed.

Staring at her husband open mouthed, she said, "You never told me that. What in heavens did he tell you? Was he the one that told you how to…?"

"No," he said in a loud whisper once they were locked in their room alone. "I came up with that all on my own and you can thank me in an appropriate manner." He pulled her into his arms for a long kiss, using all the expertise he had learned during their marriage.

"Then I applaud you on your being a quick study because I remember I didn't have any complaints," she said as she opened her mouth to his. "Not a one."

"Then I did it right," he said, beginning to unbutton her dress to help remove it quicker. "I don't know why women wear so many darn layers. It's like unpacking a gift wrapped over and over again."

"I think you answered your own question, sir," she said, shimmying out of the bustle cage and letting Seth undo the corset ties, which she really didn't need to wear in the first place. "You have too many clothes on. You should be undressing so we'll be equal."

"You are so much better than me, Callie, we'll never be equal." He stroked down her skin now exposed to him and kissed the pink tipped breasts waiting for his touch, his tongue.

"Seth," Callie said as she arched into him, urging him to enjoy her body as she enjoyed his touch. "Don't leave me tonight. Stay with me. It's been over a year since you stayed with me."

"I can't, you know I can't. I almost lost you when our son was born. I couldn't live through that. Our son needs you. I need you. I can't endanger you like that again." He trembled merely thinking of possibly losing the most important person to him.

Callie moved toward the bed, still letting Seth take his fill of her. They lay down and wrapped his big body around his petit wife. He entered her waiting silky warmth in the way he had been doing since before their child was born so as not to put too much weight on her. Always conscious of how much larger he was than she. How very fragile she seemed. He reached around and found the hidden bud, also blossoming forth to receive its attention.

Pushing herself into her husband's hips, she tipped her pelvis to get the maximum length of him, hoping this time he would stay with her, that he wouldn't pull out and leave her feeling bereft even if he made sure she had her pleasure first.

Seth felt Callie find her release and sped up his motions then pulled away, shuddering against her back, spilling his seed into the cloth he held there for that purpose. He kissed the back of Callie's neck, holding her close to him. He tried not to feel as if he had denied his wife her wish, knowing that in some way he was letting her down with his fear.

Turning to her husband, she said, "I love you, Seth. I'll never leave you if I can help it but you know my feelings, my love of children and of wanting a big family. I can have more children if you'll let yourself be a husband completely. Don't deny me this, Seth. I need you to want to have more children with me. It's what I was created for, what you were created for - everything else is to ensure the children are cared for. God wouldn't have sent me to Sweetwater without a reason and that reason was to find you, to love you. Don't renege on your duty to Him, to me. Please think about it, won't you?"

Seth felt the quiet tears roll down her face and soak into the pillow.

He knew he was behaving selfishly. He was hoping this holiday away from the ranch and their son would make Callie happy but instead she seemed to be as disheartened as she had been these last few weeks at the ranch. Could he do what she requested, what she wanted more than life with him, even if it ended what they had? He didn't understand but he knew Callie was Catholic and those beliefs were strong in Callie, in all the women from St. Michaels.

Maybe he needed to think of his wife's wants and not be concerned with his own fears, fears that were ungrounded according to the midwife. And God wouldn't take Callie, would he? Especially since she was doing what He wanted?

Callie wasn't crying anymore but she wasn't sleeping either. Seth covered her breast with his hand, cupping the soft welcoming part. "I'll try, I really will. I know deep down I'm afraid of something irrational but it's there anyway."

"I have an idea if you're willing to go along with me." At his quiet acquiescence she whispered, "Before the baby, you used to enjoy my being in control, my being on top. Didn't you like that?" Turning to him and rubbing her hands on his chest, pushing her fingers through the hair covering the firm muscles.

"Hmmm," he responded enjoying her attentions again and feeling his erection respond to her suggestion.

Feeling his capitulation, she kissed his mouth, sliding her tongue in just to feel his need of her reciprocated. She pushed him onto his back and straddled him, taking her time but feeling the need in him swell as she enjoyed the control of their lovemaking again. Seth held her waist and helped set the pace, increasing it as he found the speed that would bring them to their desired completion.

Callie bit her lip as she felt Seth build toward his climax, not even thinking about her own pleasure, worried Seth's fears would again over-come his desire of her. But she needn't have worried, Seth was so involved with her on top he allowed himself to stay with her through his whole orgasm, to be complete with her, to enjoy their union thoroughly.

Collapsing onto her husband, a joy so boundless exploded in her heart making it impossible to speak.

Finally, Seth said in her ear, "Do you think the newlyweds are having as much fun as we are?"

In that moment, Callie knew that she and Seth were going to be all right. That he didn't resent her pushing him into doing something he didn't want, that he could enjoy making love fully with her again even if the outcome was a sibling for their son. She cocooned with him and felt his arms tighten around her, just as they had for the last two years. She had never felt so blessed.

Molly and Eli tiptoed down the back staircase of the hotel. Molly trying to stifle the giggles that kept over-coming her usual calm demeanor. Eli, carrying a lamp and towels, had a big grin on his face as he asked, "You're sure this is what the girls told you to do? I've never heard of it before."

"Neither had I or I would have remembered. Here,

this one is available." She led her new husband into one of the bathing rooms of the hotel, hanging the quilt on one of the clothing hooks. She and Eli were spending the night in a hotel room, gratis, and Molly was trying to remember everything her friends had told her about the first night with their husbands.

Closing the door, she set the lamp they had brought with them on the end of a wooden bench and lit the lamp hanging on the wall. Both of them were familiar with the room since Eli spent time in the hotel before moving to the newly opened boardinghouse across the street. There was a built-in tub and brass faucets leading to pipes from the ceiling where the water heater fed all three bathing rooms. Molly leaned over and turned on the hot water lever letting it flow into the copper tub, a slight mist rising as the water cooled against the side.

Turning to Eli, she explained, "We need to feel comfortable with each other. To be able to touch and feel each other without embarrassment."

"That doesn't sound so difficult," Eli said, reaching over to unbutton the lovely white dress. "I feel comfortable removing your clothes." He smiled then leaned in and kissed Molly, something he felt he was very good at now.

Molly reciprocated by undoing his tie and pulling it off, then unbuttoning his shirt and helping him shrug out of it. His coat and vest were upstairs in their room along with their shoes and her hat.

"I feel comfortable removing your clothes, too," she told him as she hesitated at the buttons on his trousers.

"What are all these contraptions? I don't know where to start," Eli said as he found the wire cage for the bustle and the whalebone corset with ribbons.

"It will be easier for me to get out of these. Now you know what we women will go through merely to make ourselves attractive to you men." She piled the offending items on the wooden bench.

Eli took in the sheer white stockings tied just above her knees and the camisole still covering her breasts and the dark shadow beneath her waist. He stopped fumbling with his trousers and rolled the stockings, one at a time, down her slim legs. Taking each small foot in his hands as he removed the stockings completely, he tried not to notice her nakedness in front of him. He lifted the bottom edge of the camisole over her head to expose her breasts, which he touched reverently.

Molly stood perfectly still then said, "I like that."

Startled by Molly's voice, Eli dropped his hands.

Molly turned toward the levers and turned off the water, taking a cloth and soaping it with the lavender scented soap she had brought. "The girls said we need to know our bodies, each other's bodies from head to toe. We need to know what each other likes, where we want to be touched and let the other person know, too," she continued to explain what she had been told by her married St. Michaels' sisters.

She began by soaping his shoulders and down the front of his chest which had a smattering of dark hair. Taking special effort with his nipples, she found he closed his eyes when she paid attention there. Standing up on tiptoe to kiss him, she still had to ask for him to lean down a little for her to reach his lips. She washed until she got to his trousers that were unbuttoned but showed only where the light line of hair from his chest widened again.

Eli, liking this adventurous bathing took the cloth

from Molly and rewetted it with warm water and soap. He began the same journey on her body as she had on his, spending special attention to the nipples on each of her full breasts, peaking in their enjoyment of his touch again.

"Are you cold?" he asked her.

"No, are you?" she asked him in return.

"I don't think I'll ever be cold again. Do you think we're doing this right? I'm feeling great and I like everything you've done so far," he said enjoying the slippery feel of her skin beneath his hands.

"I think there's a lot more but I think I'm comfortable with you touching me, anywhere, now." She pushed his hand lower over her stomach to end at the apex of her legs.

Eli needed no more encouragement to slide his hands gently between her legs making him moan and push his hips into her stomach, trapping his hand between them, leaving Molly to rock on his hand as Eli let a finger slip into her waiting damp warmth.

Another moan and Eli bent to kiss her mouth once more.

"I don't think we are supposed to do this all standing up. That's why they had me bring a quilt." Molly said between kisses.

Hating to leave the comforts of her body, he turned and tossed the quilt to the floor. Pulling off his trousers he took care not to injure his manhood, which was larger than he had ever been. Molly lay down on the quilt without looking at her husband and lifted her arms toward him as he lowered himself to her side.

"I think we must be doing something right, Molly, because I can hardly stop touching you," he said as he placed his hand back to her cozy warmth.

Finally feeling brave enough, Molly moved her hand to touch the firmed appendage pressing into her side. Eli jumped and she pulled her hand away.

"I'm sorry, did I hurt it?" she asked worriedly.

"I don't think you could hurt me now, if you tried. Touch me again. I think I'm going to like it a lot," he urged, tipping away to give her plenty of room to stroke or grasp him. She did both.

"I think I want you to put it in me. I think I'm ready if you are," she told her husband boldly. She couldn't seem to want anything more than feeling him inside her.

"I'm ready but if I do it wrong, tell me. I don't want to hurt you," he said positioning himself over her with his engorged male member already entering the silky sheath.

Molly didn't think this was the time to tell Eli what the girls had warned her about the first time. But they all assured her the pain was worth the conclusion if she followed their advice. She closed her eyes on the pinch of pain and then opened herself to the feeling of having Eli in her, part of her, as one working toward the same goal. She moved with him trying to match his rhythm.

Eli was nearly desperate to make sure Molly was comfortable with what he was doing, if she needed him to stop or move differently. Molly assured him she was enjoying the lovemaking and then she was really, really enjoying the lovemaking.

Something began to spiral inside her, something wanted out or to be recognized or something and she noticed when her breathing changed, so did Eli's, coming faster as if he was chasing something, trying to reach that same something, too.

Finding what she had been chasing first, she let out a long sigh after holding her breath through the most explosive waves. Sensations she had never felt washed over her, rippling out to the farthest parts of her body, leaving the shell completely depleted, her toes curled in reaction.

Eli must have noticed her stiffen and he followed with a shudder, warmth spreading into her body. Molly could actually feel his life force entering her. She held him tightly as Eli lay on top of her, marveling at the perfect way man and woman were made to fit together, to bring such joy and love to one another.

He went to move off Molly, realizing he was not taking much of his own weight but Molly held him in place.

"That was amazing, Eli. I don't think it could have been better."

Eli leaned down and kissed her raised mouth. "I don't see how it could, either. I guess we figured out how to make love the first time we tried."

"The girls told me it might take some time to, you know, really be able to meet one another's needs. My needs were more than met. You surpassed anything I could have thought it felt like. Do you think maybe you're a natural?" she teased, laughing at the blush flaming across his cheek bones at her praise.

"I think we're lucky we're so compatible. I did what felt good and what I hoped felt good for you and then there was that outcome," he said, twirling a ringlet of hair around his finger, watching her eyes for any sign she wasn't telling him the truth.

"Eli, I'm so happy I found you and that you loved me in return." Molly snuggled into his chest, rubbing her nose into the chest hair there, feeling its silkiness.

"Do you think we're done with this bath business? I'd like to take you upstairs and try this all over in that big bed," he said, stroking her side from hip to breast.

"I agree with you. I feel clean enough. Let's get our clothes."

"Molly, are you going to tell the girls? I mean how I did?" he asked shyly.

"No, Eli. That is between us, as husband and wife but they may guess since I don't think I'll be able to hide my happiness," she told him truthfully.

Eli smiled and pulled her up to stand by his side. "Guessing - I can take. It's the details that make me cringe."

They went up the back stairs, Molly carrying half the items she had come down wearing.

CHAPTER 5

The telegraph operator waved to Franklin as he descended the train to the platform at the Sweetwater station. Franklin, a muscular young man of about twenty-five years old, was the bartender at the saloon for five years now. He had always been friendly but today he must have been in a hurry because he gave a half-hearted wave in the operator's direction. He kept walking toward the saloon on the main street stretched out behind the station.

Sweetwater was a small town, especially for a town on the railroad tracks but it was growing, several new buildings and business signs letting those new in town know where they could get boots or hire a buggy or even get their photographs taken. Most of these businesses had popped up in the last year or two and joined the barber shop, hotel, saloon, mercantile, butcher, and ladies dress shop already in place on Main Street.

The street itself was surprisingly clean and free of horse droppings and the usual refuse that often blows around a prairie town. All the buildings were painted and the roofs over-hanging the boardwalk that fronted the businesses well maintained. The boardwalk itself was swept clean of dirt and debris. All in all, Sweetwater was a clean little western town, not use to drama and suspense but that may be about to change.

Mary Margaret, now known to all mostly as Maggie, wore a plain cotton dress with striped bibbed apron over it as she wiped off the last table from the breakfast rush. Her sun-streaked brown hair was wound up in a bun and her face was open and free of concern.

The construction men, who were her usual clientele, had just gone to begin their day's work and she wouldn't see anyone again till the midday break when hungry men would again descend on the saloon for a hearty, square meal.

The tall man in the doorway of the saloon stood and admired the sway of Maggie's hips in her full skirt as she bent over the table. He tipped his bowler back onto his head with a drawn-out whistle.

Standing straight, she glanced up quickly and seeing who stood there, turned back to her work. "Why Franklin Johnson, you behave yourself...although you do look grand in your city clothes. Why are you all dressed up? Taking the train somewhere?" She walked across to the bar and left the wet cloth hanging on a hook over the sink.

"Not anymore, I'm not, but why don't we pretend and you can give me a goodbye kiss?" he said smiling at the pretty young waitress with her hair pinned up imagining it loose and flowing down her naked back.

"Franklin, I don't know what has gotten into you but you better remember your manners or Mason may have a word or two to say," she told him as she headed to the back doorway carrying a tray of dirty plates and cups.

The young man's long legs got him there before her and he swooped in and stole a kiss while Maggie stood there, her hands too full to push him away and a curiosity about what it felt like to kiss Franklin keeping her in place. It was pleasant but not earth shattering, which is about what she had expected.

All her friends had found the loves of their lives and she had been waiting for hers but she knew when she kissed the right man, the world would stand still, stars like Fourth of July rockets would go off in her head and she wouldn't want to ever stop kissing him. This kiss wasn't like that and she was a little sorry because she liked Franklin a lot as a friend. It would have been too much to expect.

Once the young man raised his head, he said, "Now, that was worth waiting for. How 'bout we go someplace and finish what we started?"

"We didn't start anything and I plan on going into the hot kitchen and doing up these dishes. You are welcome to join me but I'll put you to work, dress clothes or not," she stated avoiding his gaze in case she had offended him with her rejection. She had been busy all morning and still had to set the bread to rise.

"Ahh, no, I just remembered I have to do some other stuff," he fabricated.

"I figured that would cool your ardor. I'll see you about noon," she said as she continued through the door and into the hotel's busy kitchen.

The young man was about to head to the upstairs' rooms when he came face to face with an identical young man coming in the rear door from the alley. Both men stopped and stared at each other, neither breaking the silence. Other than the clothes each was wearing, they were alike as two peas in a pod. Neither smiled a welcome and both looked warily at the other, waiting for something to break the tenseness filling the space around them.

Finally, the man coming into his saloon asked, "What the hell are you doing here, Hamilton?"

"Well, little brother, I come in peace," said the man wearing the city clothes.

"Don't call me that. You're only five minutes older and a hell of a lot less mature," accused Franklin.

"You don't know that. I haven't seen you for ten years. That's a lot of time for me to have changed. I don't think I did anything all that bad for you to turn away from me. We were both hurting after Jefferson and Baldwin's deaths. The war should have been over for both of us," Hamilton said seriously.

"You don't have to remind me. I lost two brothers in that damn war. Neither of them should have been where they were. If they had just let things be, our family would still be together," said Franklin in remembered pain.

"Look, we've been over this. Jefferson went with his beliefs and Baldwin went with his. The fact they ended up on opposite sides tore all of us apart. Mamma most of all. She hated the war and she hated what it did to her family. You and me fighting over this just added to her grief," Hamilton said sadly.

"Why did you hunt me up? I know it wasn't due to brotherly love." Franklin asked bluntly, "Do you need money?"

"That's just mean, brother. When did I ever ask you for money?"

"Oh, that's right. You didn't ask, you just took my savings when it pleased you. Right out of the bank, pretending to be me. Have you outgrown that at least?" asked Franklin indignantly.

Knowing he had just misled the waitress Hamilton didn't want to answer. "Let's talk about that another time. How about I buy you dinner?"

"I'm working till midnight. Then it starts all over again tomorrow at five-thirty," Franklin informed his brother.

"Hell, you must be making money hand over fist. Maybe I'll rethink borrowing some cash from you," teased Hamilton. At his brother's scowl added, "Just joshing with you, brother. I'm doing fine. I want to mend the fences for both our sakes."

"Where are you staying? Did you plan on bunking with me?"

"That would give us the most time to be together, if it's convenient."

Franklin, defeated, waved his arm toward the stairs. "Second door leads to my apartment. Take the empty bedroom. I'll talk with you later."

Hamilton slapped his brother on the back and went toward the stairs, stopping first to pick up the carpet bag he left at the door. Franklin shook his head, trying to figure out why his brother showed up now, years after their parting.

"Who are you?" barked Sheriff Mason the owner of the saloon when he found a man loading wood into the back door of the bar.

Hamilton tried to bluff his way saying, "Why, boss, what do you mean?"

"I mean you're not, Franklin. You've just shaved off some pretty wide mutton chops and mustache in the last couple of days so I'll ask again, who are you? Franklin's twin?" Mason asked roughly.

Hamilton put out his hand to shake Mason's which the sheriff ignored since the man had tried to lie to him. "I'm Hamilton, sir. I'm sorry for trying that childish trick we used to pull on people when we were young."

"Franklin never said he had a twin and I thought his brothers were dead," the larger man said.

"Our two older brothers were killed fighting in the war. Then we drifted apart so I felt we should mend fences, you know, before we lose one another completely."

"Do you know where Franklin is now?" asked Mason not commenting on whether he thought Hamilton had a chance or not of reconnecting with his twin.

"He's been helping Maggie inside. I thought I'd help bring in the wood and then sweep up the back room," he said, showing the sheriff he was earning his room and board.

"I'll look for him there. Nice to have made your acquaintance," Mason said politely and went into the back door to find his employee.

Now Mason wasn't as puzzled about the wire from the state Marshal asking about the whereabouts of one, Franklin Johnson, and proceeded to have Franklin's description down to a T, except for the muttonchops and mustache. He stepped into the saloon and found his bartender sweeping up after the breakfast crowd.

"Need to talk with you, Franklin," he said as he got the younger man's attention.

"Sure, Mason. How can I help you?" He smiled which turned into a slight frown when Mason didn't return it as usual.

"I've got some strange wires from the state Marshal and I think it has to do with your brother."

Franklin looked toward the doorway to the hotel, hoping Maggie wasn't close enough to hear. He hadn't had time to explain to her and for some reason he wanted to be the one to tell her about his brother, about his family being pulled asunder.

"Let's go down to the office. We need to talk."

Mason went out the front door with Franklin right on his heels. Franklin turned back but Maggie still hadn't returned from the kitchen.

By the time Maggie came back to the saloon it was Hamilton sweeping the floor. Maggie looked at him asking, "Who are you?"

"Et tu, Brute'," said Hamilton, putting his most winning smile on his lips.

"Why do you quote Shakespeare? I want to know which brother are you? Franklin has spoken of his family a little but not that he had a twin, so what's your name? Baldwin, Hamilton or Jefferson?"

"So, he's told you our names. I'm his older twin, Hamilton. The other two were killed in the war so they won't be showing up and making Franklin's life uncomfortable," he replied as she watched him closely.

"Is that why you're here? To make Franklin's life uncomfortable?"

"No, I came to try to rebuild the relationship I had with my brother ten years ago, before the war tore our family apart."

"I'll wait and have Franklin tell me if he wants me to know," she said then stopped. "You kissed me this morning," she accused.

"Well, I could see you wanted me to," he said shrugging as if what else could he do but oblige.

"I did not want a stranger to kiss me," she said forcefully.

"But if I had been, Franklin, then it would have been all right? You like Franklin?" he asked, his eyelids lowered to cover the expression in his eyes.

"I don't kiss Franklin, either. You caught me off guard. Besides, I've known Franklin for months and if he kissed me it wouldn't be that surprising."

At Hamilton's raised eyebrows, Maggie added, "I mean, if he kissed me, I wouldn't be surprised. No, I mean, if someone knows someone else for a while it isn't…."

Hamilton held up his hands. "I understand. I am not Franklin and shouldn't have kissed you under false identity."

"Th-thank you, I appreciate the apology." She returned to the hotel's kitchen simply to leave the saloon and Hamilton behind.

Once at the jail, Mason motioned Franklin to sit down in the chair in front of the desk while he took the chair behind it, leaning back against the wall. "What do you know about your brother's whereabouts for the past several months?"

"You mean, Hamilton? I don't know anything about his whereabouts for the last several years. About ten years, in all. After the war ended and my Ma died, my brother and I couldn't get along so I went my way and he went his. I haven't heard anything more until this morning when he showed up saying he wanted to mend fences but I know there's more to it than that," Franklin confessed to his friend and boss.

"So, if I were to ask him, I'd get the same answers?" Mason continued with the questions.

"Mason, I don't know what he'd tell you. Probably anything that would show him in a good light, I'm sure. He always played the good son while I was a demon, born and bred. He had the habit of getting in trouble, you know, stealing a pie cooling in a kitchen window and my shirt would be found with a stain from the pie filling on it. Never failed. One of the reasons I left Ohio so far behind is because I was afraid, he'd get some girl in the family way and leave me to marry her or get shot by her irate pa," Franklin said honestly.

"He might be up to his old tricks, Franklin. I've been told to hold you for the Marshal but when he gets here, I'll probably get him to understand the situation. I mean, I know where you've been every day for the last year or so. If there was something your brother did in your name during that time, he may have misjudged you or me or the people of Sweetwater. We'll stand behind you. You're part of this town after all this time," Mason said as he let the chair's front two legs hit the floor.

Stalking back to the saloon, Franklin found no sign of his brother who had probably figured his con had been blown so was in hiding until Franklin cooled off. It wasn't going to work this time. Hamilton was going to face up to whatever he had done to get the state Marshal involved. They weren't children any longer and this was going to mean more than a whipping and being sent to bed without his dinner.

If Mason was concerned, then the problem was major. Mason wasn't one to get upset about little things. Franklin didn't want Sweetwater's townspeople to think he was involved in anything unscrupulous, which was his brother's trademark. It was a good thing Hamilton was staying out of his sight for a while since it gave Franklin time to think up how to approach his brother and get the information he needed.

CHAPTER 6

Matthew again found himself outside the neat camp site, the water puddles still frozen from the cold spell that came through during the night. His horse's breath was showing with each exhale. Matthew knew his would be, too, if his mouth weren't covered with the knitted scarf Abby made him put on that morning. "Mrs. Taylor, it's Matthew St. Michaels, again. May I speak with you?"

"Come in," she invited, trying not to keep the tent flap open any longer than she had to be polite.

Matthew entered the tent and stayed in a somewhat stooped position so as not to hit the top of the canvas. All the children were home and bundled into blankets or quilts, their large blue eyes looking out at him in fear.

He smiled, saying gently, "I have two little girls who would love to play with you and my son goes to school with you. Do you know, Thad? He's my oldest." That seemed to warm up his reception with the children but their mother was still peering at him as if he ate small children.

He turned to the woman. "Mrs. Taylor, I came to offer you a different proposition. I told you my wife owned the dress shop in town and I recently purchased the building next door to the store so I could have an office separate from our home. There is a living area in the rear of the street level so there will be room for you and your children. It already has a large stove and indoor hand pump and sink. After tasting one of your berry tarts, I feel I can offer you the street level portion of the building and have my offices upstairs.

The woman's eyes grew large as she began to realize what he was telling her. Matthew continued, "I will front you the money to buy enough supplies to bake bread, maybe some pies or tarts. There is a big need for baked bread and ready-made foods the construction men can buy. If you can see yourself as a business woman, I'll get someone to help with the budget and books, help you price out the products. Do you think you could bake enough bread and pies to keep your family together this winter?"

It was a long speech and Mrs. Taylor had been thinking from the word 'proposition'. Now she wished she had paid more attention to the one time she rode through the town to get to the riverbank.

"I would like to try but what if the men won't buy my baked bread or pies? How will I pay you back?"

"Well, I may be your best customer. My wife would rather be designing dresses and sewing than baking so this will allow her to keep sewing and not feel she isn't feeding me and our son properly," he admitted truthfully, showing his adorable dimples without realizing it.

"Can I see it? I mean, do you know how much I would have to bake and sell to make a living and pay you back with interest?" she asked him, trying to do the sums in her head without a paper and pencil.

"Well, look at that, you're already sounding like a business woman. I should have asked before assuming you had no experience. Have you worked in a business before?"

"Not really. My mother took in sewing and laundry and I helped while I was home but I've been married since I was sixteen so it's been years. I tallied up her accounts for her. I just remember things real well. I

always have. If I read something, I remember it."
Shrugging as she explained her abilities.

"You can sell a loaf of bread for about ten cents,
specialty breads for twelve to fifteen. A pie, depending
on the filling, up to a dollar with a ten-cent deposit on
the pan, which I've already found a manufacturer for. If
you can do a meat pie, you'll sell out of them every day,
I'm sure." Matthew was trying to sell the woman on the
idea of moving her family into town where she could be
watched over and protected.

"I'll need a little time to decide. I hate to leave here
without being able to tell my husband where I've gone.
He doesn't read so I can't leave a note for him. I'll have
to think on it," she said, a worried expression causing her
brows to lower.

"I understand but I'll be back with some firewood
tomorrow, either way. You'll need some bigger pieces to
burn for some real heat to keep this tent area warm." He
left the little family huddling in the cold and damp even
though it went against everything he believed in.

Mason was entering the saloon just as Maggie was
entering from the hotel when they both became aware of
loud yelling and then the sound of fist upon chin. They
ran towards the back of the saloon that opened to the ally.
Franklin and Hamilton were in a man to man brawl,
which was always the way the two brothers solved a
problem.

Mason waited for the right time to step between the
men and then threw one man against the saloon wall and
the other against the side of the feed and grain building.
"Now hold on both of you. I need some answers and I
want the man I talk with to be conscious."

Franklin was the first to speak shouting angrily at

the man holding on to the feed and grain wall. "He kissed Maggie. He can't be trusted around a descent woman, I know. I'm going to beat him till he can't stand up. No one should touch her. She's not that kind of girl."

Maggie placed her hand against his heaving chest. "Franklin, I let him kiss me when I thought he was you but it wasn't all that inspiring. Then I realized it wasn't you, which means I still get to know what it's like to kiss you," she told him, completely monopolizing his attention.

With rapt interest he watched Maggie as he wiped his mouth with the back of his hand, unsure of what she planned to do. Maggie leaned into him saying, "I'd appreciate a kiss from you, Franklin, to see if I've misjudged you in any way." Then she placed her hand behind his head and pulled him forward, towards her mouth.

He met her lips with a kiss that immediately leapt into flames. He raised his hand to cup her face and turned his head to deepen the kiss as his tongue slid into her warmth and he felt her tongue tentatively mate with his.

A loud throat clearing made the couple jump away from each other but Franklin kept a dark-eyed gaze on Maggie as she backed away, bringing the tips of her fingers to her now swollen lips.

Mason spoke up to break the trance between the couple. "Franklin, go inside and clean up. I came to speak with Hamilton, here."

Franklin looked over at his boss to see a stern expression, his lips pressed together while Hamilton looked like a cat that ate a canary, a slight grin on his face as if he knew a huge joke no one else did.

Once inside, Maggie grabbed one of the clean

towels and dipped it in the bucket of water before following Franklin to a chair. She began dabbing at the bleeding wounds on his forehead and under one eye.

"Why did you kiss me? Really?" he asked, needing to know if she really wanted to kiss him before this, before Hamilton had kissed her. Looking into her eyes, seeing the iris, pupil dilate, he smiled, thinking he had his answer.

"I, I told you. I was disappointed with the kiss from Hamilton. It-it confused me because I thought a kiss from you would be much nicer, mean more," she admitted blushing as she held the cold cloth to the cut under his eye, just along the cheek bone.

Franklin, with his boyish grin Maggie loved, asked, "Did the kiss right now make up for your disappointment? Did it meet your expectations?"

Maggie let a smile cross her lips, the color still high on her cheek. "Yes, and yes. I knew you could make my world stand still and you did. I'm afraid I forgot where we were and that we weren't alone. That is until Mason reminded us. I felt like a little girl caught by her father getting into the candy jar."

"I thought I was the only one who felt that way. I'm glad I didn't do anything else embarrassing. I mean, I felt the two of us were the only people in the world at that moment," he said watching Maggie as if he couldn't get enough of her.

"Do you want to experiment again? Maybe after you calm down and there really is only the two of us, together?" she asked, wanting to experience his kiss again and see if there is the same flare of heat between them, see if the world disappeared again. But what if it doesn't? What if it was the fight and the fear, she felt for

Franklin that caused the emotions between them? Would it still count? Did it still mean there was something growing between them as a couple?

Franklin may have been having similar thoughts because he stood, holding the cloth to his own cheek. "You'll probably be needed in the kitchen. I'll be here to help with the meal as usual but I don't think Hamilton will be around."

Maggie took the hint and went into the hotel but not the kitchen right away. She needed some place to calm her thoughts and settle herself before facing anyone else. She found herself in the linen closet.

She had been raised in an orphanage so she had been surrounded by boys her whole life. Boys she had been warned to keep away from by the sisters in charge of St. Michaels. Boys who were like her brothers and not her lover. She had found most of them irritating, not intriguing. She found them immature and not adult enough to think of them as a life partner.

Now, all these years later, in a small town in Kansas she may have found the man she was waiting to love. But she had been working with him for the last few months and hadn't, until recently, recognized him as such. All her friends, all their stories were of how quickly they had met their future husbands and knew within days he was the one. Maybe Franklin wasn't really the man she was to marry.

Mason watched the man next to him closely. "Now, I want to know why you really came to Sweetwater?"

"I already told you, to mend…" Hamilton began but was cut off by Mason.

"Bullocks! I want to know what you've been up to and how come Franklin's name is being bandied about by the head lawman in the state? I know Franklin and where he's been for the last year but I don't know your whereabouts. Should the Marshal be searching your past rather than Franklin's?" Mason said blistering the man opposite him with disrespect.

"I don't know anything about a Marshal. I showed up because I was close by and thought I could mend fences with my twin," Hamilton repeated, not swaying from his original excuse for being in town.

Mason looked at the other man's split lip, swollen eye and bruised ear. "Yeah, how's that goin' for you? The family reunion seems to be about over from my view."

"We're brothers, we've always had strong opinions from one another."

"That must make for some unusual holiday gatherings," Mason said handing Hamilton a clean handkerchief to wipe his bloody mouth.

"Not so much as you think now that there's just Franklin and me." Hamilton grinned.

"Don't leave town till I say you can go. I'd hate to have to send my deputy after you. He was a bounty hunter, you know - dead or alive. He always forgets the alive part." He strode down the alley toward the jail.

Pulling the horses to a stop near the tent, Matthew called out, announcing his arrival and was surprised when Mrs. Taylor didn't open the tent flap as she usually did. Tying the reins around the brake, he climbed down calling out again.

Mrs. Taylor opened the tent flap, wearing a blanket wrapped over her shawl with the baby tied to the front of her in a sling made from a sheet.

"I made up my mind. I want to move into town. Can

you help me?" she said, her teeth chattering.

"Certainly, but has something happened? You seem frightened," Matthew said going to the woman and taking her hand, feeling her tremble.

"I thought when I heard the wagon it was a stranger coming. Last night I heard something or someone around the outside of the tent. I'm pretty sure it was a man. I could smell tobacco and I think whiskey, he was that close. I was going to hit him with a fry pan but then what? If there was more than one, no one would be there to protect the children," she said, the trembling growing worse.

Matthew knew she meant no one would be there to protect the children if she were taken or killed. She was the only thing standing between the children and death. Matthew had known too many women in that position not to feel compassion.

"I can fit you all in the wagon. I brought wood but it will burn in the stove in your new home, just a well. I take it you didn't feel safe enough to send the children to school today?"

"No, we've been telling each other stories to keep us occupied."

"And singing, Mama, tell him we like to sing," chimed in Corabelle.

Mrs. Taylor smiled at Matthew saying, "Church hymns, mostly. It's all I know."

"You can get practiced up for church then. It's just down the street from your new home," he told the young mother. "Now let's get your things packed up."

It didn't take over half an hour to get the camp broken down and the whole little family arrived in Sweetwater in less than an hour total. Matthew pulled the buckboard into the alley and began putting the few items Mrs. Taylor had into the building next to the dress shop.

Mrs. Taylor went through to the living portion peering into the two bedrooms. "I think I want all the bedding together. The children might be afraid on their own and I always sleep by the baby."

Matthew placed the cradle, the two mattresses and bedding in one of the rooms off the kitchen and living area of the back apartment, which was cozy with a fire already in the stove and a full wood box. The Taylors also had a small table and three chairs as well as a wooden crate that held her kitchen items and food. A few clothes wrapped into a pillow slip and Matthew was done unloading the wagon. He would get his sixteen-year old son, Thad, to unload and stack the wood under the stairs on the outside of the building.

As soon as Matthew left, his wife knocked on the back door, smiling and carrying a basket for the new arrivals. "Hello, I'm Abby, Matthew's wife. I brought you some little things you may need - a record keeping book, paper and pencils. Also, a catalog of kitchen and baking pans. We have a distribution center so getting these products should take little time but you may wish to start baking bread before the pans all arrive. Anything you need, I'm right next door and I'll introduce you to the other ladies in town as soon as you're settled in," said the attractive brunette with sparkling brown eyes. She wore a fashionable dress with small waist and large bustle, trimmed with velvet ribbon at the high neck and tight cuffs and jet-black buttons down the back.

"Your husband has been more than kind, Mrs. St. Michaels. I shouldn't keep accepting your generosity. I have always been able to take care of myself."

"Please call me, Abby." Peering at the solemn children watching and listening, she continued, "But it's not only you now so let us help get you back on your feet. You may pass it on to others later, when you're able. Everyone has needed help or someone they can count on at some point of their lives. Accept help now so you may be able to help another in the future." Abby explained a philosophy she had lived her life following after someone had given her help when she had needed it.

"Thank you, I need to learn to accept help with more grace, I guess. My first name is Fran, by the way, and I do appreciate what Matthew and you have done for me. I hope as soon as Walt gets back, I'll be on my way to the new home he found for us."

"Maybe if you get a good start here, your husband will stay in Sweetwater and find a job with the construction crews," said Abby giving Fran even more to think about.

Abby left and Fran looked at her two children, both tired and a little lost at the quick change in their living arrangements. She smiled encouragingly asking, "Who wants to set the table for supper?" The two children both dropped the blankets they were wrapped in and rushed to the wooden case to get the plates.

Later that night, Fran sat at the table with the catalog and the price list of foods and began to figure out what it cost to bake a loaf of bread and then various pies, including the suggested meat pies. She tried to figure out how much time she needed to bake these items and how much loss she could plan on, keeping in mind she could feed her family with anything that didn't sell. It was well into the night when she yawned and pushed the paper, now covered with numbers and pencil scratches, aside.

In the morning, Fran dressed the children with most of the clothes they had and sent them off to school with a lunch and love. She hesitated to go next door to speak with Abby or Matthew when Matthew appeared at her door with a pot of tea.

"Abby will be here in a minute. She's waiting for Victoria, the sheriff's wife, to come and take care of the girls so she can give her full attention to getting you started if you're still willing to try being a baker." He indicated the pot of tea. "She sent me with this because she said you both may need it to keep you going this morning."

"I appreciate it. I spent long hours last night trying to figure out what it will cost to start up. It seems impossible. There are so many things to buy, set up and do. I'm a little over-whelmed," she confessed as Abby arrived with cups, sugar and cream.

"I'm not late, am I? You haven't started without me, have you? I have so many ideas and I've brought Callie's recipes to select from and they are priced out already like she always does." Abby came in like a ray of sunshine, Matthew accepting his wife's excitement with a grin.

Abby was wearing another lovely dress only this time it was in lavender brocade. Fran brushed her hands down her own worn dress and apron, then pulled out a chair for her two new friends.

Taking out her papers from the night before, Fran went through the list with the couple to see if she had underestimated her needs or missed something. All three looked them over, making some additions and then everyone was finally happy with their work.

"The most expensive item in the whole store will be the glass display case," Fran said forlornly, noting the high price of even the cheapest in the catalog.

"Not so fast. I know of a place that is closing its doors. I was looking to buy their Wooten desk and maybe some of their five-wheeled desk chairs. They might still have their cases. Let me wire them to see what else they may have. It means we can get them quicker and cheaper than through the catalog," he told the two ladies.

"I can have Faith from the newspaper draw up a design and paint the sign and there's a man in Prairieview who can paint the window sign, but what are we going to call it? Any ideas Matthew," Abby asked her husband because he goes into so many towns with his wholesale business.

"I thought the Sweetwater Bakery, nice and sweet," he said smiling.

The two women looked at him and both returned his smile and agreed that it was the perfect name.

"Good, we're agreed. I'll get the items I checked off the list. Ladies, I leave ordering the food items from the Mercantile to you until we need to order in bigger quantities. There is an account set up for you, Fran, and that is for anything your family needs, also," he told her as he began to leave.

"I'll keep a separate accounting for these items, Matthew. I never meant to be a burden or for you to have to rescue my family," Fran said firmly.

Abby laughed and said, "Fran, you are the easiest woman Matthew has ever rescued and he is pleased to do it." Which was a little confusing to Fran but she didn't ask any questions.

Later that day a pretty blond woman came to the back door, introducing herself as Faith Macgregor. She explained she designed the Sweetwater Bakery logo which was a swirling capital S followed by a cursive style lower case, then a capital B followed by the lower case. It was white with a deep-sea blue shadow that made the white stand-out even more to appear as if the words were spelled out in white-water rapids. As if the river itself was part of the words.

"I simply need your approval. I have the background wood already painted. It will be the same size as the sign over the butcher shop."

"I don't know. It looks perfect but I've never done anything like this before." Fran was hesitant to make such a decision without either Matthew or Abby approving it also.

"Abby has seen it and told me it was up to you. It's not like it can't be changed later if you decide you don't like it," Faith told her while tipping her head and studying the sign.

"All right. I like it. I like it very much." She smiled, pleased with her decision.

"Then it should be ready and dry in two days. I'll have one of the men put it up as soon as it's finished."

Abby came over for Fran and the baby and together they went to the Mercantile with the list of needed supplies. Once at the store, they placed their order, the total making Fran's head swim.

"Oh, my, Abby. What have we just done?" Fran said looking at the pile of bags and items the two ladies thought were necessary to begin the bakery.

"It will be all right, Fran. Matthew and I were prepared for it to cost more than this. We want to open with a bang and a couple of us will help. At least to begin with." Abby called to a young man entering the

Mercantile. "Oh, Franklin, will you bring these items over to the store next to mine? This is Fran Taylor. She's going to open a bakery there." Abby explained to Fran, "Franklin works for Mason, the sheriff, at the saloon."

"Nice to meet you, ma'am," replied Hamilton, not giving away the fact he wasn't Franklin as Abby thought. "I'll bring it right over."

Both Abby and Fran thanked him and then they hurried out of the Mercantile to the store across the street. The baby laughed at being jiggled and tried to pull the button off her mother's dress. Fran felt empowered, ready to tackle anything as a smile entered her life and seemed to settle on her face for the rest of the day.

Within two days, Fran had baked at least one loaf of every kind of bread she knew plus ones from the recipes Callie and the butcher's wife had given her. Abby, Matthew and a couple of others tasted and voted for their favorites.

Men had been walking slowly past the store window several times a day, peering in to see if the bakery was in operation yet. Their interest gave Fran a great amount of confidence she would sell at least something when she opened the doors for business.

Entering the saloon, Maggie saw Franklin putting away the clean mugs. She went to his side saying, "Do you want to talk about your brother? You never told me you had a twin and I can see there are still bad feelings between you. I'd like to better understand what happened."

"Since it caused you to kiss me, maybe I owe you some information," he said as he swung the towel over his shoulder and leaned against the bar.

"Have you two always been at logger heads? I mean,

have there always been contentious feelings between you? Does it have to do with being twins? Did your mother have a favorite or something?" Questioned Maggie trying to guess the possible reasons the men were alienated with one another.

"No, we were inseparable for years. No one but family members could tell us apart so we spent most of our spare time pulling pranks on people in the town and, of course, our teachers. I often took tests for both of us because I enjoyed books and learning more than Hamilton but all the pranks were always innocent, with no one losing anything or being hurt," Franklin told her, staring off into the distance, no longer in the small saloon in Sweetwater.

"That doesn't sound like enough to cause the rift that evidently occurred. So, what did?" Maggie encouraged Franklin to open up to her even more.

"He began seeing a girl I had told him I liked. She was a sweet girl I had spent some time talking to during recess. Shared some of my lunches with her and who I thought I'd get my first kiss from. But Hamilton met her at the Sunday afternoon gathering after church and kissed her behind the privy. That was the first time Hamilton had used his looking like me to my disadvantage. I started to distrust my own brother, questioning things whenever I didn't know where he was for more than thirty minutes."

"That was terrible, but what did the girl do?"

"She never spoke to either of us again. She was so mortified she didn't know me from Hamilton. But Hamilton enjoyed it so much, he started being me more than he was himself. I found myself being confronted by strange young women demanding to know why I hadn't met them as I had promised or the best one was when an older brother, built like a brick sh… never mind. He wasn't pleased that his little sister was in tears over how I treated her and I ended up with a black-eye."

Maggie's hand went to her mouth in astonishment.

Franklin continued, "He sucker punched me because I was unaware, I should have ducked the minute he came within arm's reach of me."

"That sound's awful but not enough to cause the animosity between the two of you. Didn't he finally try to stop being you?"

"It was actually our older brothers that caused the real rift. What ended up tearing the family apart. My brothers, Baldwin and Jefferson, wanted to join the army and fight for what they believed in," he said seriously.

"And you two didn't want them to go and fight, leave you and your mother to farm on your own?" asked Maggie trying to make sense of it.

"No, my mother was very political, that's why we're named after men who signed the Declaration of Independence. My whole family was very involved in politics. It was the dinner table talk every night that didn't end until we went to sleep." He spoke as if he were back at that dinner table remembering the discussions. "We were steeped in it."

"And you didn't agree with your brothers' decision? Did they choose a side of the war you didn't agree with?"

"Not really, I agreed with Jefferson who went to fight for the Union with the Ohio troops while Baldwin joined the South, with Hamilton's blessing. There was some tension in the family, of course, but mother kept track of the war, praying their two regiments never had to come into contact. That was her greatest fear. That they would have to shoot at each other, maybe wound one another."

Maggie said in almost a whisper, "They didn't, did they. That's not how they died is it?"

"No, different battles, different days but mother got the letters from their commanding officers on the same day. She was stoic but she never was the same again. Hamilton thought if we could agree then mother would come back to us." he told her, looking at her reaction to his disclosure.

"Oh, Franklin, that's terrible, what happened to your family, to your brothers. How old were you at the time?" she asked aching with his pain.

"We were fourteen, just. That's one reason we didn't join our brothers in their chosen sides. That and someone had to stay and keep the farm going for mother and for our brothers when they returned after the war ended. But mother died less than a year later and Hamilton wanted to sell the farm and split the money to make our way in the world. So that's what he did, being both me and himself to the attorney involved and signed my ownership away, as well as, his."

"Oh, Franklin. No wonder you can't forgive him."

"He did give me my share or, at least, I think he did but, by then, I had lost all trust in him. I couldn't live anywhere near him and feel safe with my good name, having people who put their trust in me feel they were safe from his machinations. I can't even trust him around a woman I care about." He looked Maggie in the eyes.

"I'm sorry I kissed him, Franklin. I knew he was different but I thought it was because you had decided to pursue me a little rather than ignoring how we feel about each other," Maggie said keeping the eye contact between them.

Franklin smiled and asked teasingly, "Are you saying I was dragging my feet? That I should have kissed you sooner?"

"Yes, I think I am," she answered blushing at her own temerity.

"Then let me start making up for lost time." He pulled her closer, widening his legs so there was room for her to stand between them facing him. He leaned down and tentatively placed his lips on hers but the same spark of desire shot through them as it had in the alley.

Franklin deepened the kiss, placing a hand on the sides of her head, holding her in place, as if he feared she was going to pull away. Maggie brought both her hands up to his shoulders to hang on, preventing her legs that were going weak of allowing her to fall.

"Well, isn't this something for the record books? Not only do I lose the woman to my younger brother, he seems to have a better technique than I do. At least she isn't running away from you like she did me," Hamilton said as he came down the stairs.

Maggie wanted to step away at the intrusion but Franklin held her in place, letting his brother know there was an understanding between him and Maggie. The glare he sent his brother made sure Hamilton understood what that meant. No poaching. No funny business.

Hamilton continued on his way out the door to the street, holding his open hands up over his head as if he were surrendering.

Franklin said quietly into Maggie's ear, "If he so much as steps in front of you or looks at you wrong, you're to tell me. Do you understand? Don't be afraid of any bad feelings it may cause. I don't want him to pester you with unwanted attentions. Promise me?"

She whispered back, "I promise."

Then Franklin let her go, standing straighter and giving her some space to collect herself while he did the same. They were still working closely together through the day and Franklin didn't want Maggie to feel he should be avoided as well as his brother.

Maggie's hand went to her hair to make sure it was still up in the bun on top of her head and said, a little breathlessly, "I better check on the kitchen. I should probably start getting ready for the meal." She hurried away, staring at the floor, not meeting his gaze.

CHAPTER 7

The Sweetwater Bakery opened for business. There was a newly purchased used display cabinet filled with several types of bread as well as cinnamon rolls with dried currants, apple tarts, and buttermilk pies. The bell over the door never stopped ringing until the men had to be to the work sites and then it started all over again when the midday break came. By that time, everything had sold out and the bread rising in the kitchen wasn't ready to bake, yet. Many would be ready by the time work let out so that's what Fran told the men.

Abby sent Victoria, who helped with Abby's hand stitching, over to help mind the store while Fran took time to feed the baby and rest, knowing the baking had begun at two o'clock in the morning.

Victoria, a pretty, young woman with light brown hair and gray eyes, took the last loaves of bread out of the oven and put in the molasses cookies she had made. Fran came out of the bedroom with the baby, both appearing much more rested than they had a couple of hours earlier.

"No one has come in to buy anything but the men aren't off work yet. I know the local ladies are holding back until you know what you're going to need to have for the men each day," Victoria said as she spooned more cookie dough onto a metal sheet.

"Oh, you even made cookies. I can't thank you enough. I didn't realize how much rest I've missed worrying about this bakery, both fear and excitement kept me awake at night," Fran said placing the baby among pillows set out to keep her upright. "Oh, there's the bell. I'll get the customer but please feel free to leave anytime you need to. I know you usually have work to do for Abby."

"That won't be a problem. I'm going to wait for the cookies before I head for home," Victoria said while taking the tray of newly baked bread to the front of the store. The men were getting off work and coming in for the fragrant goodies they had been told about.

The bread sold out again as well as the cookies, with some of the men waiting for them to come out of the oven. Fran hoped there wasn't going to be any disappointed customers but she again ran out of baked goods while men still stood in the doorway.

She apologized and took their names down so they would have first chance at the items tomorrow morning if they returned.

Matthew came over following supper rolling up his shirt sleeves after removing his coat. "I got you into this and I can get you out. I know how to knead dough, just show me where you want me," he said with his dimples in full bloom.

"I appreciate that but it is kind of an art with me, my secret I guess you could say but if you would whip these egg whites for meringue, I would truly be grateful. My arms are about ready to fall off," Fran said as she pushed the copper bowl and whisk toward him.

"I understand today went quiet well. Anything need to be changed? Have any trouble getting the deposit for the pie pans?" Matthew asked as he began a rapid, almost professional use of the wire whip.

"No, they all seemed used to the deposit except for one man. I thought he was going to skip paying the deposit I asked him for but, instead, he just stood there scooping out a quarter of the pie at a time and eating it in two bites than continued the same thing until the pan was empty. He announced to everyone it was the best buttermilk pie he had ever had and handed me back the empty pie pan," Fran said laughing, remembering the astonished expressions on the other customer's faces.

"Maybe we should put a table or two and some chairs in that front area by the window for those who want to eat here. Can you think of making sandwiches with your breads to order? Do you have time?" he asked still whipping, getting the whites to peak.

Fran sprinkled in sugar as Matthew continued to whip and then took the bowl from him when she was satisfied, they were ready. She spread the mixture over the waiting lemon pudding pies and placed them in the oven, checking the temperature on her arm as she held it in the oven for a moment.

"All right then, what's next? My sister Callie trained me well the few weeks I spent with her out at the ranch. I beat a great cake, too," he said and Fran was surprised at how comfortable she felt around this man, the whole town. Safe, protected, like becoming part of a family.

"Tomorrow I don't want any customer to go away disappointed. I want double what I had today," she said as she pulled a heavy bag of flour up onto the table to mix more bread dough so it could rise in the warm kitchen.

"Remember, it's the goal of a good merchant to run out of product so their customers keep returning for more but I understand we don't want to cause a stampede when the door opens either," he said as he dipped his finger into the cake batter stealing a taste.

CHAPTER 8

Mason met the train when the state Marshal arrived, taking the man to the jail where he could explain what he thought had happened. Mason needed to find out why the Marshal wanted to speak with Franklin and what crime his brother, Hamilton, might have been involved in outside of Sweetwater.

The Marshal, a stern looking man just over fifty was still lean and vigorous, still able to chase down any criminal element in his jurisdiction, gazed at Mason.

"Well, Mason, I'm following up on a complaint by a citizen that Franklin Johnson of Sweetwater swindled the man out of hundreds of dollars he was using to buy land through the land grants newly opening up," the Marshal began. He admired the younger man and the way he kept his town free of the sleazier aspects of a frontier town and hated having to bring in this kind of trouble.

"But those are Federal grants, aren't they? Why is the State handling these accusations?" Mason asked puzzled.

"They do, or maybe will, depending on what I find. The swindle happened in this state so I wanted to investigate the happenings first," the older man said.

"You mean you aren't busy right now and this caught your interest or you want to get a few favors owed to you by the Federal Marshal that you can collect on later when you need to?" asked Mason knowing he was closer to the truth than the Marshal wanted him to be.

"Both, probably. This came across my desk because

a Senator's son-in-law was one of those duped out of a few hundred. The young man wanted to buy a big parcel and become an important landowner so he could run for state office with all the clout of a Washington, D.C. Senator behind him," the Marshal said knowing anything he told Mason would remain with the man.

"It seems Hamilton maybe should have checked out who he was conning before he pulled the fast one on him. He seemed smarter than that but all crooks think they'll never get caught," said Mason.

"Who's Hamilton? I thought Franklin's last name was Johnson," asked the Marshal, getting up to refill his now empty coffee cup.

"That's one reason I wanted to speak with you first, before I took you to see Franklin. Hamilton is Franklin's twin brother. Franklin has worked for me for years, handling my booze and my money in the saloon. He's honest as a day is long. But he has a twin brother who makes you swear you're looking into a mirror image of the guy. I've seen Franklin every day for the last year or more and I know he's not been out of this town," Mason said adamantly.

"What if they were in on it together? You know one being here doing the job while the other is off causing good people to lose their life savings," the Marshal put forth.

"But Franklin's never had a mustache or mutton chop sideburns," said Mason reasonably.

"They might have been fake. You know like they wear on theatre stages. I knew a man that was bald as a billiard ball but no one knew cuz his hair looked so real. No one would know to this day if his wife hadn't been so jealous of his ogling a younger woman that she pulled it off in the middle of the opera screeching, 'This is what you'll get in bed you little hussy if you dare to sleep with my husband.' Quite a show went on that night. I'll never forget the expression on his face as he tried to fit it back on without a mirror. Looked like a dead skunk sitting on his head. He never wore it again," the Marshal said a smile crossing his face as he relayed the tale.

"I understand you'll need to speak with both men but I believe Franklin is telling the truth when he says he hasn't had any contact with his brother for almost ten years. He's a good man and wouldn't have anything to do with cheating people out of their money," Mason assured the Marshal again.

"I'd like to do that before we go much further. I'm a pretty good judge of people and if this Franklin is as innocent as you say, I'll lean towards his brother as the culprit."

The two men went down to the saloon just as a large group of men was leaving, the laborers carrying tools of their trade. "You got a drinking problem here, Mason?" asked the Marshal as he began to count the number of men figuring there were still more inside.

"No, there are so many men coming into town to work we needed to open a restaurant fast before they left town due to starvation. Franklin and Maggie furnish inexpensive meals three times a day. The saloon wasn't busy during those times so I let them use it. I don't know if we'll always need it. Hopefully someone will want to open a restaurant eventually that will take the saloon's place," Mason explained as he and the Marshal stepped into the now empty saloon.

Both Franklin and Maggie entered the saloon from the doorway to the hotel. Franklin saw Mason and turned to ask Maggie to give them some time and she nodded, turning back to the hotel.

"Mason, I suppose this is the Marshal?" asked Franklin as he put out his hand to shake the older man's hand.

"This is Franklin. I can tell them apart but I realize it isn't easy for someone who hasn't known Franklin for as long as I have," Mason explained.

"Well, young man, you have quite an advocate in Mason. I'm almost convinced you had nothing to do with this business but why don't you tell me what you know about your brother's whereabouts during the last year," the Marshal asked calmly, watching the younger man closely.

"As I told Mason when he asked me, Hamilton showed up here four days ago and asked me if he could stay and try to get along together. We had parted on bad terms about ten years ago and he said he wanted to bury all the bad feelings between us. That family means more than the little things that had us at loggerheads," Franklin told both men.

"Like what things? What made you two brothers at, as you say, loggerheads?" asked the Marshall.

Glancing at Mason, knowing he was going to have to disclose more than he wanted his boss and friend to know, began, "After our mother died, I wanted to stay on in Ohio and continue farming but Hamilton fooled the attorney and signed for both of us, pretending to me, and the farm was sold. He gave me half the money and we went our separate ways," Franklin said without rancor.

"Was he used to doing that? Pretending to be you?" the Marshal asked glancing over at Mason's reaction to what Franklin was saying.

"We had always done so as kids but we were fifteen and I had stopped pulling pranks by then. Hamilton still used to pretend to be me and caused problems with girls' families after telling them he was me. It wasn't very nice and I decided to put an end to it by removing myself. I ended up out here in Kansas, working for Mason for the last five years or so. I like the town and have a lot of friends here. I was planning on staying and I hope the trouble that Hamilton may have got involved with doesn't affect my life here in Sweetwater."

Mason interjected, "Don't worry, Franklin, the people who know you will know you're not guilty of anything like this."

"What exactly am I accused of doing?" he asked, slightly wary of what he would hear.

"No one died, son. A man using your name used a confidence game to swindle people out of their savings through some sort of story about being a government employee. He said he could help them get pre-signed up for the land grants that are going to be open to the public in Montana and other territories," the Marshal told him.

"It's just as bad almost. If you steal a man's life savings, he may never get to that point again. It could end up being the difference between life and death. I hope Hamilton didn't have anything to do with this." He was shaking his head but he wasn't very convincing in hiding his thoughts.

"Franklin, do you know where Hamilton is right now?" Mason asked his friend.

"No, I told him not to come around me or Maggie anymore. I don't trust him with her at all since he seems to enjoy taking what I like away from me. Me and Maggie have been getting closer in the last day or two."

This last part he told to Mason who nodded his understanding.

"I'll look for him," Mason said rising. "He hasn't left town or I'd know of it. Told everyone to keep a look-out for Franklin and let me know if he tried to get on the train or rent a horse."

Mason returned with Hamilton, told him to sit down and answer the Marshal's questions.

"So, you're, Hamilton Johnson? How'd you come to be in Sweetwater, Hamilton?" asked the older man, amazed at the identical twin's appearance. If it hadn't been Mason who brought this man in to him, he would think it the same man he had just interviewed.

"I wanted to make amends with my younger brother. We had some bad words when we parted and I wanted to clear the air," Hamilton told the older man, sticking to his original story.

"So, how many years are we talking about? Since you last spoke with Franklin?" the Marshal asked.

"Close to nine years or so, we were just teens. I thought we could meet as men and learn to understand one another, be able to listen to one another's opinion without it resorting to fisticuffs," Hamilton told both men.

The Marshal narrowed his eyes. "I noticed you have a couple of bruises healing and a cut lip. You get that in a fight?"

Mason interjected, "I've had to break-up one fight between you two already and it hasn't been a week that you've been in town."

"That was just us getting to know the boundaries again. We wouldn't have hurt one another. We used to wrestle and fight over everything. Chores, going to school, girls. It didn't seem to matter. We always ended up sitting down at the supper table as family in the end. I want that again," the younger man said truthfully.

"Where you been before this?" Mason asked.

"Oh, a little of everyplace. I've been a travelling man, I guess. No one place for very long." He smiled at the men to see if they could make anything of that. "I get bored easily."

The Marshal asked, "So you haven't been around Topeka lately? During the last six months?"

Hamilton seemed to take a minute to think and then asked, "Topeka? That the capital? I don't remember being there lately or at all. No, I don't recollect being in a city like that."

Both Mason and the Marshal had trouble hiding their frustration at the information they were getting, or for that matter, not getting from interrogating this man.

"So, if I brought in a couple of men who say someone who looks like you and was calling himself Franklin Johnson swindled them out of their money to buy land grants, they wouldn't point you out?" asked the older man.

"Am I the only man you're going to show to them or is Franklin going to be there, too?" he asked with a sly grin.

Mason wanted to slam his fist into the smug face even if it did look like his friend. No wonder the two brothers ended up brawling every time they got together for more than a minute. This one was defiantly used to causing havoc.

The Marshal, after glancing at Mason, asked, "I suppose it's pointless to ask you to do the right thing? To admit to using your brother's name during this confidence game you were pulling so we can get this cleared up without drawing him into it."

"I'm not sure what you're talking about, Marshal. I'm being cooperative and I know my brother will be as well," Hamilton said, looking like the upright citizen his brother really was.

Mason and the Marshal left the saloon without imbibing in the drink they both wanted but wouldn't take. "I'll go back to the capital and see if I can find someone willing to come out here and identify Hamilton as the man who took their money. I'll keep you posted as to when I'll be back. Meanwhile, you can keep watch on him, make sure he isn't pulling the same scam here. If he leaves town, let me know. Right now, I don't have anything to link him to Topeka let along the swindled money."

"These are the hardest crimes to bring to justice. No one wants to admit they were fool enough to give their money to a crook, yet, if they don't, the criminal gets to keep on tricking other people out of their hard-earned cash. Makes me angry since most of the folks in this town could have been taken by a con-man like Hamilton when they first came out here," Mason said as they finally reached the jail.

"We'll get him. He made the mistake of coming here so at least we can watch what he's doing. Don't worry. After all, if he's here he can't be swindling anyone else," the Marshal told Mason as they shook hands.

CHAPTER 9

Pressing his new bride up against the wall of her office in the hotel, Eli pushed up the skirts of the fashionable dress trying to get into the opening of her underdrawers. "I thought I'd come over to have a meal with you but now I find I have a different kind of hunger," he said as he kissed his wife's lips, neck and ears. Passion replacing politeness as he tried to get his fill of her before needing to return to work at the bank.

"It's a busy time here, too. I can't be gone long or Maggie will notice and come to find me," Molly said breathlessly as she helped by pushing her underthings to the floor and exposing herself to him.

Quick to take advantage of her helpfulness, Eli opened his trouser flap allowing his manhood its freedom to encase itself in Molly's silky warmth. Once there, they both settled and stilled until the urge to complete the task they set themselves overtook their wish to make it last.

Eli held Molly to him as he rose and lowered her onto his erection until she shuddered going limp in his arms. That took Eli over the cress and he too had difficulty staying upright after his climax.

"Oh, my God, Molly. Does this ever get less crazy? I don't know if I can keep this up. I can't think at work and need to be in you so badly I make up reasons to get here to you. Do you think my boss has guessed why I'm here at all hours of the day when I should be working?" he asked, letting them separate enough to put himself away and straighten his clothing while Molly did the same.

"I don't know. He is newly married, too, so is he hiding off every few hours?"

"He goes home for lunch and comes back whistling, so...."

"The girls said it can be very overwhelming. But they never said when that ends, when it becomes less important. Maybe we should have taken that honeymoon. Maybe that's why we're like this. We didn't get it out of our systems the first week," Molly said trying to see if her hair had come down from the exercise. "But you and I both had just started our jobs here in town. I still don't think it would have been a good idea to take time off."

"But it's been a couple of weeks now and I want, no need, you more often - not less. Do you think there's something wrong?" he asked as he reached and pulled her closer to him so he could kiss her neck and ears again.

Molly went willingly into his arms. "I can ask the girls, I guess, casually, you know, so they won't think anything about it."

"How do you casually bring up the subject of lovemaking and my, or our, inability to limit it to nighttime activities?" he asked stroking Molly's breasts through her dress and feeling their response to his touch again.

"Stop, you must stop touching me right now. I'll go out into the public hall and you wait and get yourself under control then return to the bank before you get fired," she warned giving him a quick kiss on the mouth and slipping out the door into the hustle and bustle of a busy hotel at noontime.

Maggie ran into Molly in the hall noting her friend's

high color. "Almost done, the men are about to finish their dessert. Then I clean up the tables and we're all set for another meal tonight."

"Don't you get tired doing the same thing every day? There seems to be no end to the work and there seems so little reward," Molly said, speaking her mind to her best friend.

"You're just missing Eli so you're getting grouchy," surmised Maggie.

"That is one thing I can assure you I am not. I admit I may be grouchy but that's because I'm just a little tired," Molly admitted.

"You resent anything that takes you away from your husband. All the girls went through it. I know because I'm the one they groused at for one thing or another. It all boils down to not sleeping enough at night and not being with their husbands enough during the day," explained Maggie with the wisdom of a much older and more experienced woman than she was.

"So, it gets better? I mean, I get better? You know, less moody when Eli's not around?" Molly asked looking for an honest answer from her unmarried friend. "And he gets less needy?"

"Yes, you both will get more relaxed less, umm, horny is a word I've heard working around here with so many men. It seems to afflict a lot of them. Must be kind of like our monthly courses, kinds of comes and goes but more often. Many go to Miss Lilies to take care of it but until they do, they get ornery and grumpy with everyone," Maggie imparted her knowledge to her married friend.

"Oh. Well, that is a little unsettling. I will need to ask Eli about that. Um, when we are at home, alone."

Maggie left her friend and went into the saloon to finish cleaning up from the midday meal. "Franklin, you don't need to help me any longer. I can do this by myself and you've been working too long of days for far too long now. You're looking tired and you never tease anymore. Is having your brother around that much of a weight on your shoulders?"

"Sorry, I've just had a lot on my mind besides worrying about why he showed up here after all this time. I don't believe it's to mend any fences, that's for sure," Franklin said, wiping the last of the beer mugs and placing them upside down on the shelf behind the bar.

"Then send him on his way. He'd leave if we weren't housing and feeding him for free," Maggie said bluntly.

"Mason asked me to keep him around. He's afraid Hamilton could disappear back east or into one of the territories if I don't give him a free room. Hamilton doesn't seem to have any money of his own so if he did have part in flimflamming people out of their savings, he didn't seem to keep any of it for himself," Franklin said with a half-smile.

"So that's what this has been all about? Hamilton cheated people out of money?" she asked, sweeping under the tables that were recently vacated.

"Yes, but it was peoples' life savings. Money they were going to use to buy land grants and such. I guess these families are devastated now, their money gone and no way to recoup the loss. I have a little money saved but probably not enough to help."

"Franklin, this is not your fault. You don't need to give up your savings to cover the theft your brother committed. Promise me you won't even offer to do such a thing. If this all ends up with Hamilton going to jail, then you'll need to let that happen. He won't ever stop doing things like this if you make it all right for him. He'll merely go and do it again since there never seems to be any repercussions for the things he does." Maggie had stopped sweeping and was staring at Franklin seriously.

"I know but somehow I feel responsible for those people's loss. We're twins and it seems what one of us does the other is as responsible for. Or that's how we were raised. Ma treated us as one so as to not play favorites, I guess." Unable to really be able to explain his feeling of guilt over what Hamilton probably did, he continued, "Anyway, I just do."

Maggie went to stand in front of Franklin. "If Hamilton kissed me again, or tried to touch me inappropriately, that would be all right with you? I should submit if you two are the same."

A fire burned in Franklin's eyes as he grabbed onto her arms. "Did he? Did he try kissing you again?"

"No. But you do see yourself as a separate person when it comes to me. It's the same with everything else he does. You are not responsible for what he has done or may do in the future just as he is not the man I care about, the man I allow to hold me and kiss me." Then she melted against his chest, allowing her breasts to press into him, to make him aware of her as a woman.

"H-m-m-m-m, I can see the difference when you put it that way," he said enjoying her closeness. He let his face lower to hers and rubbed his nose against hers, enjoying her touch more than he realized he could enjoy anything so mundane.

"Then go and take a nap. You do look tired and I

don't need your help with supper," she said moving away from him to go back to the broom. "Even with the bakery open, I can't say it has affected the number of customers we're feeding. There must be more men moving into the tent camps down by the river. Do you think jobs are hard to come by in the rest of the state?"

"I don't know. The country is still in a depression and that may be hanging on in a lot of places out west. Some of these men said they were burned out of Chicago. Said they couldn't afford the more expensive apartments being built to replace the ones that were lost to the fire."

He rubbed his eyes tiredly. "Winter usually means the ranches go down to the bare number needed and there are fewer farming jobs available, harvest will soon be over. Maybe men are coming in to fill the few additional jobs that opened up when the houses on Second Street began to go up."

Franklin climbed the stairs to his rooms, taking the advice multiple people kept telling him. Get some rest and stop worrying about Hamilton, he's a big boy who can take care of himself. Franklin knew only one of those things was true.

Maggie and Franklin were talking after lunch, the supper was already prepared so it was a slow afternoon for the two of them. It was a warm fall day and they decided to take the opportunity to enjoy what might be the last good day to escape.

"Have you ever gone fishing here, down by the river?" Franklin asked.

"I've picked berries down First Street behind Beth's house but not fished. I know Jessie and Beth fish all the time but they go out of town to a place where the river bank is less steep," Maggie said as she followed him outside to the fishing poles hung on the outside wall. The two cut across the back lots, behind Miss Lily's boarding house toward the river.

Franklin knew of a sandy spot where he could see the trout dodging under the overhanging bank that had always been a good place for him. It had a clear spot to sit or picnic while he waited for the lazy fish to take the bait. They didn't have a fly-fishing rod and reel so dropped the baited hooks and let them float downstream a little, a cork bobber letting them know if a fish took the hook.

Sitting down first, Maggie said, "That water looks so inviting I want to take my shoes and stockings off to wade like I did up at the ranch with Callie."

"That had to be in summer, I would guess. This river gets cold early and will freeze over come January. Then we can try ice fishing," Franklin said, chewing on a golden stem of long grass.

"The berry patch is just a little way upstream from here. Abby, Faith and I went a couple of times. The berries were so heavy on the bushes this summer, I've never seen them so thick before," Maggie said looking around her to get her bearings.

"Do you see yourself staying here? In Sweetwater, I mean, or would you be able to move on?" asked Franklin, watching the corks as they floated.

"I'm not sure. It's nice to have family here, someone to spend time with on the holidays, someone who has the same memories from your youth. Living in an orphanage like I did makes family very important. Callie knows that and she's opened her home to all of us at one time or another. But I'm not set in stone or anything. No matter where I go, these St. Michael people will always be my family."

"So, if I asked you to go with me…" He tried again. "If I find I have to leave Sweetwater, maybe Kansas, you'd be able to see yourself going with me?" Franklin was staring directly at Maggie, waiting for her answer as if it were the most important thing in the world to him.

Gazing at his serious face, Maggie swallowed. "I think I would, if you asked me."

Leaning over, he pulled Maggie to his chest placing his mouth over hers and kissed her in gratitude. He slid his tongue between her lips seeking and receiving permission from her untutored mouth for more.

Maggie had been kissed before, young men testing their abilities, honing their skills, but Franklin seemed to be well practiced with kissing. She was becoming acquiescent in his arms. She found herself flat on her back, Franklin over her, holding his weight off her. She felt her breasts pushed against his chest and his breathing, both their breathing, was increasing. She found her hands on his shoulders, massaging and pulling him even closer.

Franklin put his mouth over the outside of her blouse, knowing instinctively where the nipple was, increasing the moisture as the nipple peaked into his mouth. His hand slid up her leg, bringing the bottom of her dress with it, then cupped the soft furred mound, his voice harsh as he begged her to let him touch her more intimately.

Overwhelmed with desire and sensations, Maggie wasn't sure what he had been asking for. He seemed to be touching her very intimately already.

Pulling away first, he kissed her forehead then

leaned his forehead against hers. "I didn't mean to get so carried away, it just seemed so natural for us to do more. Sorry, I got so far ahead of us. I don't think we should be doing this anymore, not right now. I can't offer you anything until I know what's in store for me. How much trouble Hamilton has brought to me."

"I don't care. What Hamilton's done is his problem. It shouldn't have any power over you." Grasping his back, she tried to pull him over her again.

"I know it shouldn't but it always seems to. His bad behavior always ends up affecting me. I can't make plans for us until I know I won't be in jail or running from the law," Franklin explained as he began to kiss her again, this time laying alongside her.

Maggie, relaxing again, enjoyed the attention. Finally, Franklin leaned back and still lying beside Maggie, started pulling out his shirt-tail and unbuttoning his trousers.

"Wait, Franklin, I'm not ready to, to…." said Maggie as she started to scoot away from the now partially undressed man.

Franklin looked at her as she began to panic. "No, oh, no, I'm not, ah, I just wanted to show you something. If anything happens to me, if someone needs to make identification, I wanted you to know I have a birthmark Hamilton doesn't have. I want you to see it so you'll know if it's me."

"You mean if you're dead. If it's just the body?" Maggie asked guessing at why Franklin wanted a disinterested person to know about his birthmark. "Do you think Hamilton would harm you and pass your body off as his?"

"I don't really think Hamilton would do anything to

me but he might be tempted to take advantage of my demise. He's not bad, not really, but he is manipulative. If something works to his advantage, he won't hesitate to use it," replied Franklin, his hands still on his trouser buttons.

With a deep breath, Maggie said, "Alright, I'm ready if you're sure. I don't think this is something I'll need to know. Nothing bad is going to happen to you."

Franklin pushed down his trousers on one hip, just above the hair line and on his left side, where the hip hallows to the leg, was a tan patch. Maggie thought it looked like a bird flying and stopped herself from touching it.

"I'll remember what it looks like but I still can't believe anyone would hurt you, plus I can always tell you from Hamilton. I think Mason can, too."

Redoing the buttons and tucking in his shirt, he said, "We better get going. It'll be time to begin setting up for supper. Besides, the fish aren't biting." Pulling in the lines, he found the bait gone. "I guess we were too busy doing other things and missed seeing the corks go under."

"Um, we did get a little distracted but I think we had more fun than catching a stinky old fish." Picking up the can of worms, she brushed the grass from her skirt.

Maggie followed Franklin, thinking how quickly things changed for her. She found she did love him enough to leave Callie and the others. She could move and begin again only this time she would have Franklin beside her.

CHAPTER 10

"Mrs. Taylor, I just wanted to stop in and let you know we haven't given up on finding your husband. I'm still waiting for a couple more sheriffs to get back with me. With winter coming on, there's a lot of unemployed men coming into the towns seeking work and housing. So not hearing doesn't mean anything bad at this point," Deputy Wilder explained, sorry he didn't have better news for this hard-working mother.

"Well, he'll be surprised when he does get back here. I mean, we have a place to live and the bakery is really doing well, I think. I sell out of everything most days. What the men don't buy, Abby and Matthew will at the end of the day. I keep increasing the baking and it keeps selling."

"I'll take that lemon pie if no one has their name on it," he said reaching into his pocket for the correct coin.

"Certainly, I won't charge you the deposit for the pan. I know you'll bring it back. Or send it back with the children from school."

"Thanks, I'll get it back to you, probably tomorrow. I tend to have a sweet tooth."

"I found most men do. I can't keep cookies in the case at all. They seem to fly out of here. I set a couple aside for the children just so they'll have them in their pail for school."

"I'll make a note to myself to get in here earlier then. My wife doesn't get time to bake much when she's teaching. I like to bring bread and pies home to her," Wilder explained, his dark good looks simply dismissed by the young wife.

"I'll see you some morning, then. You might like to try the meat pies, called a pasty, originally eaten by the Cornish miners. I got the recipe from a woman when we were in Michigan."

Fran finally locked the front door. The case was empty besides for a few crumbs that she wiped out. Taking a broom, she swept the floor then went back to the living area. Matthew's son, Thad, was reading to Corabelle and Walter as their eyes drooped. The baby was sleeping but would wake again for an hour or two before going down for the night.

"Thank you, Thaddeus, it makes it so much easier to do this with you helping by watching the children for me."

"They're good kids, Mrs. Taylor. I don't mind and half the time I'm reading my homework to them. They listen to anything, even if they don't understand it all. By the time they get to my grade though, it will seem like they always knew it." He picked up the two books and paper he had been working on earlier.

"I'll see you tomorrow. Take a couple cookies with you, you earned them."

"My Dad pays me enough but I'll take the cookies for school tomorrow." Taking a bite out of one of them, he smiled leaving through the rear entrance to walk to his home next door.

Fran helped her children get undressed and into their nightclothes then tucked them into their little beds. She made herself a cup of tea and checked the meat in the oven roasting for the meat pies and pasties she will make early the next morning.

After looking in on the baby, she began the process

of mixing up the dry portion of the bread dough, it was a little too early to put them out to rise, yet. The pie dough was next, Fran had an order for five apple pies and a mince and she would need to bake some for the case, as well.

Rolling out the dough was cathartic for her. She could think about her husband but only in good terms. That he would be home soon, that he would be surprised at what she had been doing while he was gone, that he would come home and be her husband again - the children's father again. She would not think about what it would be like if he never returned.

Fran hummed a hymn as she finished placing the dough in the pie pans and filled them. She could only fit four in the oven at once so it was time consuming to bake that many pies but it was what the customers wanted.

The baby began to squirm and make little fussing noises. Fran washed and went to gather her youngest daughter up and changed the wet diaper. She sat and fed her, rocking in the chair Matthew had brought for her. The baby was soon full and ready to sit up. Fran placed pillows around her so she could stay in an upright position and watch what Fran was doing. Fran talked to the baby, keeping up a continual conversation as she finished the pies and started on the bread doughs.

CHAPTER 11

Mason reread the two telegrams in his hand that, Tom, from the telegraph office had just delivered. He wasn't sure what he should do about the first one. This whole case had been handled by Wilder from the very beginning. He would wait until his deputy got in and then discuss it with him.

The other was letting him know the Marshal was returning to speak with Hamilton and, possibly, Franklin. Mason knew Franklin would be here but he wasn't sure where Hamilton was most of the time. Letting out a loud sigh, he leaned back in the chair, stopping as it came to rest against the wall. He was thinking how easy this job used to be before Sweetwater began to grow with the train stopping a couple times a day. The visitors had increased the profits to the hotel and saloon but it meant more people coming and going. More people for him and his deputy to keep track of. So far there hadn't been much to worry about. Some fights between men who had too little money and too much beer. Petty theft out at the tent cities popping up near the river but what could he do about that? Jobs were scarce and men got bored having nothing productive to do. He hoped that wasn't always going to be true but for now, it was the way of things it seemed.

Mason thought about all the other changes happening in the same time - meeting his wife, hiring Wilder as a deputy, the town doubling in population, a new school and civic building. He guessed he was lucky to have this job, to be part of this growing community.

Now he had to keep Franklin from going to trial with his brother and help a family reunite. Not a problem - it was just a normal day in Sweetwater for its sheriff.

Wilder read the message. "Well, there doesn't seem to be any mistake that they've found Walter Taylor. Should I go and collect him or do you think you need to go."

"No, you can go fetch him. We'll wait to let Fran know when we're sure ourselves. You'll be able to tell after you've seen him. I think the boy looks like his dad," Mason told Wilder who nodded and went to buy a ticket to the town mentioned in the wire.

The Marshal returned to Sweetwater, not happy with the outcome of his investigation and sat in the sheriff's office with Mason. "I don't know what I'm supposed to do. I've never met victims who have been so hard to find and then once I do, can't get them to formalize a complaint. They've been a skittery group, even that Senator's son-in-law that began this whole mess. He wants to stay out of it saying he doesn't want people to know he was swindled. Say's it will make the public doubt his ability to do a good job once in office. I don't know why he just doesn't come forward and give his evidence. It would make things much easier for me."

"So, there isn't even a real complaint? I mean, nothing a judge would sign or anything?" asked Mason, considering their options as lawmen.

"Not really, still working off the information I got in the beginning. I know something illegal happened but I need people to tell me exactly when and how. I asked for them to come and identify Hamilton but no one had the time," complained the Marshall.

"I'll help you all I can but there doesn't seem to be

anyway besides getting Hamilton to confess."

"But to what? I know it has to do with land grants and getting people special treatment but then that's it. No proof of anything illegal occurring."

Getting up from his chair, Mason said, "Let's go see if we can get anything out of Hamilton."

"And that, Franklin. He may still know something. It's his brother after all." The Marshall snatched his hat off the peg while following Mason out of the jail.

The two men found Franklin where he usually could be found, the saloon. It was between meals so the bar was empty. The Marshal looked over at Mason and asked, "You're sure we're talking to Franklin and not Hamilton? I can't tell them apart."

Mason had to agree. "They are very similar, in how they move, too, but I know Franklin and I know Hamilton when I catch him. He seems to stay clear of me, always finds somewhere else to be if you know what I mean."

"Mason, Marshal, how can I help you?" Franklin asked as he finished pulling chairs off the table tops and back onto the newly mopped floor.

The Marshal asked, "Your brother tell you anything more about where he's been the last few months?"

"No, I would have told Mason if I had learned anything. Hamilton's been closed mouth about everything except that he wants to stay on here and build our relationship again. I'm not sure that's the real reason for him staying here," Franklin told the two men honestly.

"So, what's he doing most of the day? I don't see him around much," Mason inquired.

"I told him to stay away from here, from Maggie for

sure, so I think he's been helping Matthew at the distribution center. I warned Matthew to watch him, not to confuse Hamilton with my work ethics. I didn't want Matthew coming up short or anything," Franklin explained knowing the other two would understand his worry.

Mason's brows lowered in thought. "I'll look over at Matthew's place and, Franklin, you go to any of his other hangouts. Bring him back here to speak with the Marshall."

As Franklin left through the rear door, he noticed the fishing poles were gone so he headed toward the river bank where he and Maggie had fished. As he got past the end of the houses on First Street, he felt someone watching him. He turned as a burly man knocked him to the ground, using his brute weight to take Franklin down. Franklin wrestled with the man, trying to get on top where he would have a better advantage with his strength and long arms.

Just as Franklin thought he could leverage the man off him, two other men came up and instead of helping as Franklin expected from his friends in Sweetwater, the men each took one of his arms and held him so the first man could pummel him with his big, beefy fists. Taking great care to hit a different place on Franklin's face with each blow.

Franklin's eyes were already swelling but he saw the big man, now tired out and breathing hard from the punishing blows he dealt, swing his booted foot back and aim for Franklin's crotch. The boot landed with a terrific thud to his upper thigh just as Franklin twisted in time to protect his most sensitive parts.

"A-w-w, Charlie, you missed. Remember the man

said to be sure to hurt him bad, to remind him that takin' a man's money was one thing but to take his wife was another," said one of the men holding Franklin up.

"Then hold him tighter, this ain't easy work. You two got the simple part," complained Charlie.

"All right, try again," said the man, holding the now weakened Franklin still to get his just desserts.

A shotgun went off nearby and the three men jumped, looking toward the danger. And danger it was. Miss Lily, a lady of indeterminate age, stylish white hair and dressed elegantly held a shot gun, now pointed toward the group.

"Let him go and get out of here," Miss Lily yelled threateningly. "The sheriff will be here less than a minute after hearing this shot, sooner if he hears more."

The three men glanced at one another then the two dropped their bundle as they both ran towards the river and the brush that concealed their horses waiting there.

Franklin crumpled to the ground, every muscle and bone in his body screaming with pain. The big man took one last look at him and kicked Franklin in the head, right near his temple. Then he too ran to the waiting horses.

Miss Lily rushed up to see what care she could give before the doctor arrived. She had sent one of her working girls to get him and the sheriff. She knelt beside the man saying, "I'm not sure which of the twins you are but only Hamilton would have done anything to make men so angry at him."

Hamilton checked the last of the cases that arrived earlier that day by train. Nothing looked tampered with, the seals all still in place. He initialed the shipping report then placed it on the sharp spindle. Done with this day's work Hamilton thought with satisfaction.

Just as he turned to lock up the rear barn door, two men, dressed in typical cowhand attire right down to the leather chaps and boots and wearing worn ten-gallon hats approached him. Hamilton was on his guard immediately.

He warily watched the men and knew they meant no good towards him. He tried to get to the door and slide it closed but they came at him in a rush. Each one taking a side and slamming their fists into his face and head, then body as Hamilton tried to get in a few punches of his own.

It was the kick to the groin that caught Hamilton unawares and he crumpled as the pain reverberated through his body to end centered at his core. The thought that God had played a very un-funny trick on man by placing his genitalia right out front and unprotected raced through his mind. But was replaced with the much more serious thought that these men may end-up killing him.

Unable to stand and protect himself any longer, the two ruffians continued their assault by kicking him in the ribs, kidneys and any spot not protected by boots or arms. Hamilton, a mound of humanity covering his head from the furious blows until he couldn't think any longer.

Mason strode across the street from the saloon. He stopped to speak with Matthew since he was around before searching for Hamilton. Matthew pointed him towards the distribution building but Mason heard the commotion before he saw it.

Running through the darkened building, he saw the barn door was still open and went toward the sound of a fight. He got there in time to see two men kicking the life out of Hamilton, he was pretty sure.

"Hey, you two, stop right there," Mason yelled as he

was half-way through the building, still yards away. The two men turned and began running down the alley behind the houses. Mason didn't dare fire at them. There were too many citizens out and about in that area.

Instead, he bent to examine the bloody-faced man lying in the dirt. He was totally unrecognizable and Mason couldn't say that it wasn't Franklin who he knew had gone looking for Hamilton, too.

Then he heard a shotgun blast from across town, probably near the jail and Mason knew he would be pulled in two directions.

Calling out to Matthew who had stayed handy in case he was needed to find Hamilton, Mason yelled, "A man's down behind your building. Get the doctor and some help."

Matthew had heard the shotgun, too, but did as Mason asked. Sending his son for the doctor and calling out to a couple of the men to help him bring in Hamilton.

Maggie, her heart beating at twice its normal rate ran up the stairs in the saloon to Franklin's private rooms, rooms she had never seen before this afternoon. She had been in the kitchen when news came that an injured man was being brought up to the rooms above the saloon. Fearing it was Franklin, she dropped everything and ran to see if she could help.

Stopping in the doorway, she saw not one but two men, both beaten, both unconscious and both in need of medical help. She looked down at the man in the bed and couldn't be sure it was Franklin with so much of his face swollen and misshapen, other injuries showing through the torn clothing. No one had done anything for their comfort other than taking their boots off. They were waiting for the doctor for orders before touching the men.

Mason and the Marshall entered as Mason said, "We can't find any sign of the two men who did this, I'm afraid. They high-tailed it out of here as soon as their work was done. Matthew's gathering a posse to look, though. Thinks they may have come from Preston but Miss Lilly said there were three. I only saw two, so the other one might have been waiting with the horses."

"But why did they beat both of them? I don't understand. Franklin never did anything to warrant this," Maggie said to no one in particular. And no one seemed to have an answer.

"Maybe they didn't know the difference so beat both of them or they think they were both part of the fraud. We don't even know if this has anything to do with the case I'm working on," offered the Marshall, shaking his head at the damage done to the two men in front of him.

Maggie went to the man she felt was Franklin and began to undo his trousers, having the Marshall say, "U-m-m, young lady, I don't think you..." But he stopped when Mason laid his hand on the Marshal's arm.

When Maggie saw the bird shaped birth mark, tears came to her eyes and she told the others, "This is Franklin." She began to wash her hands and wet a cloth to sooth the cuts and scrapes on his face. "Can someone get some ice from the kitchen? And vinegar and more clean towels. We may need more light if the doctor has to stitch which looks entirely probable."

More lamps appeared and a bowl of ice, more water and towels also so when the doctor showed up, he grunted his approval and began on Franklin since his wounds had been cleansed already.

Maggie took as much care when tending to

Hamilton. After all, no man deserves this kind of a beating - no matter what he may have done. And Franklin insists his brother wasn't evil, simply a little lazy when it came to making a living.

Maggie was amazed at how non-emotional her tending to Hamilton was. How she could touch his body, cleanse the blood and dirt away, cut off his shirt to give the doctor better access to his wounds - yet not have an emotional connection of any sort.

While doing the same things to Franklin had torn at her heart. She had to force the tears back so she could do what was needed. Even now, she wanted to be with Franklin, holding his hand, ease his pain in some way, placing cold compresses on the swollen eyes and chin, placing vinegar-soaked clothes to the bruises on his ribs and shoulder.

"This one's done. Let's see what we have over here," said the doctor as he left one brother to tend to the other. Taking the same slow care, looking over every cut and scrape, noting every sign of bruising or swelling, the doctor made his examination.

Finally, he said to the group all waiting for the verdict, "The first man has a definite concussion. We'll have to watch him for the next few days to see how much damage has been done. He's gonna feel and act like a man that got kicked in the head by a horse. The second has a less severe head injury along with the cuts and usual bruising, although I think he got...." Here he glanced at Maggie then said, "The family jewels seem to have sustained damage."

At this declaration every one of the men in the room winced and some crossed their legs unconsciously.

Mason asked, "Do you think they'll be awake

anytime soon? Maybe identify the men? Miss Lily said they weren't from around here and she'd know. But maybe Hamilton knew his assailants."

Just then a man called out for Mason and the Marshall to come downstairs, that Matthew and the posse he had formed were back. Mason told the doctor, "Whatever you need just let me know. Franklin is like family here."

Maggie sat next to Franklin, taking her place, with no one denying her right to be there, an unmarried woman with two unmarried men. The doctor told her he would be back that evening but if either one woke to send someone to get him. He patted her shoulder as he left. A little morale support for her long vigil.

Molly came up and hesitantly looked at the two injured men, "Oh, Maggie, you're going to need help here. Let me see if one of the housekeepers has any experience with this sort of thing."

"No, I'm staying. I may need you to bring me clean clothes but I'm not turning their care over to anyone. I want to be here when they wake up. Can you get someone to handle the meals? I won't be able to do those until they're better," Maggie said indicating both men.

"All ready handled. I've got one of the waiters working the saloon and Thad is acting bartender. I'll help with breakfast and the midday meal. The customers will simply need to get used to the change," Molly told her friend.

"We St. Michaels graduates stick together. I know and I appreciate it all."

"Let me know if you need anything. I'll bring up some food for you and broth when the patients wake up. Do you need more ice or water?" Molly asked peering around for things that may be needed.

"No, but will you find Matthew and ask him to bring me a gun? In case those men come back to finish the job?"

Without hesitation, Molly said, "Certainly. I'll get one for you right away. Just so you'll know Mason and the Marshall have been in the saloon pretty much since they came downstairs. You're not here alone."

"That's good to know. I'll still feel better with a gun of my own. I don't know where Franklin's is and I don't want to search through his things. I don't know if Hamilton has one but it's not in view, either," Maggie told her friend as Molly left to get Matthew.

Matthew came with the requested pistol, making sure Maggie knew how to cock and fire it.

"When I was at Callie's, she made sure all of us knew how to fire a rifle, shotgun and hand guns. The cowhands were eager to teach us, at least us females. Seth might have taught the men if they didn't already know. I know the cowhands were well trained with rifles because of the coyotes. Handguns were carried but I don't think anyone had ever shot one other than for practice. I'll be fine. I was actually quite a good shot," she boasted.

"I'll remember that when I make up a posse next time. You may ride lead," he teased his little sister from St. Michaels.

"Matthew, thanks for trying to find the men who did this. It will mean a lot to Franklin when he wakes up."

"I just wish I could have gotten their trail but when they hit the main road, I really wouldn't be able to beat them to Preston. Once there, they could melt into their normal haunts," Matthew explained. "Do you need me to come to spell you tonight? So you can get some sleep?"

"No, I wouldn't get any sleep anyway. I'll stay here, that's why I wanted the gun. Franklin is completely helpless in his condition."

"I understand. I'll be back in the morning unless you send for me," Matthew said watching the pretty women with so much worry on her face. One last glance at the two badly beaten men made him wince knowing how much pain they would wake up to.

In the early morning, Maggie was woken from her brief nap on the sofa by a man's mumblings. She pushed the blanket off her legs and went to the bedroom where the men were. Hamilton was moving his head and mumbling, like someone talking in their sleep.

"Hamilton, Hamilton can you talk to me? Do you know what happened?" she questioned as the doctor had told her to do.

"An angel, you must be an angel. Give me a kiss to make me feel better," he whispered.

"Hamilton, you are seriously hurt. You have at least one broken rib and look like a horse stomped all over your face," Maggie told him gently, not taking the opportunity to berate him for his foolish talk.

"Get Franklin, I have to tell him something. He needs to know these guys mean business. I'm sorry to have led them here," Hamilton confessed, showing more sense and logic than he looked capable of having.

"Franklin can't hear you right now. He's across the room in the bed and in as bad or worse shape as you. The doctor says he has a concussion so I'm watching over you both till you're better. Do you want some broth or water?"

"What do you mean he's across the room? Where am I?" he asked but moaned with pain when he tried lifting his head.

"Mason had your cot pulled into Franklin's room so you would be easier to watch and probably protect. We don't know that these men won't come back and finish you both off. It looks like they tried really hard the first time." She got him a cup of cold water and helped him raise his head enough to take a drink.

"I think I may have to get some kind of tube or something so you can drink. That lip is so swollen much of it went down your neck," Maggie explained needlessly, wiping his chin and neck gently, patting away the water that escaped his lips.

"I need to see him, help him. It's my fault he got hurt. They were after me, for things I did before coming here, in another life. I swear I'm through with that existence but I can't seem to completely shed it, yet. People still coming after me I can accept, maybe I deserve it but not Franklin. He's the good to my bad, two sides of the same coin but one lucky the other not so much."

"Sh-h-h-h, rest again. I'll let you know if there's any change in his condition. The doctor said it might be days before either of you would wake up. We'll know how injured he is then."

Maggie checked on Franklin but saw no eye-movement under the lids so went back to the sofa and lay down. The sun wasn't up yet and there were a few more hours to get some rest. Having Hamilton wake-up without any lingering damage to his mental facilities gave Maggie hope for Franklin's recovery.

CHAPTER 12

Fran finished replenishing the showcase from the noonday rush of customers. Only the baby was home with her, the two older children having gone to school that morning as usual with Thad.

Looking up as the door chime rang announcing a new customer, she saw Wilder but before she formed the words of welcome, she saw the man hobbling on crutches behind him.

She rushed to her husband, tears of joy running down her cheeks. "Oh, Walter, Walter, I missed you so much." She threw herself at him, almost tipping him over as he dropped one crutch to grab his wife to him and kissed her thoroughly.

Wilder stood there, half-expecting he would end up witnessing an embarrassingly personal reunion when he brought Walt Taylor back to Sweetwater. He didn't intrude and, instead, studied the baked goods lining the glass shelves in the case.

Trying not to hear the soft murmurings and responding reassurances behind him, he knew when Fran finally realized they were all still standing in the front of the shop.

Bending, she picked up her husband's crutch saying, "Where are my manners? Mr. Wilder, would you care to come back to the family section and have a cup of coffee and a baked good? I actually set aside a meat pie for you."

Walt got his crutches back where he could use them to get himself to the area his wife indicated.

Wilder told her, "No, I better check in with the sheriff. I understand a lot has gone on while I was out of town."

"Well, take the meat pie, at least, and some cookies. I owe you so much for bringing my Walter home." She went to the case and retrieved a wrapped package. Gathering some ginger snaps to wrap up, also.

"I can't just take them, ma'am, wouldn't be right. I was only doing my job. But I'll gladly pay for them. They smell wonderful, like my grandmother's own favorites," he said taking a couple coins out and leaving them on the top of the glass case.

"Then thank you for doing your job so well. I had almost given up hope," she said, her voice breaking with emotion.

Wilder tipped his black hat and left with his goodies, leaving the newly reunited couple to get all the misunderstandings worked out.

Once in the rear living area, Walt gazed around. "Fran, you've done quite well for yourself and the children. Wilder said they're doing good in school and people here have been helping you get set up." He lowered himself unto the short sofa Abby had recovered and given them.

Fran poured him a cup of black coffee without asking if he wanted one. Walt always wanted a cup of coffee. "I have some stew made up or I can get you some cold chicken. Of course, there's plenty of fresh bread and there's pies and cookies out front. What can I get you?" she said nervously now she was alone with her husband after all these weeks.

Walt didn't say anything, peering around at the neat living area with the flowered curtains, the large amount of stored goods, jars and cans Fran used to make the baked goods she sold.

He was placing a cost to everything he saw and then said sadly, "Maybe I shouldn't have come back. I mean, you're doing better now than I could ever provide you with."

"Didn't you want to come home to me and the children? Did Mr. Wilder force you to return? I never asked him to do that. He offered to look for you, is all. I thought something bad had happened to you to keep you away from me, from us," she said worriedly, maybe Walt wasn't back home. Maybe he was only here to say goodbye properly.

"No, I tried to get back to you. I knew you couldn't make it alone. Rather, I thought you couldn't but here you are, a business woman living in a nice place, the children in school. What could I offer you that's more than this?" he asked hurt by the realization he wasn't as needed as he thought.

"Don't talk like that, Walt. I love you and the children love you. You are needed and you shouldn't think badly of yourself just because some good people found me in desperate straits. They offered me a safe, honest way to feed me and the children and I took it. And I'm good at it." She told him reasonably, "But that doesn't mean you're bad at it,"

"I don't know, Fran, I love you but what am I to do? I mean you don't need me. When I left to find us a place to live, I couldn't afford to pay the six or eight dollars a month rent they wanted most places. Then the horse tripped up in the mud and broke a leg. I had to put her down but my leg was broke, as well. A local farmer and his wife took me home but it was harvest time and he couldn't get away to ride into town to tell anyone about me. He finally got done with slaughtering the hogs and getting them in the smokehouse so then we could go into town. I gave him the other horse I took with me in payment for his care of me. He had set my leg and found the town's doctor who said I'll be out of this cast in a few more weeks."

Hesitantly, Fran asked, "So what are your plans after you get rid of the cast?"

"I don't know. I had planned on coming back and getting you and the children. Work a little until I could find a place for us." Again, he looked around the room and shook his head as he took in all the bakeware and bowls, then the ice box.

"I love you, Walt. The children missed you so. They attach themselves to any man that comes near them they so miss having you around. Are we worth nothing to you then?" she asked bluntly keeping her tears at bay.

"You're worth the world to me, all of you but maybe I was the one holding you back all along. I don't want to be an anchor, something holding you all down," he told her, the honesty hurting him like a knife cut.

"Right now, the neighbor boy takes care of the children after school while I finish up things for the day. Sometimes other women come in and bake during the afternoon so I can lay down and take a nap with the baby since I begin my day at four in the morning and that's after working till ten or eleven at night. I don't expect them to keep doing that. I mean, they're exceptionally generous people here and when I'm able I plan on repaying their kindness by re-paying them in kind." Fran decided to let her husband know that what he felt she accomplished without him was really something the community helped her attain.

"How did you get all this? Did you sell the wagon?" he asked still not sure how it all happened in a few short weeks after he had spent years trying to get ahead.

"Matthew came to me with this proposition after he found out I was living alone with the children in the wagon. We were almost out of food when we received a basket from the towns' people. I made a tart for Matthew, which he thought was so good I could open this bakery. He helped me with everything. I wouldn't be here if he hadn't forced me to make the decision. I promised Matthew I would pay him back everything he put in initially, my start-up costs and all," Fran explained.

Walt's face got red and he almost snarled, "Who the hell is this, Matthew? Why has he been so helpful?"

Fran stared at her husband worried if she even knew him any longer. Then answered knowing she needed to keep her anger under control if she wanted to save her marriage. "Matthew is the neighbor who is married to the most beautiful and kind lady you will ever meet. I am sure everything I have, everything I have become, is due to Abby's manipulation of all the men around her. It's her son that watches the children in the afternoon for no more than a couple of cookies in payment. I resent your assumption I would stoop to…to forgetting my marriage vows to get financial help from a man."

Walt, rubbed his hand over his face saying, "I'm sorry. I don't know why my mind went to thinking those thoughts. I had no reason to think such a thing."

Fran stared out the window and then decided to be completely truthful with her husband. "It could have gotten to that, Walt. I mean selling myself to feed the children. We were down to nothing to eat and the weather was starting to get so cold the water in the bucket was freezing over some nights. I couldn't find enough wood to burn to keep the tent warm so I sent the children into town to the school. I thought, at least they would be warm during the day.

"Mr. Wilder's wife is the teacher. She knew the children were underfed and sent Mr. Wilder out with a basket of food. Once I got noticed, the rest just snowballed. The people of Sweetwater couldn't do enough for me and the children."

She turned and looked directly at her husband and said, "But don't ever think I wouldn't have done the unspeakable to get food or wood for my family. By the grace of God, I didn't have to."

Walt tried to stand to go to his wife's side, tears in his eyes as he realized what dire straits his leaving to find them a home left the rest of his family in. Of course, he couldn't have foreseen his breaking his leg but still he left them unable to fend for themselves and then condemned his wife for accepting the charity so many people had offered.

Fran went into his open arms and cried out all the evenings of being alone, all the days of worry over being unable to feed her children and not knowing if her husband had abandoned his family, turned away from all the responsibilities she represented.

He knew he should be as thankful as Fran was for their good fortune. "I'm sorry, I'm even more of a fool than I thought. You've been working harder than any man and all I can do is worry about myself, how others will view me," he admitted, letting his wife settle in his arms as he took it all in.

"No one ever blamed you for any of the problems,

Walt. They made plans with the idea that you would come back and we would be a family, that's why there are two bedrooms here. I pay rent and I pay for the ingredients now. I have a small savings to go toward paying Matthew and Abby back for the start-up costs. Can you see yourself living here in Sweetwater? I need another person to work with me but if you would rather do something else then there are jobs to be had here now. Not just in construction but there's a distribution center that's hiring," she said hoping he wouldn't discard her offer without thinking about it.

Wiping the tear streaks from her upturned face, he told her, "I think I like this town. It seems to have a big heart and that's always attractive for a family man. I want to help you, be close to the children since I've been away for so long - in their short lives, anyway. I'm a little slow getting around but I'm willing to help with anything you need." He hugged her to him, kissing his wife again, beginning to realize the good-luck that kept his family together for him to return to.

"I'll teach you to beat egg whites. You can do that sitting down," she teased and wouldn't tell Walt who had taught her the secrets in the first place. Once Walt found out how handsome Matthew was, he might get a little jealous, especially if he realized how often the tall, dark man had been alone with Fran and the children.

Young Walt and Corabelle came through the rear door just then, seeing their father and squealing as they ran to him, jumping around their mother to reach him.

Thad was right behind them so Fran said, "My husband is home, Thad, so you won't have to stay and watch the children after school anymore but take your cookies anyway. You've earned them."

Everyone had tears in their eyes as Walt held his exuberant children and Fran was confirmed in her assumption the children had missed their father as much as she had.

"Thank you, Mrs. Taylor. My Mother and Dad will be glad to hear everything is okay now. A family is the most important thing in a kid's life," Thad said, a much more adult youth standing in front of her than she had realized before.

CHAPTER 13

Maggie helped Hamilton back into bed after using the bedpan behind the screen Molly had brought up to the room for that purpose. "Hell, I'm still weak as a kitten. How can getting beat-up take all your strength? I mean, I can see hurtin' but why can't I lift my own di...I mean, I can hardly hold a cup of coffee."

Maggie's eyebrows rose at his questionable language but answered anyway, "Probably to make sure you listen to the pain and rest until all of you can be moving at the same time. Besides, you lost blood and those ribs need rest to heal."

"Hamilton? Is that you?" Franklin's voice cracked after not using it for so many days.

Maggie rushed over to Franklin's bed to see him looking out at her through the still swollen eyes, both a swirl of purple and brown. "Oh, I'm so glad you're awake and are all right. It's almost a miracle. I was so afraid you wouldn't wake up, you were in such bad shape," she informed the somewhat conscious Franklin.

"Thank you, have you been taking care of me?" he asked.

Maggie, all smiles, said, "Of course, who else would I allow to do it? I let someone else handle the meals in the saloon."

Franklin became quiet before asking, "How long have I been out? When did they get meals in the saloon? While I was sick?"

"Franklin, you're not sick. You got beaten by three men and left for dead. You have a concussion and broken ribs and a few new scars. That was days ago. We started the meals in the saloon months ago, don't you remember?" Maggie asked worriedly, thinking she needed to call the doctor.

"You said, we? Should I know you?" he asked and then Maggie fell apart. She told Hamilton not to let Franklin move, to keep him talking if he could before rushing out the door and down the stairs, grabbing her shawl as she ran out.

Hamilton asked, shuffling closer to Franklin's bed, "You remember me though, little brother?"

"What a question. Of course, I remember you. It's like looking in a mirror." When he got a closer look at his brother, Franklin asked, "Do I look as bad as you? No wonder that girl ran out of here like the hounds of hell were chasing her."

"We look pretty much the same. Although I think you got beat up by a different group of men than I did, their handy-work appears the same. Only I didn't get concussed. I've been awake for the last three days while you just woke up for the first time." He informed his twin as that man closed his eyes, finally finding that daylight caused his head to hurt even worse than it had when he first heard Hamilton talking.

When the doctor returned with Maggie, he examined Franklin thoroughly, asking him some questions. Then pronounced, "I think our patient is out of the woods, Maggie, but he has residual loss of memory. It may return to him little by little or it may come back all at once like a lamp being lit or he may never remember that lost time at all."

Hamilton watched the reaction from Maggie as she stoically took in the doctor's information. Then she asked, "What else should I do to help?" She took a deep breath then finished, "To help the patient, doctor?"

"Well, it seems what you've been doing is working so continue with doing that. When you think they're ready you can add more solid foods, meats and eggs and things like that to build up their strength. They can move around these rooms some. Don't let their muscles get atrophied, need to use them," the doctor said while putting his instruments away.

"I'll see they follow your directions, sir. Thank you for coming so promptly," Maggie said taking on the persona of a nurse and not of an emotionally attached woman.

Hamilton tried to keep talking with Franklin, letting Franklin ask questions, bringing up things from their childhood but there was always an underlining of friendship and love between the two men. Hamilton didn't really want Franklin to regain his memory since this Franklin didn't remember the rift between the twins. He was the same friendly boy he had ever been.

Maggie made sure both men received meals and clean clothes but had one of the porters help them bathe since now both men were mobile. She felt it might be deemed improper since there wasn't any real connection between her and the brothers any longer.

When the men were considered well enough to spend the nights alone, both mobile enough to make it to and from the bedpan and able to feed themselves, Maggie returned to working the meal times.

Hamilton felt badly for not trying to help Franklin remember Maggie but he was enjoying having his brother back too much. Before she left them the final time, Hamilton said, "I'm sorry, Maggie, that he doesn't remember everything. Maybe someday he will and then he won't want to talk with me."

With tears in her eyes for her own loss, Maggie said, "I'm so grateful he woke up at all. I'm not going to ask for more."

As she worked in the saloon beneath the man she loved, she thought about all the times they had done this job together. From the first morning when he had jumped in to help her take orders from men who couldn't read the bill of fare she had so painstakingly printed out on a chalkboard. Franklin had not hesitated to make the meals run smoother and the work lessen for her. The only part he stayed away from was the actual preparation, telling her he knew what his cooking tasted like and knew no one would pay anything to eat it.

And she knew he reminded the men to leave a little extra for her, which he made sure she took for her own. Separating it from the money he collected to pay for the meals. She insisted on sharing it with him although she thought he may have been adding it back into her portion.

She was thankful for his help and his friendship. To ignore her feeling of loss for what that friendship was growing into would be stupid. It would be like cutting off a limb. But if he didn't remember their kisses or their afternoon at the river bank or the plans they had made together, she would need to forget them, too.

Maybe not forget them. More like put them away to take out and think about when they weren't such a painful memory, when the loss of him wasn't so fresh.

The Marshall returned one last time dealing with Hamilton's case. After telling Mason a long story he ended with, "Well, Mason, I guess this means it's over.

I can't get a case against Hamilton because all those involved were in essence participating in a criminal act themselves."

"Let me get this straight. Hamilton was presenting himself as a federal employee, telling folks he was going to be in charge of the land grants in the territories when they opened to the public and would welcome bribes. So, in reality, these men thought they were enlisting the aid of a federal employee for a fee to have their application placed nearer the top of the pile. So they would be ensured of getting the piece of property they wanted. And many of these men represented trusts or corporations that were going to use these properties for commercial profit. Land that should be used to set up homesteads," Mason said making sure he had all the pertinent information.

"That's it. So, although Hamilton was offering to do something for the bribe, he had no ability to do so. His was the least criminal of all the acts involved. An attorney could actually argue what he did prevented legitimate agents from being approached by these same men and bribed into committing a crime," the Marshal said as he stood up, putting on his sheepskin coat and wool scarf.

Mason, putting his coat on and following the Marshall out, said, "I'll go down to the saloon and let them know. It may make things a little less tense. Franklin still hasn't remembered parts of his life. I want to kick him in his saddle-warmer for hurting Maggie but then he can't help not remembering."

Maggie was washing the last of the beer mugs after the midday meal. The men still preferring beer to coffee, even in this cold weather. She heard the hesitating steps on the stairs and turned to see Franklin coming down each step gingerly.

"You must be feeling better to try to come down here on your own," she said conversationally.

"Hamilton's been doing it for days now. Why am I expected to be any different?" he asked finally making the landing and walking over to where Maggie stood on the near side of the bar.

"I don't know. I guess because you were out longer than he was. You are looking better. Hardly any signs of the bruises and the stitches look all healed over now, too. Just a little scar that is almost hidden by your hair," she said trying not to run her fingers through his hair which needed to be cut.

"Now everyone will be able to tell Hamilton and me apart. Our scars are different from one another," he said watching Maggie's expression. "I was speaking with Mason earlier and he told me something extremely interesting to me. He said you could always tell me from Hamilton and that when we were brought in, both of us beaten to a pulp, you could identify me by identifying a birthmark I have in a very intimate area."

Franklin finished as Maggie turned bright red listening to him describe his birthmark and her knowing it was there.

"I-I, ah," Maggie tried to find a plausible answer to his comment but couldn't even meet his gaze as she stammered.

"Maggie, were we more to each other before the beating? I mean, were we intimate with one another?" he asked, taking hold of the hand Maggie was chewing her nail on.

"Yes."

At her answer his eyes darkened with a passion she had not seen there in weeks and quickly said, "I mean, no." At Franklin's confusion, Maggie clarified, "I mean we were more to each other than what we are now, but we were never - intimate."

"Tell me. I need to know. I have these feelings when I think of you or like this, when I touch you but I can't seem to grasp them. Like something from a remembered dream." He whispered quietly, "So tell me about us."

She wanted him to know, to possibly remember what they had together, what they wanted together before the beatings. "We met when I began the meals here for the men who couldn't afford the hotel restaurant's meals. You helped me when you didn't need to, working long hours for no increase in pay but we did share the gratuities. I think we did but you may have been putting yours back into mine...I'm not sure."

Franklin was rubbing her wrist with his thumb, paying attention when her heart pulses changed, and he teased, "I must have thought a lot of you if I worked extra without pay."

"Well, I did feed you, too, so that might have had something to do with it," she said as she began to relax in his company once again.

"And I take it we became more than just friends? That at some point I showed you my birthmark?" Then with a glimmer of the old Franklin's humor asked, "Did you show me yours?"

Again, Maggie was embarrassed and couldn't find an answer to this teasing, funny Franklin. "Maybe I should check for it now, since you aren't acting like yourself," she informed him.

That was enough to have Franklin pull Maggie into

his arms as he placed his mouth over hers, evidently remembering how to kiss just fine. He pulled her body up against his, stroking her back from shoulder to below her hips, taking care to caress the soft curves of her fanny thoroughly. His tongue slipped between her lips and sought solace with hers, her soft moans exciting him into closer culmination.

The two jumped apart as Hamilton closed the upstairs door rather loudly. "If it were just me, I would have slipped out of here quietly but you're kind of right out there in the open. You can be seen from the hall of the hotel. I suggest you go upstairs where I will be sure to stay away from for the next, umm…" He checked the watch in his pocket. "Three hours."

"Would you go upstairs with me if I promise not to take this too fast? I would like to be alone with you to investigate what we have together, what we are to each other," he said beginning to kiss her lips again and then down to her neck and ear.

"I don't know if I should, Franklin. This is more than we've ever done before and I don't do this kind of thing normally. It's simply that I still remember you, what we were, the plans we made to be together."

"So, we weren't on a closer physical kind of relationship? You sure? Because my body seems to remember yours real well. Even when I first woke up, I knew something was between us. I just didn't realize how much," he said as Maggie stepped back from him giving them some space apart.

"Did Hamilton tell you? Say something about me? He tried to pretend to be you when he first came to town, kissed me and tried to get me to go someplace quiet with him. Is this your way of doing the same thing?" Maggie asked beginning to distrust her own feelings toward this new Franklin.

"No, he failed to tell me any of that. But that's like him, only showing himself in a good light." He seemed to remember his brother's shenanigans from their youth.

"You used to mistrust Hamilton in pretty much everything. You've changed in that respect. You seem to trust him again and I'm worried that might be your downfall," she warned him honestly.

"After coming out of that coma or whatever, I realized all that was past. What mattered was that Hamilton and I had a chance to start over, to forgive each other, to live as brothers like we used to. But one thing I will never allow is for Hamilton to mess with what you and I have. I know it was strong and I think I can get back to where we were really quickly. Just having you near me makes me want to know you better." He tried to hold Maggie's hand, which she placed behind her back.

"I think you need to heal a little longer before you start making any new plans. You may not remember us but I'm not forgetting anything. When I see the man I loved, then I'll think about going further with him." She turned before she lost her nerve after saying such a thing and went back towards the kitchen, leaving Franklin standing at the bar.

Maggie ran right into Molly as she stepped out of her office, closing the door quickly and placing a hand up to check that her hair was still in place.

"Oh, Maggie, you startled me," Molly said nervously.

Maggie was still up-set over her talk with Franklin and wasn't thinking straight herself. "I was heading for the kitchen but can we talk?" she asked her long-time friend who was much wiser in the ways of men having worked in a big hotel before as a manager.

Before Molly could answer, the door behind her opened and Eli stood there, looking guiltier than a small boy with his hand in the cookie jar. "Ah, hello, Maggie," Eli said in his usual polite way.

"Hello, Eli, nice to see you but you may want to tuck the other side of your shirt in before you go back to work." Maggie smiled cheekily at the red-faced couple and headed for the kitchen, deciding not to burden anyone with her worries and fears.

CHAPTER 14

As the weeks progressed, Sweetwater readied itself for the holidays. There had been days of snow and a few days too cold for many of the construction crews to work on the houses going up on Thompson Street. A few men had returned to their own hometowns and the families they left there. The meal times were less busy due to this change in the number of workers.

On the other hand, the bakery's business increased. Orders for special pies and cakes were coming in on a regular basis, the local women taking the extra time this gave them to do other things. Of course, many of the women in town had jobs they did as well as keep house for their husbands. The handy, ready-baked items became a convenience for the families living in Sweetwater as well as the men still living in the single tent city.

A Christmas Day party was planned in the saloon, the bar being closed due to the holiday. This gave a place for those men down by the river and in the tent camp set-up nearer town a place to go during the cold daylight. The men from the boarding house across the street were going to attend as well as the employees of the hotel and any guests staying there.

Fran and her family were attending the Christmas Day's festivities, too. Walt had baked bread for the potluck dinner and was very proud to be the town's baker, leaving all the fancy pastry baking to his wife. After all, he told everyone, the best bakers are men. And after tasting his bread many were in agreement.

The food was all being donated, even Callie sent premade items like fruit cakes and hams. Matthew sent over some wine and imported candy, Molly was donating a large pan of macaroni and cheese as well as scalloped potatoes from the hotel's kitchen. Jars of mincemeat would be made into pies and there would be bread pudding with raisins smothered in a warm brandy sauce waiting on the hotel's stove.

Mason would be donating cider, sarsaparilla, coffee and tea. Mayor Thompson, one of the town founders, donated a beef quarter and the butcher added a half-dozen dressed chickens. Oliver, the hotel cook, would roast them to perfection for the group. It was going to become an annual event, much like Callie's Christmas Eve party, which was open to all St. Michaels Foundling Homes' previous residents and close neighboring ranchers.

Hope Wilder had the children make Christmas decorations that she used to decorate the schoolroom but then sent over to the saloon to be used there on Christmas Day. Snow flake cutouts dusted with glitter and long swags of paper rings hooked together in bright colors along with hand-drawn pictures of scenes of the manger and angels, camels and kings colored by the children. These would be retrieved after the party by the artists.

Christmas Eve was not a silent night. The winds started early afternoon and blew across the plains and water troughs froze solid. The horses in the livery were warm and well fed but any others out in the tent camps were as miserable as their owners. Tents were waving like flags and men had piled into nearby standing tents as their own went with the winds to be retrieved when the weather calmed down. Then the snow began to fall and anyone in the town that had planned to travel out to the Harrison ranch for the annual Christmas Eve party put their time and attention into making the party at the saloon even better.

Maggie carried in the clean plates to leave overnight so they would be ready for the next day. Flatware and cups were also in place at the end of the long trestle table set-up to hold the food. It was placed so there would be lines down each side of the food and people could help themselves to what they wanted. Starting with the breads and side dishes then ending with the meats and gravy just as Callie had taught them.

Hamilton hung the decorations on the wall, swaging the paper rings while Thad tacked up the children's artwork. Franklin added boughs of greenery and red bows Abby had sent over to act as center pieces on the tables and bar. There were already paper snowflakes on each of the panes of glass in the windows facing the boardwalk. A holly wreath wrapped in red ribbon and finished off with a large bow was in place of honor over the bar.

Molly added jars of scented wax that would be lit in the morning, making the aroma of cinnamon and other spices spread throughout the room, covering the smell of tobacco and beer the place usually reeked of.

Finally, Maggie was satisfied the room was as ready as they could make it the night before the gathering. She sat sipping hot spiced cider and nibbling little balls of sugared dough cooked in oil. Hamilton came up, stole one of the sweet morsels and popped it into his mouth.

"Are you ever going to forgive me?" he asked nonchalantly.

"I have no reason to hold anything against you. You

don't need to wait for my forgiveness," she said, sitting up straighter and getting ready to walk across the street to her room.

"Come on, you know you hold me responsible for Franklin getting hurt and losing his memories - his memories of you. I'd change it if I could, you know. You made him so happy it was hard to watch you together," he admitted to her.

"That's in the past, I'm moving on and so should you. Talking about that, when are you planning on moving on? You never stay in one spot too long, I thought. You ran out of people to fleece, I suppose, and since we were all forewarned, there's no one here to fool." The bitterness coming out easier on this strange night, nothing being as it usually was.

"I'm not leaving, Maggie. I don't want to make things any more difficult for you but Franklin and I have come to an agreement. I've got a job with Matthew at his distribution center. This is the season for miracles so I'm hoping you'll forgive me and give Franklin another chance. He wants to make it up to you, go back to how you were together."

"But he doesn't remember how we were. All he knows is what you tell him and I don't trust that and I don't trust Franklin anymore. He's different and the sweet man I was falling in love with doesn't seem to be around any longer. But you made me think. Franklin and I spoke about leaving Sweetwater together. Perhaps I'll continue with those plans and then you and Franklin can do whatever you want." She stood, grabbed her cape, pulled the hood over her head, then ran into the snowy night to her room above the newspaper.

"Damn," said Hamilton as Franklin got closer. "I

think I just made it worse."

"How could you do that? I thought her ignoring me was bad enough," complained Franklin.

"I thought since she seemed so happy tonight, you know humming Christmas songs and getting all these decorations up…. I thought I could put in a good word for you. I thought the Christmas spirit would soften her up a little," Hamilton confessed.

"Doesn't seem to have worked. She looked angry when she left. I was hoping I was wrong." Frustrated, Franklin glared at his brother. "Just stop trying to help me. She's either going to accept I am the same man she knew or I'm going to have to show her I'm that same man. I have strong feelings for her, probably love her, but she isn't in any frame of mind to believe me and it's been weeks." Franklin watched making sure Maggie got back to her room through the snow.

In the morning, everyone in town attended the church service and then most of the town's population and that of the tent camps went directly to the saloon. Games were set out, some of the children bringing their Christmas gifts to show off and share. Miss Lily and her two ladies came accompanied by trays with a variety of cookies. Everyone else came laden with food and warm wishes for all. It had become an inside Fourth of July gathering and everyone was full of goodwill to men - all except Maggie.

No one would have noticed unless they saw her face when she thought no one was watching. The smile dipped at the corners. The eyes weren't shiny with laughter but with unshed tears from the evening before. She ached to be with Callie or sister orphan, Mary Beth, her constant companion up to a few months ago until that friend married a lawyer turned newspaper editor.

But Franklin noticed and felt guilty knowing he and Hamilton were the cause. He had wanted this holiday season to be a new starting point for them. The end of her distrust of his motives, the beginning of starting over. Now he wasn't sure she was ever going to accept him with his memories of the two of them gone. He had tried to remember, tried to find anything familiar in the saloon's restaurant but couldn't remember anything for months before the beating. Couldn't remember when Maggie came into his life.

Molly came over to sit with Maggie. "Are you feeling all right? You look tired."

"I'm fine. I didn't get to sleep right away last night. I guess I was too excited about today." Taking this excuse to escape any well-intentioned questioning, she said, "Oh, look, I think they're bringing in the food from the kitchen. Save me a seat at your table, will you?"

"Of course, Eli already is sitting there," Molly said pointing to the tall well-dressed man.

Maggie waited at the food table, getting anything people asked for that didn't appear to be there. She finally felt everyone else was through the line when she took one of the last plates and filled it sparingly.

As she approached the table Molly and Eli were at, an empty seat was there next to Franklin, his plate of food still untouched. Maggie sat in the empty chair and took the compliments from some of the others over the event's success with small nods and many thanks. She was extremely conscious of Franklin and the glass of cider he had brought to the table for her.

Trying not to be discourteous, she said, "Thank you for the cider but you needn't go to the bother."

Franklin firmed his lips. "It was no bother. After all, you spent all this time on getting the food and everything organized. I wanted to let you know I appreciated it. No hidden plan, I promise."

"I'm sorry if I'm surly. I must not have gotten enough sleep. I'll go to bed early tonight," she said but that didn't seem to make Franklin happy either as she noted his downturned mouth.

"I'll help you clear up." He stood, leaving most of his food uneaten as did Maggie.

She excused herself and disappeared into the kitchen where she could take a deep breath without being afraid, she would break into tears. What was she going to do all day this close to him? She couldn't leave unless she feigned illness and everyone would want to help and bring her soup or some other aid. Then she would feel guilty and really would get sick.

Franklin came in carrying a stack of dirty dishes. "You can't keep running and if you leave Sweetwater then I'll be right behind you. We need to get this out into the open." As others came in with more used plates and to refill coffee pots, Franklin gave a stern glare at Maggie. Taking her arm, he escorted her into the supply room where they could be alone.

"I am not going away easily. I think I love you, no, I know I love you but I need to know if I have any chance of getting you to love me back. I don't want to make you feel like I'm following you around all day. We work together and I like that. If you really feel you'll never return these feelings that I have for you, I'll try to live with that, as long as you stay."

"You don't even know me. You've forgotten me and moved on. You're not the same and I can't explain the difference but I'm no longer part of your life," Maggie said trying to explain her feelings.

"I can't say anything as to whether I'm the same of if I've changed. I know when I look at you, I feel different. You were holding Abby's baby today and something, almost like a punch to the gut, something visceral hit me and I wanted to claim you right then and there. Haul you upstairs and put a baby in your belly and I admit, I don't think I've ever had such an urge before," he confessed watching the emotions play across Maggie's face, one of surprise and then desire.

That softening expression had Franklin telling her everything, even if it wasn't exactly what he should be saying. "I may have forgotten our first kiss but I remember our last one and it only made me hungrier for more of you. You responded to me in the saloon that day and I'm asking you to stay and investigate those feelings. The ones that make me melt against you like a second skin, the ones that make me lose my breath, the ones that make me wish with everything I have I'll remember those first sweet months of knowing you, of falling in love with you." He held her against his body as he leaned against the barrels stacked on the floor.

"When we're together and it's only you and me, I feel like I've always felt about you, Franklin. I'm just not sure you're serious. I mean, that you aren't simply trying to, well, bed me and then move on," she finally told him honestly.

"I can't say the part about bedding you hasn't been on my mind, a lot, but not moving on. I see us married with children, sitting in front of a fire and getting old together. Along the way there's a lot of bedding and such but we are always together. It's always you and me and

I think I've always thought so because I found this in my drawer. I know without having to remember that I bought it for you. Ask Abby, I got it there, I'm sure." Franklin took out a small box and opened it to show off a ring with a blue sapphire built-up on gold filigree.

"Oh, it's beautiful, Franklin. It's lovely but are we ready for this commitment? Are you ready?" she asked wanting him to tell her the truth.

"I'm sure. I've been sure. Some things can't be forgotten, honey. We can wait a little while if you need to but I want to make sure you and everyone in town knows I intend to make you my wife." Then he slipped the ring on her finger knowing it would fit, knew somehow, he had bought it for her finger.

Maggie rested against his body, tears running down her cheeks, letting all the pain and misery she had felt for the last few weeks wash away. "I was so sad, like I had to start all over. That I was the only one who knew we loved each other."

"I may have forgotten some of the time we spent together but not the love part. I knew we were supposed to be more to one another than nurse and patient. Hamilton actually hinted at more, saying if I hadn't been so head-over-heels in love with you, he'd have gone after you himself. But I didn't need him to push me in your direction. I used to hope to hear your voice when you came into the saloon while I was relegated to my room upstairs. I got jealous the day I heard you take care of Roy's injured finger until I saw which one Roy was. Thirty years too old and fifty pounds too heavy," Franklin teased.

That got the response he was looking for. Maggie, drying her eyes with her hankie, smiling and saying,

"You were jealous of my doctoring a festering splinter on a wizened old man? Really?"

"To my defense, I couldn't remember who he was and you were being so damn nice to him. I thought, why didn't you just slap some salve on it and be done. I almost came down stairs to do it myself but my sore body kept me back. I did finally have Hamilton point out which one he was and that's when he teased me about having it bad." Shrugging his shoulders, he continued, "I thought, so I have it bad. I know how to take care of that." He covered her mouth with his.

The young couple spent half an hour longer locked in the back room until Franklin pushed Maggie away. "Honey, we're gonna' have to stop this or slip upstairs and I know that would be a bad idea after all the righteous talk of waiting until you were ready and all. Here, let me fix your hair and I need to straighten up, too. Go on and join the singing and I'll be right out, I promise." He kissed the tip of her nose and pushed her through the door.

Franklin stood after Maggie left and tried to pull on his trousers to get more room for his erection. Opening the rear door, he took a deep breath, hoping the ice-cold air would help him get his raging body under control. He couldn't return to the saloon in this condition. It would only take a couple of minutes to cool off, though, and then he could control himself enough to be around Maggie again.

Slipping back into the saloon, Maggie began clearing dessert dishes from the tables and refilling coffee cups. Miss Lilly was playing the piano and leading the group in signing Christmas carols and other popular songs as someone in the crowd called them out.

Everyone seemed to be enjoying themselves, the men from the tent camps most of all. They didn't have much entertainment and finding themselves among the town's families seemed to raise their spirits as they sang loudly, if not well.

Maggie finally realized several minutes had gone by and Franklin hadn't come out of the kitchen so she lifted the large pan now containing the gathered plates and carried it to the wash sink in the kitchen. She found herself curious as to what was taking Franklin so long so she opened the door to the back storeroom. After all, he had said he would be right out.

The room was empty, of people anyway. There were small piles of snow at the rear door leading outside. Maggie opened that door to see if Franklin was outside and was disappointed to find the area empty, too. She called his name but there was no response.

Returning to the saloon, Maggie tried to make sense of Franklin's disappearance. Had he changed his mind? Decided he had been too hasty? Maggie hid her fisted hand with the ring on it in the folds of her skirt. Maybe no one had noticed and she'll be able to slip it off before it became town gossip. She looked around and found Hamilton standing next to Matthew and Abby but he didn't seem to be worried about anything.

Maggie glanced up the stairs to the closed doors, knowing Franklin couldn't have gotten there without her seeing him but had the urge to check anyway. Suddenly she felt a hand on her arm and she relaxed, guessing Franklin had gone around the building and came in the front saloon doors.

She turned with a relieved smile which caught part way. "Hamilton, it's you." The disappointment almost brought tears to her eyes.

"What's wrong? Where's Franklin? Did you two fight again?" he asked worriedly.

"No, just the opposite. We've made up, not that you will be happy about that," she said jerking her arm away from him.

"I told you, I am not your enemy. You are the best thing to happen to my brother. I truly believe that or I would be fighting you for control." Keeping his voice low he asked, "So, where is he?"

Fear for Franklin overcame pride as she said, "I don't know. We were in the back storeroom behind the kitchen and then I came out here. He was going to follow me but never came back. I went to look for him but all there is are a few boot prints in the snow. Now I'm thinking he feels he made a mistake in giving me this." She showed him her hand with the ring still placed prominently.

"I'll be right back. My brother didn't just get engaged and then hide off. I'll find him." He weaved his way through the singers to the hotel's doorway.

Maggie was surprised at how much calmer she felt now that Hamilton knew about the engagement and his acceptance of it. Hamilton was the only person she felt held any sway over Franklin and if he approved, as he seemed to, then Franklin wouldn't have any conflicting emotions over giving her the ring.

Franklin returned but by-passed Maggie to get over to Mason who leaned toward Hamilton to hear what he was saying. Then Mason leaned over to his wife, Victoria, and whispered in her ear. She nodded and Mason went out the door with Hamilton after grabbing a couple of coats.

Matthew said something to Abby, who looked up at him from her sitting position, then she nodded as her gaze searched the room. When she spotted Maggie, she smiled and returned to singing, glancing every once in a while, towards the bar where Maggie stood.

The singing ended and everyone applauded Miss Lily and her girls who had led the singing and were simply pretty to look at. The men got out the checkers again and the children returned to playing with their Christmas gifts or toys they had brought. It was beginning to get dark and women were packing up their empty bowls and pans, getting ready to go home.

Abby came over saying, "I noticed Franklin had finally given you the ring. He was very worried you wouldn't accept him since you hadn't known each other very long. I assured him it wasn't the length of time you knew one another but how well you knew one another. I told Franklin I knew I loved Matthew the first time he stepped into my shop selling me the new corset from Kalamazoo. Franklin told me he knew he loved you on your first fishing trip. That was before the beatings, of course."

Maggie blushed as she remembered what they had done on that first, and last, fishing trip. "I remember that day, too. It was very, umm, enlightening," she told the married woman who saw way too much.

"I'm for home. Matthew said he'd be back but the girls are too tired to wait." Then she called to her teenage son, "Thad, come help me get all this home, will you, please? Both of your sisters are going to get crabby and no one wants that." She laughed, trying to stuff a wiggling baby into the hooded bag that would protect her from the cold.

Maggie helped get all of the babies' toys and belongings into the cloth sack Abby carried for those items and Thad took one baby and Abby took the other and left like a conquering army.

Then one by one families began to leave. The coats on the pegs soon dwindling to belonging to the men from the tent camps who were trying to prolong their visit in the heated saloon for as long as possible. Maggie didn't blame them. Now that the sun was going down, frost was forming so heavy on the windows, not even the street lamps shown through.

She went into the kitchen to help the scrub boy wash the last of the cups and dessert plates, which they stacked on the counter to air dry. Making sure all the stoves and lamps were either banked or turned down, she locked the back door. Molly and Eli had left early to celebrate their first Christmas together at home so Maggie had told Molly that she would lock up.

Returning to the saloon, she found the men smoking and had the cards out now the women and children were gone. Maggie hesitated and then climbed the stairs to Franklin's rooms. They hadn't changed much in the last couple of weeks. A little cold since no one had added wood to the stove so Maggie did.

She sat on the sofa she had spent so many nights on waiting for Franklin to wake-up and then while taking care of both men. The room was rather plain, a small table with two chairs, an upholstered striped arm chair and a table with lamp which she was debating whether to light. She knew what the bedrooms looked like, now returned to having a bed and bureau used as a washstand in each. Franklin's the only room with a window besides the living area.

Finally, she heard heavy steps coming upstairs, sounding like someone was taking them two at a time. She looked towards the closed door, hoping it was Franklin but something deep inside telling her it wasn't.

Hamilton came in, his hair covered with melting snow. "I need to dress for the weather and get my gun belt. Someone has taken Franklin. We'll be back by morning, I hope."

"What do you mean? Someone t-took Franklin? Who would want to take Franklin? How do you know?" she asked all at once.

"It looks like someone came by the road, hid in the livery and then dragged Franklin to a horse and took him. We're gonna' follow them since we know about when he was taken and how fast a horse can go in this new snow. The men responsible aren't well fed so they won't be real alert for a posse to form so soon," he continued as he pulled on another union shirt and an extra pair of socks undressing and dressing in front of her without embarrassment.

Maggie had no illusions of his modesty. After all, she had taken care of him for several days until he was able to do so for himself. "So, this boils down to what you were up to before coming here doesn't it? Franklin is paying for your sins again?" she accused.

"Of course, doesn't it all boil down to that? I was the bad seed. I have never denied that but I didn't see this coming, either. I don't have the money anymore. If I did, I'd return it. Besides, it wasn't their money, anyways. Most of the cash came from syndicated groups or corporations of men with money. This is just being downright vindictive now." He stomped his feet into his boots and left pulling his gun belt around his waist.

"I'm staying here until you bring him back. I hope he won't need me to care for him again but I will if he's injured," Maggie told Hamilton as he went back down the steps.

The men downstairs hardly looked up to notice them.

Maggie took the extra blankets off the shelf in the bedroom and made up her bed on the sofa. She wanted to lay down on Franklin's bed to feel closer to him but thought he might need it when they brought him home. She hoped not, she simply wanted him back where he belonged - with her.

CHAPTER 15

The four men were quiet as their mounts trudge through the deep snow following the path left by the three horses less than an hour or so ahead of them. The other horses had the harder job and it was beginning to show. Wilder, a good tracker, saying they were getting closer to the first group.

Mason nodded he had heard but didn't pull down the scarf covering his face and nose. These were the times he was sorry he didn't grow a beard in winter but the only time. Matthew said nothing but he had heard, the same as Hamilton had as he checked his gun still resting on his thigh.

The weather was cold and snow was still falling but not one of the men complained. They had all volunteered for this and all knew Franklin and could guess why he had been tossed on a horse like a sack of grain. Wilder had informed the group of that right from the start, saying the rear horse was being led not ridden, that horse walking closely to the one directly in front of it.

Hamilton had his face down into the collar of his sheepskin lined coat, a knit scarf over his ears but covered with his Stetson that kept some of the snow from landing on his face and melting. He was worried about Franklin's comfort and warmth. His brother's hat and coat were still in the saloon's back room. Franklin had been dressed in his shirt and waistcoat since he thought he would be staying in the warmth of the saloon all day. Now Hamilton had to face the fact his brother may be out in the elements, snow piling up on his body, some

274

melting as it sucked his body's warmth from him.

Wilder put up his arm and all four riders came to a quiet stop. He pulled the knit scarf away from his mouth and said quietly, "These guys are right ahead of us. I think if we rush them, they'll run, leaving the trailing horse so they can make a faster escape. I don't think one of us can get in front of them without them being alerted, not enough brush with leaves for cover and the snow's too damn deep off the road. Any other ideas?"

Mason said, "I think if we come at them like a bunch of banshees, they'll run. If they wanted Franklin dead, they would have killed him back in town. They're just paid abductors. They won't stand and fight against an armed posse."

Matthew and Hamilton agreed so they all took out their guns spurring their horses into as fast a gallop as they could, whooping and shooting into the air, making enough noise to be twenty men.

As everyone thought, the two men up ahead, dropped the reins to the horse carrying an inverted Franklin and pushed their horses to a faster gait, forcing their frightened mounts to leap over the snow drifts only to find more in their path.

Mason and Wilder glanced at one another after catching up to the horse carrying Franklin. They realized the other two men's mounts were too tired to get through the snow and being frightened wasn't helping. Those two men continued to spur their horses as Matthew and Hamilton tried to see to Franklin's care.

Franklin had a horse blanket thrown over his body, but he had been tied, hands and feet under the horse. Matthew cut the ropes with the knife from his boot while Hamilton lowered his brother off the horse, searching for wounds or other injuries.

Franklin moaned through his nearly frozen lips and then shivering took over, racking his whole body. Hamilton swung his jacket off and forced his brother's arms into the still warm coat, warmed from Hamilton's own body. When Hamilton tried to wrap his knit muffler around Franklin, Matthew put his hand out to stop him then unwrapped his own scarf winding it around Franklin's neck and face.

"Franklin, can you hear me? Franklin wake up or I swear I'll leave you and go back and claim Maggie in your place," Hamilton threatened, trying to get Franklin riled enough to fight the cold.

Franklin mumbled something that sounded rude. Matthew and Hamilton smiled at each other and hoisted the half-frozen man onto the waiting horse. Hamilton took the reins to lead the somewhat upright Franklin back to town.

It wasn't long before Matthew and Hamilton realized Mason and Wilder were a little way behind them with the two criminals tied to their horses and heading back to a warm jail cell. Hamilton took great satisfaction since he planned to be in on any questioning to find out which of the men, he had conned was continuing to try to get him.

The first three and the second four kept up a steady pace, following their original path back to Sweetwater. They let the horses set the pace in the moonlight reflecting off the snow which had finally stopped falling.

The mounts began to speed up. The horses from Sweetwater knowing their warm stall and share of grain was close. The others picked up on the excitement, keeping pace with the locals. The men were eager to be home and warm again, too. Hamilton made no complaints although his two union suits and shirt weren't much protection. He accepted his punishment as just knowing he had gotten off much lighter than Franklin – again.

After leaving their horses with Andy at the livery, Mason and Wilder went directly to the jail to put their prisoners in the cell and indicated they would go home to their wives and a warm bed. Neither one admitting which was more important.

Matthew and Hamilton rode on to the saloon and practically carried Franklin up the stairs to find a sleepy Maggie sitting up on the sofa. As soon as Maggie realized the man slumped between Matthew and Hamilton was her fiancé, she jumped up and hurried into his bedroom, pulling down the covers to let Franklin lay down. Then she took over removing the coat and, realizing it had to have been Hamilton's, she gratefully handed it back to the brother. She finished taking off Franklin's wet, cold clothes making short work of them and covering him with her blanket off the sofa as well as the blankets already on his bed.

After making sure Maggie was all right, Matthew left to return to his family. Hamilton went to his own room to remove his wet gear after putting a couple more pieces of wood into the stove.

Maggie had examined Franklin as she undressed him and found a new bump on the front of his head. She felt it had probably been cold enough not to need an ice-pack and picked up his hand only to find it as cold as it was when he was brought in. Franklin had curled into a fetal position, trying to keep his body warmth to his core. Shivers racked his body with their strength, his lips and eye lids tinged blue.

Taking a couple of towels, she laid them right on the stove, moving them around quickly to keep them from scorching. When she felt they were warm enough, she took them into Franklin and tucked them against his chest. Taking one big breath, she then disrobed. Down to the naked skin, which was warmer now than she had been before thinking about what she was doing.

Crawling into the far side of the bed, she curled her body against the frigid backside of Franklin, feeling the cold from his body leave it and attack hers. She let her warm breath fall on his neck under the blanket, adding to her body's warming of the man in her arms. Finally, she matched his even breathing and they both fell into a deep sleep.

When the sun finally made its way into the room, Maggie found herself facing the opposite way. She went to move before Franklin woke but arms like tight bands held her in place as she realized there was a very warm, very male body curved around her naked one.

His face was nestled into her neck, then she felt little kisses along her shoulder and she said, "Franklin, let me up. I shouldn't be found in bed with you like this. I didn't mean to fall asleep. I was just going to warm you before going back to the sofa."

"It worked, I'm very warm right now. Maybe we can try for something else," he said as he moved his arms and cupped one of her breasts, thumbing the nipple, bringing it to life, eager for more of his attention.

"Franklin, you told me you would give me time," she pleaded, hating the way her body was betraying her.

"I said a lot of things but it was all based on my not remembering our time together. Like the first time I saw you walk into the saloon wearing your flowered yellow dress that always makes me think of summer or our first breakfast and how relieved we were when it was over or our first kiss down by the river." He pressed his hips and arousal into her backside.

She turned to face him, surprise bursting inside her. "You remember. You remember me, us, how we fell in love!"

"I do. I had a little help, I think, from a hit on the head by one of those two thugs, then hanging over the horse mile after mile. I kept waking up and remembering everything," he told her, looking down at the female parts she inadvertently was showing him.

"And now? What do you remember now?" she asked so happy he seemed to remember their whole time together.

"Everything, I think. There doesn't seem to be anymore dark areas. I remember us and that's the most important thing, anyway, isn't it?" He kissed her, returning his hand to keep one of her breasts warm.

A light knock on the bedroom door had both people in bed stop dead in their tracks as Hamilton said through the door, "I piled the clothes up, a lot of clothes, in front of the door out here. I told Molly earlier you were too busy to do breakfast this morning so she has one of the waiters doing it and I have to be at work across the street so you're on your own."

Franklin smiled at an embarrassed Maggie and said sarcastically, "Thanks, oh, I'm all right by the way. Nice of you to be worried for me."

"I figured with the way these clothes were thrown all over out here you were doing better than I was," Hamilton teased in return. "Bye."

"I forgot all about breakfast. I'm never going to live this down. I mean, before I could look anyone in the eye and tell them I was nursing both of you, but now...," she moaned, trying to hide her face into his neck.

"I'm not going to lie and tell you Hamilton won't tease you unmercifully for the next few weeks but only when you're alone. He won't say anything to anyone else."

"So, all I have to do is hide whenever he comes near so I won't be a target?" she asked still chagrined she had been found in a man's room, in his bed, naked.

"No, only until you marry me. Then he'll lose interest and he'll go on to something else," he said watching her response to his remark.

"Marry you? Soon?" she asked, not disliking the idea.

"Before the end of the year. That gives us up to a week to make plans. Is that a problem?" he asked hoping she didn't think he was rushing her.

"I, ah, yes, I'll marry you before the end of the year," she answered and was pulled close to his chest as he kissed her lips with all the passion he had been holding back.

"I should let you get dressed, as much as I hate to say so," Franklin said as he tried to let Maggie go.

"I think I want to stay, make an honest man out of you. You say you remember, then let's see if you remember what I like," she teased, offering him everything he ever wanted.

"I'm not sure we should, it's going to hurt, I think. You, I mean, it's going to hurt you and I'm not sure I can do that," he confessed, kissing her to let her down easily.

"It's going to hurt no matter when we make love. I

don't want to go another day and have something else keep us apart. Once we make love, we will be joined fully for life and no one, nothing, will be able to tear us apart. We will be one no matter what happens after this." She brought her hand up and rubbed his chest, pulling him towards her again as she pushed her hips into his still present arousal.

Franklin's mouth left her lips and placed it to the eager peaks of her breasts, turning them into hard pebbles, needing to be touched, licked, sucked. His hand moved down her body and found the warm channel waiting for him, already slick and the usually hidden nub waiting impatiently to be soothed.

Maggie pulled him onto her, letting him hold some of his weight off her while enjoying his pressing down on her mound, his soft velvety crown waiting impatiently at her entrance.

"It's all right, Franklin. I want this. I want to be with you," she whispered, raising her hips to meet his. That movement alone pushed him over the edge.

He let his erection slide unhindered into her silky warmth, the softness of her enclosing him. Her body eagerly pushing back in response to his movements. Franklin felt that this had been what he had been seeking all his adult life, like home only more so. He tried to get closer but realized they were as close as possible, already. Maggie had committed herself to him and that was all that really mattered as he tried to reward her for the joy he felt. He brought them both to a culmination neither expected to be so intense.

Franklin collapsed on Maggie but tried to slide to the side after a minute or two. Both were having trouble getting their breathing under control.

"Oh, honey, that was worth waiting for. I've never been so close to anyone in my life. We were made for one another. You have to believe me."

"I'll take your word for it. All I know is it was unbelievable, nothing the girls could have said would have explained what happened. No wonder they keep saying its indescribable. I thought they were being coy but I couldn't describe it and I just went through it."

"Maybe that's what it's supposed to be, kept only between the two people. I mean, I don't plan on telling anyone but I sure am going to participate again. With you, honey, only with you." Franklin pulled her in front of him again so he could cocoon her body with his once more.

Hamilton let himself into the unlocked jail's office, leaning against the wall since Mason and Wilder were already sitting in the only chairs. The two ruffians sat morosely on their cots. "Get any information out of them?" he asked nodding towards the jail cell.

"Not much, their names and I wired the Marshall since this all seems to be part of the trouble that followed you," Mason relayed.

"Yeah, I'm kinda tired of that, too, and the fact they keep pulling Franklin back into it when he didn't do anything. I mean, what good is it to take me back there when I don't have the money any longer? If someone wants to take it out of my hide, that's one thing but why try to take Franklin, um, me?" Hamilton continued.

"I can take them out back for a while. I need practice with the bull whip," Wilder offered casually.

Mason hid his smile knowing Wilder was just pulling their chains, trying to get one of the men to start talking.

"So, we're waitin' on the train then? Is it running?" asked Hamilton getting frustrated with the wait already.

"I guess so. Marshal may already know who these boys work for, where they hang out. We might be able to get at whoever hired them that way. Otherwise they'll stand trial for attempted murder and kidnapping, so we'll be having a hanging by the new year," Mason said making sure the two in the cell heard every word.

One of the men, the youngest, spoke up saying shakily, "Hell, I didn't know anyone was gettin' kilt. I was told to pick this guy up and take him back to Preston where some other guy wanted to beat him up. No one said he was gonna kill him."

The other man in the cell glared at the younger one with yellowish eyes but didn't contradict him or tell him to shut-up, Mason noted. So, no loyalty to the man who hired them. They were simply two guys willing to do a job for money.

"So how much you get paid this time?" Mason took a shot in the dark.

"Same as last, twenty when we git hired and twenty when we bring him back. Last time we didn't get him back. Some ol' woman stopped us. Thought she wuz gonna shoot us so we ran," the younger man told them, not holding anything back.

Mason realized who they had and asked, "Where's the third guy, then?"

"Oh, Bull, he don't travel well in winter. There ain't a horse that would put up with him on their back and still be able to go through the snow. Only the boss didn't know so paid us for three men anyways," the man said proudly.

"Well, he's going to know now, so unless we hear a

name real soon, this won't end pretty for you two," threatened Hamilton, losing all patience, balling his fists in anger.

Finally, the older man looked right at Hamilton and asked, "How many married women you been poking behind their ol' man's back that you can't figure this one out? We told you last time why we wuz beaten on ya. Still need more hints?"

"You told me? I don't remember...." Then Hamilton realized Franklin didn't remember anything from the beating' so whatever was said was lost to them.

"I wuz to tell ya, after you wuz short of breath from the kick to your sacks that Mr. Hinze says hi, and to bring his missus back or else we'd be back for ya. Well, we cum back," explained the older man as if speaking to someone without his full mental capacities.

Mason and the quiet Wilder turned to stare at Hamilton with interested expressions, waiting for his explanation of things.

"It, it was only one wife and not something I usually do. But we had an understanding. She wanted to leave her husband, who she had many reasons to leave, but, ah, needed a little help doing so." Hamilton tried explaining and still not be thought the kind of man who breaks up a marriage and then dumps the woman.

But Mason and Wilder remained silent, yet expectant, so Hamilton felt he needed to explain more. "Mrs. Hinze, she wanted, no needed, to get away. Her husband was, ah, abusive, especially when he drank, which was often. We played poker together so I was around some, you know, dragging him home afterwards and stuff. Then one night, I brought him home and Mrs. Hinze thanked me, ah, properly. After that, I brought

Hinze home most nights and I, ah, got thanked each time. Then one night, Mrs. Hinze asked me to help her get away. That she could get some money but didn't know how to get out of town. That a lone woman travelling would bring attention and she was known in the political circles so needed a man to be with her, sort of to look like a travelling couple. I told her I would do that. One day she said she had the money, her trunk packed and it was convenient for me to be elsewhere, too, so we got on the next train east."

Wilder couldn't help asking, "You call her Mrs. Hinze, even after....?"

Hamilton took a minute to think about it and answered, "Yeah, I guess I always do. So as I didn't slip up when we weren't alone. Anyways, it doesn't matter. When we got to the City of Kansas, I went my way and she went hers. She had family in St. Louis and once there she said they could protect her while she filed for divorce."

Wilder shook his head, as if how dumb does a guy have to be to mess with a married woman of a powerful man? Mason took pity on him.

"All right, so this woman is still in hiding and this Hinze thinks you have her and his money. I think she may have taken quite a stake when she left." Raising his hands in surrender in case one of the others thought to argue, he continued, "Not that she hadn't earned it, of course. Just makes a man mad as hell when both his wife and his money are gone. He have any connection to the other thing?" Mason asked Hamilton.

Hamilton shook his head. "No, nothing, the two things have no association to one another although Hinze is pretty politically connected."

"Pretty busy boy, weren't you?" Mason said trying to figure an end to things. "Maybe we should just let Heinz know you don't have his wife or his money." He looked to Hamilton for confirmation.

"I haven't heard from Mrs. Hinze since we parted company in Cow Town and I didn't help her for the money. She seemed to have enough to continue on with so I left her," Hamilton said honestly.

"That dog don't hunt, lucky. Hinze knows you got her hold-up in the saloon with ya. Someone said he saw you and her gettin cozy. She's livin upstairs with ya," the older man in the jail cell informed the room.

All three men outside the cell looked dumb-founded at the last remark and then Mason's face relaxed as he told the others. "He means, Maggie. Someone told Hinze about Maggie, not Mrs. Hinze but there must be some resemblance to the two of them."

Hamilton shrugged and said, "Not much. Size maybe but Mrs. Hinze's hair is from a bottle so much brassier, bust is larger and hips wider and she's several years older."

"I don't know if I find your description so disturbing because you know these things about Mrs. Hinze or about Maggie," said Wilder, his silver eyes glittering at Hamilton shrewdly.

"I'm just observant. In my line of work, you have to be. I mean my former line of work. I'm legit now," he told both law officers.

"What are we going to do about this mess? I mean, how do we let Hinze know Maggie isn't his long missing wife?" asked Mason thinking out loud.

"I have more bad news. Franklin and Maggie are engaged so getting her out of the picture, out of danger isn't going to be easy. I don't think any of us can talk Franklin into sending her away. Not after yesterday's kidnapping. He's going to want to keep her close to protect her," Hamilton informed the others.

"Well, that's good and bad, I suppose. Do you think if we come right out and send this Hinze a wire, telling him about Franklin and Maggie that he'll back away, go and try another avenue for his wife? He may not really care about Hamilton if he isn't cohabitating with the woman. He may think you've been rubbing his nose in it, you know. Maybe knowing she dumped you will be a balm to his self-esteem," Mason said, trying to find ways out of this predicament.

"I suppose it can't hurt coming from you. Then if you mention you got his name from these two." He pointed over to the cell with his thumb. "It may make him think twice about trying to get his hands on me again or grabbing Franklin by mistake. I don't know where Mrs. Hinze went, I swear on my brother's head." He raised his right hand into the air.

"Hell, it can't hurt, I guess, but I'll run it past the Marshall when he gets here, first," Mason said and then told everyone to get out of his office, he had work to do.

Hamilton went to the saloon for lunch, having put in very little time at work, worrying about how to protect Franklin and maybe even Maggie. He found his brother behind the bar, looking no worse for wear except for a new red bump on his left temple.

"Should you be up? What if you have another concussion?" asked Hamilton bringing his filled plate up to the bar to eat.

"I'm fine. Everything's fine," he said smiling. He had trouble keeping the smile wiped off his face all morning then decided he'd let people wonder what put it there. He wasn't going to tell anyone the truth.

"Yeah, I figured you were fine this morning. I take it you and Maggie are fine, too? I saw the ring yesterday, the one you bought for her weeks ago," Hamilton said between forkfuls of food.

"Yeah, and you're to stay out of it. I don't want you scaring her off. I finally got her to trust me again. It helped I remembered meeting her and our first kiss and things like that," Franklin said, drawing another beer for a paying customer.

"If you remember everything, do you remember what those men beat you up the first time told you?" asked Hamilton as he stopped eating to hear the answer.

"No. Oh, wait one of them said the beating was for taking some guy's wife." Then looking at his brother asked, "Is this all over a woman? Did you steal some man's wife? The guy that was hitting me said something about taking a man's money was one thing but taking his wife was another. Then he tried to kick me in my crotch but missed, thank God," Franklin said wincing at the memory.

"I didn't steal anyone's wife. She left him at the same time I was making my bow to Topeka and heading here. There was a mix-up is all and he thinks she's living here with me. They think Maggie is the missing wife," Hamilton said realizing how this could sound to a man in love.

"Who the hell is THEY? Is she in danger here? Will they try to take her next?" Franklin said loudly, angry that not only had he been abducted by mistake, now Maggie could be in danger, too. The saloon quieted as the customers stopped eating to listen to the drama.

Hamilton stood back from the bar so Franklin couldn't punch him and explained, "Mason is sending a wire to inform the man in question his wife is not here in town, has never been in town and that I left her in the City of Kansas to continue to travel eastward. I think that should clear up all confusion and let the man know he isn't unknown to Mason, so any more trouble will bring the law right to Heinz's doorstep. Which he won't want because he is interested in running for public office. That's probably why he wants his wife by his side. A divorced man, especially one divorced with cause, isn't going to do well in the political arena."

Then Hamilton finished, saying, "I gotta get back to work. Kiss Maggie for me. I wish you two only the best."

Franklin bit his lower lip so as not to swear a blue-streak once his brother left. He picked up the plate and gathered several others on his way to the kitchen. As soon as he saw Maggie putting away the leftover food, his smile returned. He was just so damn happy, even Hamilton's escapades couldn't make him angry for very long.

"Is everyone gone then?" she asked, eager to be alone with Franklin although she had promised herself, she wouldn't succumb to his touch again, not until they were married.

"Yeah, that's about it. A few mugs left is all and we'll be done for the next few hours." Passion flared in his eyes.

Maggie took a deep breath, then said in a whisper for his ears only, "We promised no more of, of, of anything until after the wedding."

"I don't think I promised. I just agreed it would probably be the more cautious way to go but there was no vow or anything," he said, holding her hand, pulling her towards him.

Maggie shook his hand off hers and looked around at the almost empty kitchen except for the dish scrubber. "We agreed, then. Now don't try to pretend you have a concussion or some such nonsense. I can't spend any more time upstairs with you. It simply isn't seemly and you know it," she whispered harshly.

"Then will you go into the back room with me? What can happen there?" he asked innocently.

"Oh, I don't know, maybe we can both get abducted?" she teased which had the unexpected result of Franklin pulling her close to him, holding her tightly.

"Never let anyone take you. Scream bloody murder, I'll always be close by."

The scrub boy stopped working to watch the couple then but with one glare from Franklin, the young man went back to washing the dishes without saying a word.

"What's wrong with you, Franklin? Did last night upset you so much you're worried about me, now? No one wants me and for that matter no one wants you, either. They'll figure it out at some point or the men in the jail will tell someone," she told him reasonably.

"It's just that I worry, now we're engaged. I don't want anything to prevent us from getting married, that's all. I'm simply being foolish. I know you're safe here." He held her a moment or two longer before letting go.

When Hamilton came home for supper, Franklin jumped on him for information. "Well, did Mason hear back? Did the guy get the wire?"

"Better than that. The Marshall knows the damn man and said he would personally deliver the message and explain about you. That I have a twin. Then warn him if anything more occurs to cause the Marshall to return to Sweetwater about us, then Hinze will be first in line for an arrest - evidence or not," Hamilton said, almost proudly as if it was his doing.

"So, you don't think Maggie is still in danger?" Franklin asked pointblank.

"I think you're both out of danger because I'm out of danger. I really am sorry this has brought you so much pain, both physical and emotional. I did only want to start over with you. I got tired of running and grifting. I like it here. I like working with Matthew but I'll leave if you want me to, if you think it's best."

"No, we discussed this before and Maggie will get over being angry at you. I think you should stay. At least this way, I can keep my eye on what you're doing."

"Do you think Maggie wants to introduce me to any of her unmarried friends? You know, to give you some private time?"

"I'm not allowed any private time," Franklin said sadly. "At least, not until after the wedding."

Hamilton looked at his brother in commiseration, then said, "Well, you said the wedding would be soon, right? So, it won't be too long before you'll be locked in your room again with clothes thrown all over."

Franklin glanced around to see if anyone was close enough to hear them but everyone was busy eating their meals and talking among themselves. "Don't start in with the teasing or I swear I'll, I'll bust you one in the face. We can't make Maggie angry or she may leave me. I mentioned what you told me about people thinking she was a runaway wife and I thought for a moment she was going to join the woman."

"All right, I'll be so polite she won't recognize me.

She'll think we're triplets."

"Whatever you do, give me a chance to make it all up to her before you ask for any favors like finding you a girl to step out with," warned Franklin.

"Not even for the wedding?" Hamilton asked, never one to take anything too seriously.

CHAPTER 16

The small wedding turned into a very large wedding without any effort from the bride and groom. First, Seth Harrison and his wife, Callie, wanted to be at the church to represent the family for the bride. After all, Callie had brought Maggie to Sweetwater with Mary Elizabeth who was already married to Jessie Macgregor, the newspaper editor. This was merely seeing another St. Michaels Foundling Home chick properly married.

Matthew and Abby and their three children were there because Maggie was another sister from St. Michaels and the groom's brother and best man was Matthew's employee. He wanted to show his approval of new families setting up households in town.

Mason and his wife, Victoria, attended since Mason felt part of the reason Franklin and Maggie found each other. They were working together in his saloon when they fell in love.

Molly and Eli were there, because Molly hired Maggie and was responsible for the bride and groom meeting and working together, plus, she was a St. Michaels' sister, also.

Fran, Walt and the children were there because Maggie had been one of those women who had helped the young mother when she was first trying to get the bakery started. The married couple consider the bride a good friend.

The banker, Paul Weaver and his wife, Colette, getting large with child sat quietly in a central pew. Paul felt he should give the couple his congratulations since he was so blessedly happy in his own marriage.

Wilder and Hope were sitting behind Callie. Hope was another St. Michaels' sister of the bride as was, Faith, wife to Jeremy Macgregor the architect and Charity, wife to Will from the Harrison ranch and Mary Elizabeth Macgregor, sister, part-time midwife, and friend who was the matron of honor.

Then there was row after row of construction workers, dressed neatly, hair slicked back and beards trimmed as they watched two of their most favorite people marry one another.

Miss Lily played the organ and sang a requested love song for the couple. The Reverend Daniel Walters officiated, while his pregnant wife, Rebecca, with their young son, Jacob, on her lap sat in the front pew.

Maggie and Franklin pledged their vows. The groom added a plain gold band to the lovely sapphire keeper-ring. The newly married couple kissed and the entire church burst into cheers, making some wonder if there had been bets on whether or not this couple would ever make it to the altar.

There was a large reception held in the saloon with all the food and beverage furnished by the bride's family. Callie and her helper, another Mary from St. Michaels, had baked and decorated the cake when they got to town yesterday. Fran was looking in awe at the perfect frosting flowers and asking the co-baker, Mary Francis, how they were done.

The men were all lined up for a mug of the beer being given out freely, while the women held either glasses of lemonade or Champaign. The long table usually reserved for the food-line was covered with linen and lace and held an array of savories and sweets, much like what Callie served at her Christmas Eve parties. Platters of smoked salmon and oysters, olives and pickled water melon rind, dried meats and unusual cheeses from both goat and cow's milk, and caviar with special crackers all the way from Russia. There were also salads and breads as well as cold chicken, duck and venison. Back up platters were waiting in the kitchen to be brought out as needed.

Hope, the schoolmistress, was sitting near her deputy sheriff husband. She turned to him and confided, "Wilder, I can't wait any longer. I need to tell you there will be another population increase in a few months."

Wilder's eyes lit up then burned dark with passion.

Hope placed her hand on his arm in contrition. "Oh, I'm sorry," Hope said. "That was clumsy of me. I meant both Faith and Victoria are going to give birth."

As Wilder held his smile in place, Hope gave up her own secret. "It's really too soon, Wilder, but we may be having our child soon after them."

Wilder grabbed her to his side saying, "I thought maybe, but I wasn't sure. It's just that you haven't, I mean, we didn't need to stop for any reason the last month or so." But his smile was wide and his eyes full of love for his woman.

"I wanted to wait until I was certain, so you wouldn't get disappointed. The midwife can't say for sure this early," she went on to explain.

Wilder gazed into his wife's eyes. "That's all right because I know." He had to stop himself from crowing to anyone within hearing that he was going to be a father.

He looked over at Mason and Jeremy and saw a similar look of pride but a little farther down, Jessie had his arm around his wife, Mary Beth, the midwife's assistant. Just the protective way he held her made Wilder realize there was going to be more than a population increase - it was going to be more like an explosion.

"Isn't the midwife expecting, too?" he asked his wife quietly keeping the panic that swamped him under control.

"Yes, but she'll have delivered by the time the rest of us are due and besides there's always Mary Beth to help," Hope explained.

"I'm not sure we can depend on her, Honey. Is there another girl out at the ranch who can maybe take over?" he again asked quietly remembering how protective Jessie was being.

"If there is, I think Callie is going to have need of her," Hope whispered back.

"Damn, is anyone not expecting a baby?" he asked incredulous at the number of new citizens and the need for another midwife.

Hope giggled and answered, "I don't think the bride is yet but I can't say if that will be true in a week or so. You Sweetwater men are simply too single minded, I'm afraid."

Then Wilder pulled her into his arms and said loudly, "That's because you Sweetwater women are so damn lovable." He kissed her right there in front of everyone making the crowd stomp for the bride and groom to kiss which had every expectant father kissing their respective wife.

A word about the author...

Author Susan Payne has always loved to read which meant she often found herself reading books she was too young to fully understand. That didn't stop her. She found a dictionary and looked up anything that she questioned. She still thinks reading a thesaurus is a good way to spend an afternoon.

Raising a family of five children kept her busy but also allowed her time to read. Often more than fifty books a month with her children playing at her feet. That's where her love of history met her love of words as she read the new historical romance genre.

In her forties, she decided to try her hand at writing but became discouraged when she never reached the conclusion to the many stories she began. She 'retired' even after joining the local chapter of Romance Writers of America and saw how many of them seemed to write with ease.

Later, Susan found her mind filled with characters all clamoring to tell her their stories. All wanting to be heard. All wanting her to tell the world how happy they were with their chosen partners. How they had gotten through loss and survived as well as thrived.

At over eighty manuscripts, Susan is still hurrying to get the words down so that she can write the next. All stories of men and women who made their mark on life and then moved on. The stories keep coming and the couples keep finding their happy-ever-after.

You may contact Susan at:
http://www.authorsusanpayne.com or
authorspayne@gmail.com